Naïve & Lethal

NAÏVE AND LETHAL

(A NOVEL MYSTERIOUS AND ROMANTIC IN NATURE, BOOK 1)

BY NINA R. RICCI

Naïve and Lethal

Digital Edition published by Nina R. Ricci Books, 2018.
Copyright © 2018 by Nina R. Ricci
Cover Design by Jigs Designer
ISBN 13: 978-1-7325063-1-2
LCCN: 2 0 1 8 9 1 2 2 5 9

Content Advisory:
This book is intended for mature audiences and contains strong language, violence, and sexual and adult situations.

This book is the work of fiction. Names, characters, places, and incidents are products of the author's imagination, or the author used the information fictitiously. Any resemblance to actual events, locales, business establishments, or persons living or dead, is entirely coincidental. Certain long-standing institutions, agencies, and public offices are mentioned, but the characters involved are wholly imaginary.

Printed in the United States
First Printing 2018 / First Edition
Publisher's Cataloging-in-Publication Data
Ricci, Nina R. Stolen Naïve and Lethal,
Mystery / Suspense
T X 0 0 0 8 5 5 5 2 5 2

DEDICATION

Dear Reader,

For every line your eyes travel, fingers trace or ears hear, thank you.

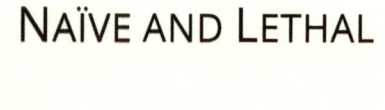

NAÏVE AND LETHAL

CHAPTER 1

Mindlessly pedaling down Johnson Boulevard, Storia couldn't seem to wrap her mind around what just happened. Tears streamed down her face impairing her vision. Suddenly, out of nowhere, the blast of a horn shattered her thoughts and tires shrieked. Her eyes fluttered as she took one last look at the bluest sky. She closed her eyes to the darkness she now saw behind her eyelids.

"Call an ambulance, will you!" shouted the man behind the silver four-door sedan rushing to help Storia. "She came out of nowhere," he cried.

"Don't move her," a second voice cautioned. "Don't move her. You might cause more damage."

Moments later a crowd of people gathered around trying to see the young girl lying on the ground. Soon after, the police arrived followed by the ambulance. As the first arriving officer made his way to the accident, he tried to disperse the crowd. Moving the people away, he stretched his arms out heading towards the young girl. This act caused the people to back up slowly. He and other arriving officers pushed the crowd back. The paramedics came with a gurney and medical kit in hand. Another officer followed behind them asking the onlookers to make room.

"What happened here? Did anyone see what happened?" the arriving officer asked moving his way through while speaking to the crowd.

"The young girl shot out of nowhere, and the man over there by the paramedics hit her," a woman replied.

"What's your name?" the officer asked.

"Beverly Silas", answered the woman.

"You saw what happened?" the officer continued.

"Yes", Beverly answered. "I was about to turn left when she came barreling around that building over there. I blew my horn along with many others, but she didn't hear the horns because she continued almost like she wanted to get hit."

"You can't make that assumption lady. I saw the whole thing too. The girl was riding with her head down, and she looked like she had earphones on," a guy said looking at Beverly.

"Okay. Calm down, everyone. I'll need all of your statements. What's your name?" the officer asked walking towards the guy. (Speaking into his radio)"Dispatch we're going to need additional assistance at the Johnson Boulevard Planning Street pedestrian-vehicle incident."

"Roger 216. I am requesting additional units."

"Copy that dispatch."

"What's your name son?" the officer asked the guy.

"Yehonatan Pope. That's Y-e-h-o-n-a-t-a-n, not Jonathan. Yeah, my mother named me after the friend of David, son of Saul. You know, in the Bible."

"Son, just tell me what happened?" the officer requested.

"Yeah, the girl came 'round Pete's. You know, like between those buildings over there (pointing). I was crossing the street and was just about in her path when she, like the other person said; came barreling down the road. I thought someone was chasing her. She was upset. I could tell by her facial expression, and SHE HAD ON HEADPHONES," Yehonatan looked over to Beverly who was talking to another officer.

"Shut up," she shouted over the other officer's shoulder.

"Hey!" the officer yelled and grimaced. "Yehonatan with an H, let's not be a hindrance to this process. She, like you, is stating what she saw. It is perspective; got it?"

"Yes, sir, but hey, I'm telling you there's no way she heard the horns," Yehonatan continued.

"Okay. I have your information. If I have any other questions, I'll contact you. And kid lay off the weed," the officer instructed.

"Like, I was with some friends who...."

"Did you hear what I said?"

"Yes, sir."

"So the guy you were named after had an H in his name too?" Yehonatan's friend asked walking next to him.

"Actually, it is the original spelling before the letter J was formed. God girl, don't you read the bible?" Yehonatan answered as he watched the paramedics put the girl in the ambulance.

"Why are you staring? She's pretty gross looking," Yehonatan's friend asked.

"That girl looks familiar. I think I've seen her around." Yehonatan answered.

CHAPTER 2

"Hi. I'm looking for my daughter. I was contacted and told she is here."

"What's your name, ma'am?" asked the receptionist.

"Jessi Greer, my daughter, is Storia DeLuca."

"Wait just a moment, please."

"Is she OKAY?"

"Please, just a moment ma'am."

"Just tell me if she's OKAY. Answer me!"

"Ma'am calmed down," said the officer sitting at the desk.

"Is your daughter here? Has your daughter been in an accident? Do you know what is happening with her right at this instant? Do NOT flipping tell me to calm down!" Jessi yelled.

(Just as the officer is about to reply to Jessi, the doctor walked up.)

"Ms. DeLuca?" the doctor asked respectfully.

"Mrs., Mrs. Greer," Jessi said sharply.

"Sorry. Mrs. Greer. I'm Dr. Budding. Is Storia DeLuca your daughter?"

"Yes."

"Your daughter arrived moments ago. She was struck by a car and has not regained consciousness."

"What?"

"That is how she arrived. The impact knocked her off her bike. The protective gear helped her somewhat, but she took a pretty big hit. She has suffered quite a bit of damage to her right side. As soon as she is out of testing, we will come and get you. Okay?"

"How did this happen? Where was she when this happened? Who did this to her? WHO DID THIS TO HER?"

"Mrs. Greer. I'm sorry. I don't have those answers, but please know that we are taking care of your daughter as best as we can. She is not in a coma as far as we can tell. The body has its way of dealing with shock and pain. We will give you more information once we are finished running test. As soon as she is out from testing, we will come and get you and take you to where she is, okay?"

"Okay," Jessi dropped her head. She wiped the tears from her eyes.

"Ma'am, I'm sorry to have to trouble you, but can you fill out these forms? We will need to know about any allergies and current drug use," the nurse stated.

"My daughter is not on nor does she do drugs," Jessi said snatching the forms from the nurse's hand.

"Ma'am, I know you're upset, and I hate having to gather this information knowing that you're deeply concerned about your child. I am not trying to say that she is on drugs; however, we need to know if she's taking any prescription drugs so when we administer something for her, we won't have to be concerned with any adverse reaction due to drug mixing. That's all," the nurse stated compassionately.

"Oh my god! I apologize. I am a wreck," Jessi cried.

"That's okay, no need for apologies. I understand. I'll come back for those documents, or you can give them to the receptionist once you finish filling them out."

"Thank you," Jessi wiped the tears from under her eyes with her fingers.

"You're welcome."

(Jessi's phone rings)

"Hello. Oh, hi. I'm at Saint Thomas Hospital," Jessi replied to the caller's question. "Well, I haven't found out yet. They just know she was hit by a car pretty hard. She's unconscious Bill. My baby hasn't been awake since the accident," (Crying) "No please Honey, stay for your meeting. I will see..." (She is interrupted) "...no, I just don't want you to fly back and miss..." (interrupted) "Well if you insist. No. Maria will pick up the boys. Okay. I'll see you in a few hours. I love you too, Bill. Be careful." The call ended.

"Mrs. Greer?" The nurse called.

"Yes."

"Let's go to see your daughter now."

"Excuse me." A man followed Jessi and interrupted her as she followed the nurse.

"Yes," Jessi replied.

"My name is Michael Edwards. I couldn't help but hear the back and forth with you and the..."

"What do you want?" Jessi interrupted.

"I hit your daughter," Mr. Edwards said sorrowfully.

"What have you done to my baby? Why? You son of a bi...," Jessi slapped the man repeatedly across his face.

The man stood still. He did not stop her. He felt he deserved her reaction.

"Ma!" Carlee shouted. She ran towards Jessi.

Carlee pulled her mother's arm shouting for her to stop. The security guard pushed himself between Jessi and Mr. Edwards.

"I didn't mean to hit her. She came out of nowhere. I didn't mean to hit her!" Mr. Edwards cried. "I had to come. I have to know how she is doing," He whimpered as the security guard escorted Jessi away from him.

Jessi's eyes grew big as she realized what the man was saying. She sank to the floor in tears.

"Ma, what are you doing?" Carlee kneeled down beside her.

"I'm never there for you girls. God is punishing me. I know he is," Jessi exclaimed.

"Mom, come on," Carlee helped her mother from the floor.

"Can we see her now?" Carlee asked the nurse.

"Ma'am we're going to go back there, but you must realize this is the intensive care unit. You have to calm down and be quiet so that you won't disturb or upset the other patients, okay?" The nurse said as she looked at Jessi with concern.

"Yes. I'm sorry for losing it," Jessi said.

"Does dad know?" Carlee asked.

"He's flying back; he should be here in a few hours.

"No mom. My father - Storia's father. You know the man you were married to before this guy?"

8

"I wish you wouldn't call that low life son of a..."

"Oh, is everyone an S.O.B now? Is that what we're doing now?" Carlee interrupted.

"If you think I'm about to entertain your sarcasm today, think again," Jessi tilted her head slightly and looked at Carlee.

"Please keep it down, or I'm going to have you escorted out!" the head nurse said.

"Well, I guess she told you," Carlee smirked, rolling her eyes.

"Hello," Carlee dropped her phone as her mother pulled the curtain back. "Oh my god! Oh my god! Storia. Wake up. Why isn't she waking up? What happened to her? Why does she look like this? Why does she look like this?" Carlee cried. She placed her head on Storia's chest. Her hands touched Storia's bandaged wrapped head. "He did this to you?" Carlee cried.

"What do the tests show nurse?" Jessi asked.

"The doctor is reviewing them now. He should be in momentarily to let you know what's going on."

Carlee's phone rings, but Carlee didn't answer.

"Carlee, can you turn your phone off?" Jessi asked.

Carlee continued to cry. She didn't answer her ringing phone and ignored her mother altogether.

"Carlee! Can you turn that phone off?"

There was still no reply.

"CARLEE TURN THAT GOD FORSAKEN PHONE OFF!"

"What the hell is wrong with you? Can't you see she's upset?" Grandma Ellie said hobbling into the room on her cane escorted by a nurse. "Oh dear heart, Storia has a big family. She'll need a much bigger area than this."

"Oh, really? Is that what Storia needs? Who is going to pay for that? Am I guessing it is going to be You? Are you going to start throwing your bogey, hillbilly mafia money around now?" Jessi barked.

"My son's best accomplishment besides these girls and Daniel was divorcing you, not his six-figure salary, not his stack of degrees, not his debt-free living, or that beautiful chateau with those breathtaking views. NO! His best accomplishment by far – to this date – is when he divorced your repugnant, self-loathing, self-righteous, egotistical, and diabolical behind. You..."

HEY!!! This very moment is the last time I will warn you! Another outburst and you all must leave," the nurse said sharply.

"Put her out now. Don't wait," Carlee said to the nurse.

"If there is another outburst from any of you, you're out. I'm serious!

"What do you mean? No one is putting me out. I'm her mother," Jessi said whispering.

"See what I mean?" Carlee rolled her eyes and looked back to Storia. "She needs a bigger bed. Nurse, can we transfer her to a big bed? I'm not leaving until she wakes up," Carlee asked the nurse who is checking Storia's medicine.

"That's not possible. Storia is in this size bed for safety. Once we move her, clearly to a bigger room, we can put an extra bed in the room for you or one of your family members if you like."

"What is that you're giving her anyway?" Carlee asked puzzled.

"Oh, this is just saline to keep her hydrated. This one is Benadryl for this one, which is iron. Her iron stores are meager. She had a bit of a reaction to the iron.earlier that's why we're giving her Benadryl. It takes about an hour or two to administer the iron," the nurse explained.

"The name on the bag doesn't say saline, and that one doesn't say iron..." Carlee informed.

"Oh come on. If the woman says it's saline and iron, that's what it is. Are you about to go CSI on her?" Jessi grew impatient with Carlee's questions.

"I am talking to the nurse. Why are you talking to me?" Carlee responded curtly.

"Yeah, leave her alone and let her ask what she wants. Was she bothering you? Grandma Ellie exclaimed.

"Sigh!!!" Jessi searched in her purse for her ringing cell phone.

"Can you turn that phone off?" Carlee yelled sarcastically.

Jessi answered her cell phone as she stormed out of the sliding door.

"I thought she would never leave," Grandma Ellie said hobbling toward Storia.

"Can you continue, please, nurse?" Carlee asked.

"Well, the technical term as stated on the bag is Sodium Chloride. It is used to hydrate and carry medications into the bloodstream. It is in essence salt water. Saline is also used to push meds through the body. You will know when this medication is fully distributed when the color representing this medication becomes clear and only the saline remains. The "iron" Sodium Ferric Gluconate – Ferrlecit is being administered to treat anemia. I say saline and iron because it is easier to understand," the nurse smiled.

"Oh, it was," Carlee chuckling.

"Dr. Budding, what is going on with my daughter?" Jessi asked anxiously. She rushed in behind the doctors.

"This is Dr. Melvin; she is a neurologist. (Pointing) She is Dr. Patterson, she is a GYN, and this is Dr. Analyn, she is a psychologist," Dr. Budding introduced the team of doctors to Jessi.

"Oh yeah, (Pointing) that one over there is my ex-mother-in-law, she needs your help Dr. An-ah-lynn. Did I pronounce your name right? That's my daughter Carlee. What's wrong with my daughter and why is she here?" Jessi asked pointing to the GYN, Dr. Patterson.

"Um, well," Dr. Budding said looking at the psychologist.

"Does your daughter live with you, Mrs. Greer?" Dr. Analyn asked.

"What the fu..." Jessie yelled as she is cut off in mid-sentence.

"Answer the question moron," Grandma Ellie yelled. "Yes, Storia and Carlee live with her, angels in heaven help them."

"Well, Storia is pregnant," the psychologist revealed.

"Yes, she's about 15 weeks along," the GYN followed as she showed Jessi the sonogram stills in her hands.

"Give me those," Jessi tried to snatch the images.

"You don't know how to read the information on that thing. You're such a dumb ass. I, for the life of me, don't see what my son saw in you...big tits and a dick house you call a mouth," Grandma Ellie growled rubbing the left side of Storia's face. "This baby is 15 – 15 by a couple of days Jessi. What is she doing pregnant?"

"Well, I can't keep a watch on her 24 hours of the day," Jessi replied.

"I've had enough of your excuses, Jessi. 24 hours of the day is your response? 24 hours of the day? How about 16 hours Jessi? How about 8 hours? Two major things account for 16 hours on any given day - sleep and school. Are you suggesting she got pregnant at school, so you don't have to account for the 8 hours left in a day?," Grandma Ellie argued as she rubbed Storia's lower abdomen.

"She won't continue with this pregnancy," Jessi said as she looked to Dr. Patterson. "You can fix that while we're here."

"We don't offer that procedure here at Saint Thomas. Perhaps you'd like to consider adoption, we can assist with that service," Dr. Patterson looked at Jessi and Grandma Ellie.

"Hell no, we won't consider adoption. I'm the law in this room when it comes to decision making for MY daughter," Jessi claimed as she pointed to herself.

"Dad!" Carlee screamed. She ran to her father as he walked through the sliding door. "I wasn't sure you if you knew about Storia."

"How's my Pumpkin?" Devon asked. He kissed Carlee on the forehead. "What's this about you making decisions? For which daughter are you making decisions?" Devon asked. He looked at Jessi.

"Oh, that's right. You don't have any girls with Mr. DeLuca, huh?" Grandma Ellie asked smugly hobbling over to a chair.

"Let me help you, grandma," Carlee grabbed her grandmother's arm and helped her to the chair.

"When can she be moved?" Grandma Ellie asked. "And there won't be any abortions had here."

"Abortion?" Devon stated puzzled. He frowned at Carlee. "Honey you're 17," his voice cracked.

"No, dad. Not for me, for Storia."

"STORIA'S PREGNANT?" Devon yelled. He glared at Jessi.

"Why are you looking at me? I didn't have anything to do with her being pregnant... What the hell?"

"Okay, okay, okay," Dr. Budding interrupted. "Storia is in terrible shape. It is a miracle the accident didn't cause a spontaneous abortion. Look, this is the least of our troubles. We are very concerned about her coma-like state."

"Coma?" Jessi asked startled.

"Coma-like. She is unconscious and has been unresponsive for hours, but there are minimal signs of brain damage or injury. We at this point have to assume that when she fell off the bike, she took a great blow to the head, which is why she is unconscious. We believe this is what is causing her brain to function at its lowest stage of alertness. Her heart is fine. There are no signs of seizures or drug use. So at this point, we have to assume she hit her head at impact and although the helmet absorbed most of the force, she is obviously reacting perhaps subconsciously. These tests, except the

14

pregnancy test, are preliminary. We will continue to analyze her results and compare for a complete assessment. As you can see, Storia broke her right arm and leg. She dislocated her left tibiotalar joint of the ankle with a distal fibular fracture. We're looking at about 2 ½ months if not longer with the weight of the growing fetus for that to heal. The orthopedic surgeon will be in to explain the procedure. The ankle is troubling but, she's young; up to 18 weeks for sure for a good heal, but she'll have to stay off it assuming she regains consciousness and is mobile," Dr. Budding explained.

"So, what are you trying to say, doctor?" Jessi asked unpleasantly.

"I am not trying to say anything. Storia's pretty banged up Mrs. Greer. Besides the unconsciousness, which is our major concern, her injuries, overall are minor. She is anemic. Her blood count is leveling out at about 7.5. The growing fetus will demand most of that which will place a lot of strain on her body. We recommend transfusions of blood at levels 7 or less. We are hoping while she is here that the Ferrlecit injection will help build her iron stores and the absence of her menstrual cycle will help to crank out some red blood cells and cause those levels to increase within a matter of months. She'll need to take a supplement at least three times a day. We'll help with that while she is here," Dr. Budding continued. "We will run more tests on her brain to monitor the activity."

"I am recommending prenatal vitamins with iron. We will inject it into Storia's I.V. for the time she is unconscious," Dr. Patterson said.

"I recommend some family counseling as soon as possible to help deal with the accident, the divorce, the new marriage, the verbal abuse, and the pregnancy assuming it will be viable," Dr. Analyn suggested.

"Oh, so you want to talk to us about liking each other for the baby's sake, huh?" Jessi asked sarcastically.

"No. You all should want to get help for your sake," Dr. Analyn said. "The ones who reject it are the ones who usually need it the most."

"You called that one right doc," Grandma Ellie said laughing. (Devon laughing with her)

"Mr. DeLuca, can I see you for a moment," asked the psychologist.

"Sure." Devon walked out of the sliding door with Dr. Analyn.

"Mr. DeLuca, your mother, and your ex-wife's relationship are volatile, and you have these things going on right in front of the other child." Dr. Analyn remarked.

"I have it going on?" Devon's eyebrow rose.

"You're the common denominator. I believe you're the one who can defuse the situation between the two women."

"The last time I got in the middle of those two, I ended up at Madison Edwards with a concussion. I assure you I won't be interfering in their disputes ever again."

"Well, something has to give," Dr. Analyn added looking for a sign that Devon would assist.

"Ump! On my father's, whom I love and adore, life, it won't be me," Devon concluded.

CHAPTER 3

The hospital staff moved Storia into a larger room. She is still unconscious, but the doctors are optimistic.

"This room is beautiful. The view is perfect. Storia will love it when she wakes up. Of course, we'll need to stock the refrigerator and get some color in here. Carlee, could you be a dear and order some flowers for me?" Grandma Ellie asked.

"Yes, ma'am."

"Dig in my purse. Any of those cards will do."

"Okay."

(Frowning) "Oh yeah, that's right start throwing around your money, barking orders, yeah, we're all at you beckon call," Jessi sucked her teeth and then rolled her eyes.

"Oh boy, here we go. Can you please not start with my mother, Jessi?" Devon smacked the sides of his legs with his hands.

"Forget that! Why should I play nice? She's done nothing but insult me since she arrived. She said some terrible things to me. Did you know she said I was nothing to you but big tits? For god's sake, she told me that my mouth was your dick house! Did you know she said those things to me? Did you know that's how she felt about me? Jessi cried.

"No." (Smirking)

"It's not funny. Those are awful things to say to anyone."

"Well." (Trying not to laugh loud)

(Emotional) "It's not funny Devon! You never stood up to her for me."

"I mean "dick house" is pretty funny," Devon, laughed; he was embarrassed. "Mom, where – how do you come up with these names?"

"That's your question? You want to know how she came up with dick house?"

(Laughing) "Well yeah," Devon said with a big awkward grin. He tried to look at Jessi with a straight face. "I've just never heard that term, but the visual makes it real on some erotic level that is turning me on. The fact that my mother said it is grossing me out. I'm confused." Devon's attempt at humor failed miserably.

"Nice going dad," Carlee rolled her eyes and put her earphones in her ears.

Carlee shook her head, sat on the windowsill and scrolled through her musical selection.

"Well, isn't that what caused you to make the worse mistake of your life?" Grandma Ellie asked Devon.

"Mom, I am not about to discuss dick houses with you. Being married to Jessi wasn't bad. For the eight years, there were a total of 160 weeks of extreme bliss for me."

"Oh really, when was that?" Jessi and Grandma Ellie practically asked simultaneously.

"Well, it was the conception and birth of Daniel, Carlee and my sweet apple, Storia. Those three are the best of me," tears filled Devon's eyes.

"Hey, what was that for?" Carlee asked responding to the kiss on the forehead her father delivered.

"I love you, kid."

"I love you too dad, what's wrong?"

"My baby here in this bed unconscious is what's wrong."

"Oh, dad, Storia's gonna be fine. God said." Carlee said happily.

"Okay Pumpkin. I'm counting on it," Devon hugged Carlee.

"God said, and you believe that?" Jessi blurted out.

"Are you about to question the works of God? Oh, what am I talking about when it comes to you? Of course, you are you, motherless whore," Grandma Ellie said hoping to get her goat again.

"Oh, mother. Not in front of the girls," Devon pleaded.

"Not in front of the girls? Not in front of the girls? Fu.." Jessi yelled.

"Go ahead and say it. That's certainly why this girl is laid up here pregnant. It is how you feel, right? A pile of white trash the sanitation worker didn't even want to pick up, but my son the idiot virgin, oh, she's just fine for him. I'd say the thoroughbred and the mutt, but that analogy is too insulting to the mutt because even the mutt has more character than she does," Grandma Ellie said heatedly.

"Mother cut it out! You do the same, Jessi. I will take my kids off your hands so you can ride off into the sunset with Bill if that's how you feel Jessi. That was an awful thing to think about saying about my kids," Devon barked.

"They are children Devono Gabriele DeLuca – children!" Grandma Ellie fussed.

"Mother – please!" Devon begged.

"I can hear you people up the hall. What is going on in here?" Jessi's husband, Bill asked as he walked through the sliding door.

"Oh honey, she's so mean to me," Jessi said running into Bill's arms.

"What's going on in here?" Bill asked again.

"William," Devon spoke.

No one answered his question.

"You know when you enter a room William you don't enter it asking questions, you speak," Grandma Ellie lectured. "I've always said you two come from the same pod."

"Mother!" Devon looked with a firm face at his mother shaking his head slowly with a frown. "Oh my God, she's moving. Get the doctor," Devon yelled. He ran over to Storia.

CHAPTER 4

"Storia, Apple, Honey. Hi," Devon kissed her forehead.

"Daddy, what - - - - happened?"

"I'm glad you're awake!" Carlee placed her face on Storia's face.

"Grandma, is that you?"

"Yes. Thank heavens child, it's me," Grandma Ellie cried.

"What happened daddy?" Storia asked again.

"Well, is that all you see?" Jessi stood at the foot of the bed with her arms crossed.

"Honey," Bill moved Jessi out of the way of the doctors.

"He's not there like I am, and it's him she's happy to see?" Jessi cried.

"You can't worry about that, Love. Aren't you happy she's awake?" Bill comforted Jessi in his arms.

"How do you feel Storia?" Dr. Budding rushed in excitedly.

"Daddy?" Storia called.

"I'm here Apple," Devon answered. He walked to the left side of Storia's bed.

"Why is she calling for him?" Jessi asked jealously.

"Be happy she's awake, dear," her husband answered.

"Tell the doctors how you feel, Apple," Devon requested.

"I feel tired and sick and hungry."

"All of that, huh?" Grandma Ellie laughed.

"Yeah. How long have you been here?"

"Well Baby Doll, I got in on Thursday of last week. You've been here at Saint Thomas since that time. Today is Tuesday, honey. Your daddy has not had a chance to tell you. Honey you've..."

"Why does daddy (mocking Grandma Ellie's voice) have to be the one who tells her?" Jessi interrupted Grandma Ellie.

"Honey calm down," said her husband, Bill.

"No! I'm tired of calming down," Jessi snatched away from her husband.

"Security," the nurse called from the door.

"Security my ass! Storia is my child; I'm the one who has taken care of her without you and what boy got you pregnant, Storia?" Jessi screamed.

"Ahh," Storia looked surprised.

A nurse walked into the hospital room with security.

"Remove this woman," the nurse ordered.

"You weren't there, and you haven't been there. Now you walk in like the white knight, NO! Jessi yelled at Devon. "Get your hands off me," Jessi yelled at the security guard. "Who got you pregnant Storia? Answer me! You are not keeping that baby!"

"Shut the hell up. She just woke up. Do you want to upset her?" Grandma Ellie snarled.

"Not that you don't know, but for the record, I have been there. Carlee found me and has been texting and calling for weeks. What? Did you think you would be able to hide them from me forever? Did you think the girls would continue to believe your lies about me?" Devon said smugly.

"You son of a fat bitch! You will be sorry. I'll make sure of it," Jessi promised.

As the security guard ushered Jessi out of the door, she continued to yell down the hall.

"I apologize you all. You all know how Jessi gets; she is distraught, that's all," Bill said in shame.

"No William, I'm sorry you have to be a part of this mess," Devon pat William on the back.

"Yeah, I'd better go. Hey, Storia, I'm glad you're back with us," Bill, head hung, turned to walk out of the door.

"Hey, thanks, William. Take care." Devon said.

"Take care of her," Bill waved bye as he walked out of the door.

"Now that she is up, we'll run a series of test to make sure everything is okay," said Dr. Budding. "You had us baffled for a while there Storia."

"Hello?" Mr. Edwards shouted as he walked through the sliding door.

"You must have the wrong room," Devon said.

"It's the man mom beat up in the emergency waiting room," Carlee said. "He's the one who hit Storia."

"Cotton picking', you don't say," Grandma Ellie looked around the curtain.

"I just wanted to apologize," Mr. Edwards said sadly.

"You were trying to, I remember. You look a mess, and you're wearing the same clothes. Do you have a home?" Carlee asked.

"Pumpkin, don't be rude," Devon rebuked.

"Sorry."

"That's okay. I haven't been home since the accident. I just wanted to know that the girl was okay. She came out of nowhere," Mr. Edwards cried with flowers and a teddy bear in his hands.

"Hey buddy, listen, she's fine. Thanks for your concern. Did you want to give those things to her?" (Mr. Edwards nodded) Devon assured Mr. Edwards. He took the flowers and teddy bear from him.

"I haven't been able to sleep. All I see is your daughter darting out from around the mailbox. It happened so fast." Mr. Edwards confessed.

"I'm okay sir," Storia replied though her voice was hoarse.

"Is that her? I heard she was unconscious. Is that her voice? So, she is alive? Is she okay? Yes? Yes? No one would tell me anything about her condition," Mr. Edwards anxiously noted.

"Yes. Storia is good," Devon assured.

"Mr. Edwards, what are you doing in here? Have you been checked out sir?" Dr. Analyn directed Mr. Edwards to the door.

"She's talking. She's awake. They said she's going to be fine," Mr. Edwards said excitedly.

"Yes, I heard. Isn't that beautiful?" Dr. Analyn asked.

"God heard me. He heard me," Mr. Edwards suggested. "Can we stop by the chapel? God is in there. He heard me.

I want to tell Him thanks," Mr. Edwards requested as he walked alongside Dr. Analyn.

"Well, you know Mr. Edwards I read from a valid source that God is everywhere. He would hear you if you said thank you from anywhere in this building," Dr. Analyn declared.

"Well, that might be true, but I was in the chapel when I asked Him to make the little girl okay. I think it's appropriate to thank Him there. Can I know what the little girl's name is? Is it okay, do you think?" Mr. Edwards asked Dr. Analyn and waited for an answer.

"Well, Mr. Edwards, God answered your prayers, so He already knows what little girl you're thanking Him for, but her name is Storia."

"Storia. Okay. I'll be back," Mr. Edwards walked into the chapel.

"Okay, Mr. Edwards. I need to see you for evaluation. I believe you might have suffered a psychotic break of some sort," Dr. Analyn said concerned.

"I don't think he has suffered a psychotic break at all," a voice said from the background.

(Turning around) "And you are?" Dr. Analyn asked.

"I'm his wife. I've been looking all over for him. He left a message for me but didn't mention the location. I believe he's tired and is a little hysterical at least that's how he sounded on his message. You should understand that – doctor," Mr. Edwards's wife argued.

"Hysterical?" Dr. Analyn said puzzled.

"Yes. You know - when shock meets fear that met uncontrolled emotion, panic, and perhaps delirium?" Mr. Edwards's wife was snippy.

"Hysteria?" Dr. Analyn questioned.

"Why yes. My husband hit a child. We've lost three. The thought of him hitting a child is a bit more than he can handle, but he's going to be fine" Mr. Edwards's wife confessed.

"Are you a doctor?" Dr. Analyn asked.

"Yes. I am," declared Mr. Edwards's wife.

"Claudia," Mr. Edwards called. He ran towards his wife.

"I have a practice out of Blackbrium Medical. I'm a Breckenridge Alumni. It was either that or medicine. Psychiatry seems more intriguing. You know Dr. Analyn; I admire your noble deeds. Were you going to "cure" my husband with your theory? No thanks. You know what I'm going to do? I'm going to take him home, run a nice bath for him, assist him into it, feed him a nice meal, give him a couple of diazepams, relieve his stress, if you know what I mean, and put him in the bed. Would your theory prescribe - oh that's right your degree is scientific and theory-based, you can't prescribe anything. Next time you try to get someone to voluntarily admit themselves to a psychiatric hospital in hopes that it will become an involuntary situation so you can align your pockets with insurance money, think about this conversation. Moreover, while you're in this chapel, thank God you couldn't get my husband to self-admit because now you don't get to witness the wrath of his wife. (Walking towards her husband) "Oh yeah, I will file a formal complaint with management," Claudia concluded. "Come on sweetheart," Claudia said to her husband. She held his hand and guided him out of the chapel.

"Honey, the little girl's name is Storia," Mr. Edwards said happily. "I asked God to fix her, and He did."

"He did? Baby, that's great!" Claudia answered. She looked at Dr. Analyn as she and her husband walked towards the door.

"I'm so tired, but I feel better knowing that Storia is okay," Mr. Edwards said calmly.

"Oh, I have some things that will make you feel much better dear," Claudia kissed her husband.

"Umm, I can't wait. You smell good; that perfume you have on smells like my favorite," Michael kissed his wife.

Dr. Analyn watched as the couple walked out of the door. She put her hands in her pocket, turned around and shook her head as she thought about how weird that exchange was and how she was glad it was over.

CHAPTER 5

"So it looks like she had some swelling," Dr. Budding said to Devon.

"But she's fine, right," Devon asked.

"Yes. Storia appears to be doing much better. We are going to keep her a few more days for observation. If all is well, we'll send her home. Now I'm curious, will she return to her mother's home? If so, I'll have to contact CPS, well, child protective services for evaluation. I don't believe the child will be safe in your ex-wife's home."

"Oh, don't worry, doc. My granddaughter is coming home with me," Grandma Ellie declared.

"We'll straighten it out, doctor. Thank you," said Devon. "Mom, she's my daughter. Don't you think it's fitting to let me decide along with my daughters and Jessi?"

"No, especially not with Jessi; not at all. You haven't even revealed the biggest secret of them all since we already know about the baby."

"What secret is that?" asked Carlee.

"Yeah," Storia followed.

"Well, I was going to tell you both the day the accident happened," Devon said.

"What daddy?" asked Storia.

"Tell us what? Out with it dad," Carlee said.

"I'm getting married?" Devon said quickly.

"You're WHAT?" Jessi asked as she walked into the hospital room.

"Call security," yelled Carlee.

"Give the tramp a chance," Grandma Ellie said.

"Screw you, Ellie," Jessi said. She looked at Devon.

"Too many people have had you, Jessi, you whore, I don't want to screw you, sweetie," Grandma Ellie laughed.

"Mother, stop it!" Devon yelled.

"What's going on in here? I can hear you people down the ...oh, it's you again (the nurse asked as she walked through the sliding door. "Security!"

"You dumb bitch. How dare you call security? I have every right to speak with and see my daughter," Jessi barked.

Security walks in

"Escort this woman out," the nurse instructed.

"So you think you're gonna marry some bitch for my girls to call momma?" Jessi yelled at Devon as security escorted her out. "Let me go damn you! Let me go!" Jessie shouted as she fought with security. "Devon, you will not get away with this! You won't steal my grandchild and turn it against me! You son of a fat, dog-faced bitch! Isn't that appropriate – dog face bitch!!! Jessi screamed down the hall.

Grandma Ellie ignored Jessi this time though she wanted to say something to her badly.

"You did good grandma," Storia giggled.

"You're such a dummy," Carlee said. She continued to brush Storia's hair.

"Carlee, don't call your sister a dummy," Devon fussed.

"Why do you two hate each other so much anyway?" Storia asked her grandmother.

Grandma Ellie and Devon looked at each other, neither wanted to answer her question. Grandma Ellie changed the subject.

"Well, let me ask you this dear," Grandma Ellie hobbled over toward Storia's bed.

"Why haven't we met this woman you're going to marry dad?" Carlee interrupted her grandmother as she wrote on Storia's cast.

"Yeah, daddy, why not?" Storia followed the line of questioning.

"Storia, we know you've been with a boy," Grandma Ellie said focusing on her facial expression.

"Grandma, I don't want to talk about it," Storia said looking towards the opposite wall.

"Hi," the lab tech entered the room. "I'm here for some blood, honey. How are you?" The lab tech asked.

"I'm feeling better," Storia answered.

"Oh, whatcha crying about?" the lab tech asked.

"Bad memories that's all," Storia replied as Carlee wiped the tears from her face.

"It's just the notion that guys are such assholes," Storia cried out.

"Hold still honey," the lab tech drew blood from Storia's vein.

"And by the way, watch your mouth Storia. I can see you're upset, but those are not the words you use to describe people or situations. Don't be like your mother," Devon said loosely.

"Well, I mean it, daddy," Storia said continuing to cry.

"All done. Well, I hope you get some good memories to replace those bad ones soon," the lab tech stated smiling.

"Thank you," Carlee said looking at Storia.

"Yeah thanks," Storia added.

"Can we talk about how this happened, Apple?" Devon asked Storia compassionately.

"Yeah dad, let's talk about how this happened. How do you come to be getting married?" Carlee asked.

"No," Storia answered.

"I'm serious," Devon said.

"Me too," Carlee replied.

"So all we're getting out of this is that he's an asshole?" Grandma Ellie asked.

"Grandma," Carlee called shaking her head in a quick back and forth motion.

"What else is new? All boys till thirty are assholes," Grandma Ellie continued. "They like a lot of houses, you know, for their little man in the pants," Grandma Ellie added.

"Oh my god, Ma. Whatever did you get such a term? Eloise asked laughing as she walked into the room.

"Hi Aunt Eloise," Carlee said from Storia's side.

"Still not talking to me Storia?" Eloise asked.

"Nope, she's not talking to you, auntie. Good to see you though," Carlee said answering for Storia. "You betrayed her. Remember?" Carlee added.

"Okay," Eloise said moving the corner of her mouth slightly as she shrugged her shoulders.

"That was easy,' Grandma Ellie said.

"So, are you getting married or not?" Eloise asked Devon.

"You're here for the wedding too?" Carlee asked looking over at her dad. "Seems like we're the only ones who didn't know," Carlee added folding her arms across her chest and looking towards the window to avoid looking at her dad.

"Yeap and if it's off, I'm out," Eloise answered.

"Still hanging out with black people, huh?" Grandma Ellie asked looking at Eloise not caring to hear the answer.

"Yeap mom, I'm still married if that's what you mean," Eloise answered looking for a response to her question from Devon.

"I'll be sure to gift you a dick house rejuvenation certificate once it's all said and done'" Grandma Ellie said with a smirk.

"That's okay. I'll just find someone with one that is..." Eloise was interrupted.

"You people are insane. In flipping sane," Devon said interrupting Eloise to prevent the girls from asking questions regarding the content.

"So, dick houses and the little man in the pants, is that what we're talking about right now? Storia asked as she looked around the room.

Carlee and Storia laugh.

"Okay, your results are coming back very good," Dr. Budding said as she walked quickly through the hospital door smiling.

"Do you ever go home?" Carlee asked Dr. Budding.

"Well, not when I have a patient with a broken arm, leg, and ankle, who is just regaining consciousness, and who also happens to be pregnant with a low blood count," answered the doctor.

"Pregnant?" Eloise said looking around the room. "How old is she again?"

"I guess you have a point," Carlee looked at the doctor then over to her dad.

"Why are we pregnant?" Eloise hoped to get an answer to her second question.

"Cause we do the things that it takes to get pregnant," Grandma Ellie said with sass.

"We aren't pregnant, Storia is," Carlee said.

"Once she is out of the hospital, who is going to take her to the doctor for her prenatal visits? Who has to pay for it? Is she keeping it? Who is going to take care of it? That's why I say we. She is not going to do any of what I just said by herself," Eloise said with an attitude.

"Okay you've made your point – we," Carlee noted.

"Ump," Eloise said madly.

"When can she go home doc?" Devon asked.

"Where is Storia going to live? I know Jessi is pissed," Eloise asked.

"My house," said Grandma Ellie.

"Yours?" asked a surprised Eloise.

"We want to hold on to her for observation. She still has a lot going on," answered the doctor. "We'll see."

"You cool with that Devon?" Eloise waited for an answer this time.

"No, but," Devon paused.

"That broad won't go for two teenage girls from your past," Grandma Ellie said.

"But, what? Does she know about Daniel? By the way, where is Daniel?" Eloise asked with concern.

"She knows about them. She thinks they are in school like Daniel," Devon answered.

"She thinks all of them are in a boarding school? Why is that – Devon?" Eloise asked with her hands on her hips.

"Quit asking so many questions," Devon snapped with his head down, his hand in his pants pocket turned towards the window. "Daniel will be out of school soon."

"She can't help it. She's nosey. That comes from her hanging around her in-laws," Grandma Ellie declared.

"You are a boob mom. Do you have a problem with black people?" Eloise raised her eyebrows.

"No. I have a problem with people who don't do anything with their lives; live off the white wife, brag about their WIFE'S degrees and speaks like they've skipped primary, junior high and high school English classes not to mention college courses some claim he, I mean, they attended."

"Why don't you tell me how you really feel Ma?"

"Eloise, please don't give her permission. Please, mother, don't tell her how you really feel." Devon pleaded.

"Well," Grandma Ellie started.

"Oh my blessed Lord," Devon said facepalming.

"I told you to marry your kind," Grandma Ellie argued.

"My kind, ma he is a human being just like me," Eloise explained.

"Yes, he is a human being, but he's not the educated kind. He doesn't appear to be the employed kind, not to mention the responsible kind, fatherly, faithful, or damn it; he is even kind?" Grandma Ellie said touching a finger for each offense.

"Mother come on. She loves him. She chose him," Devon interjected.

"She chose him, huh? She chose him. What a choice. In what category did he get chosen? He is not successful. Many men are nice and have very nice packages that are successful. Why couldn't you pick one of them that happened to be black by the way? I don't appreciate you calling me a boob because I don't approve of your husband. Your husband could be gray, but if he speaks as though he wasn't educated properly and he doesn't have a job, I'm going to have a problem with him," Grandma Ellie explained.

"Mom, your tireless attempt at making off-color references to prove you don't have a problem with black people while you mention common stereotypes, is old and it's dumb. If you don't care for black people, so what, just say that so we all can move on with life," Eloise said grimly. "Not that you care, but for the record, I am the one who can't hold a job in my field. I was a substitute teacher for years because I didn't have the credentials. The schools I worked for laid me off because other teachers that came in after me had degrees. Joey bragged about my degrees because I went back to get them with his help not because he was living off me. I didn't have a job at all for two years, and he supported me. Joey is college educated, employed, and makes forty-three thousand more than I do. He does have two sides. He has a professional side, and then there is his at home with family and friends side. So, yes, he does speak with street slang, but our home is paid for, my children are in private school, and dance, and classical music appreciation, and they're in an elocution program, thank you very much for having your facts straight. To be perfectly honest with you, I got pregnant on purpose because I thought I was losing him. He married me ONLY because I was pregnant. That's why I hate coming to visit. You are a dysfunctional mother. You! You have spawned dysfunction!" Eloise was both angry and hurt.

"Have you not heard anything I said?" Grandma Ellie said confused.

"Yes, I heard you, but did you hear me? By the way, I don't believe you... if he were gray... who even says that?" Eloise said somewhat loudly.

"Okay, where are we going with this pointless conversation? I know Joe and his family took you and Emily into his home and has been instrumental in your success, but you two arguing the semantics, I mean, what are you all hoping to conclude? Where are we going with this conversation?" Devon asked.

"No - where," Eloise answered. She pulled the skin under her eyes wiping the tears.

"And fast," Grandma Ellie added.

There was total silence in the room.

"Okay, so can someone please confirm for me what a dick house is?" Storia asked growing impatient as though she had been waiting for the answer the whole time.

"Sigh, I'm outta here!" Eloise stormed out of the hospital door rolling her eyes.

"What did I say? I mean, I really want to know," Storia said.

"Storia, do us all a favor," Carlee suggested.

"What?" Storia asked.

"Shut up!" Carlee yelled.

"Well! That was rude," Storia said crossing her arms.

"Are you mad?" Carlee asked not caring.

"Well..." Storia was about to answer until she was interrupted.

"Because being pregnant is proof that you not only know what a dick house is, but you had no problem letting company over and invited them in," Carlee stated rudely.

"Daddy! It is not my fault grandma is mean to Eloise because she married a black guy," Storia said.

"Carlee, don't be mean, and Apple, let's not mention why your grandmother and aunt argued," Devon instructed.

"Really dad? Do you not question in your mind who she is pregnant by and what is she even doing pregnant?" Carlee asked.

"Pumpkin, your sister has been in a serious accident. We have plenty of time to get to that," Devon said calmly.

"Dad, oh my god, what is wrong with the present? She's pregnant. Now she's fine. Why can't we ask?" Carlee inquired.

"What is wrong with you, Carlee?" Storia barked.

"You're sitting here acting so naïve trying to be funny about grandma's term when you know what it is."

"How do you know what I know? For your information, I like that it is shitty that even though I am not talking to Aunt Eloise, no one went after her. She was clearly upset."

"Come on now girls. Apple, watch your mouth," Devon chimed.

"Ump," Storia pouted and placed her arm on her broken one.

"Who impregnated you Storia?" Carlee asked.

"None of your business," Storia shouted.

"Oh no! Your pregnancy is going to take parenting time from me. So, it is my business!"

"Carlee, you are selfish!"

"I'm selfish because I'm supposed to be understanding when I can't get someone - - one of my parents to help me with a crisis I may be going through because now my sister and her baby need the attention. Oh, but that's selfish. Get over yourself. I've been here since you arrived. I sat here praying for you while you were unconscious. Now that you're awake, you have been acting like you don't know anything, saying all of this stupid stuff and asking all of these silly questions. Then, when asked a question, you clam up as if no one is speaking to you. You're 15, Storia. 15. I'm 17. I was in the same family meeting when mom and dad talked to us about sex, birth control, communication, and honesty. I know you were there because you sat next to me."

"So! So damn what! So fucking what! Did I ask you to be here Carlee? Did I? Did I ask you to stay here with me? Did I ask you to do anything for me? If you did whatever you did when I was unconscious, was it because you wanted to or because you wanted to have something to throw in my face because you did it? There is the door, and you're free to use it because I don't care! When did mom and dad talk with us about sexual matters? What was I 6? And please don't talk to me about mom! So, anything else?"

"So, why are you pregnant? So, why didn't you use birth control? So, who's baby are you having Storia?

"Daddy, can you please tell Carlee to leave me alone?"

"Well, Apple, we have to have this talk sooner or later. What were you planning to do about the baby, honey? When were you going to tell someone?"

"Grandma, can you tell your granddaughter and son to leave me alone?"

"Sweetheart, I've been begging to ask these questions myself. I mean, hell, this is not a joke. Your pregnancy is a serious matter, Baby Cakes. What did you think we were going to do, roll over and ignore it?"

"You people think you know everything and especially you Carlee. You are not even considering how I feel right now. For your information, I am over my head, and I don't know what a dick house is; I've never heard of that, so I am not acting. For a long time, I saw black, and I couldn't talk even though I could hear your voices, so excuse me for being happy to be awake. Not long ago, I wasn't saying anything, and I wasn't asking anything, so for you to have the nerve to say that what I am saying or asking is stupid – well, you're dumb. Don't talk to me, none of you! I don't want to talk.

"Oh Apple, don't feel like that. We are here for you. Carlee didn't mean any harm," Devon tried to calm Storia.

"What do you know daddy? How long have I been here two or three weeks? You've been in Carlee's life a total of two to three weeks, and you think that you know what Carlee means when she says the crap she says? I mean jeez. She is not the boss of me. I didn't ask any of you to do anything for me. Leave me alone," Storia said. She was irritated by Carlee.

"Honey, you have to know that it is a complete surprise that you're pregnant that's all. I mean, I didn't realize you were into boys. I haven't been out of your lives that long, honey. You were about nine when I left. I have been fighting and looking for your mother for at least two years trying to see you and your siblings. You cannot go to the courts without an address," Devon tried to explain.

"Daddy you know what? I'm tired. I need to take a nap. So please, leave me alone. Can you all, please just leave me alone?"

CHAPTER 6

Storia adjusted the bed slightly and tried to go to sleep. Devon walked over to Carlee and yelled at her through his teeth trying not to disturb Storia. Carlee made hand, face, and body jesters in response to what Devon said. The two went back and forth while Grandma Ellie dozed off in the hospital style lazy boy. Devon and Carlee couldn't get their points across by speaking on the matter the way they were communicating, so they started to whisper while they argued. They were interrupted by Storia's sniffles.

"What's the matter Apple? Are we disturbing you?" Devon high tailed it towards Storia. He woke Grandma Ellie from her doze.

"He told me he loved me. He told me he wanted to be with me forever," Storia confessed crying uncontrollably.

"Oh, Apple, don't cry," Devon tried to console Storia.

"You don't understand. He said that he would take care of me and when he kissed me down there he said it would be okay," Storia explained devastated.

"Wait a minute. What?" Carlee looked as though no one else heard what she heard.

"How old is he honey?" Grandma Ellie asked.

"I don't know. Daddy, how old are you?" Storia asked.

A gasp filled the air.

"Well – Honey – Apple. Why do you ask my age? Is this boy you're talking about my age?" Devon asked not sure he wanted to know the answer.

"Well, daddy, I don't really like him. I just like hanging out at his house because he has all of these cool things there," Storia said reluctantly.

"What? His HOUSE? With his parents' right?" Carlee looked at her dad frightened.

"No! Who's asking dumb questions now, Carlee?" Storia said blowing her nose.

"How did you meet him?" Grandma Ellie asked.

"Well, Mrs. Gloria, Rachel, and I went door-to-door selling the cookies we got from school," Storia explained.

"Yeah, that was some time ago," Carlee said remembering the time.

"Well, when I got to his house and knocked on the door a girl came from the back, and she looked upset, but she told me Tommy was in the back. When I got to the back, he was in a really cool looking tree house, so I talked to him about buying some cookies. He came down from the tree and ordered a bunch of them. He gave me the money and told me to bring the cookies to him when they got in. He asked about the project I was selling the cookies for, and I told him, and then, he ordered more cookies and gave me money. He said he would give them to friends. He asked me if I wanted to see the inside of the tree house, and I said sure but Mrs. Gloria came and thanked him for the cookie order and the money, and we left," Storia explained innocently.

"Okay, wait. Tommy? --- as in Thomas, Tommy? --- Mom's friend, Storia, how did you get pregnant by him?" Carlee asked prematurely.

"Carlee, how do you know he is the one? Can you shut up and let her tell us the rest since she's TELLING us?" Grandma Ellie said bitterly. She gave Carlee an evil look while pressing her lips with a mean face.

"So, Carlee, you know this boy?" Devon was fearful and confused.

"More like man, but I'll shut up," Carlee rolled her eyes.

"What else happened, Honey?" Devon asked gently.

"Well, I went to his house the next day..."

"Damn it," Grandma Ellie said shaking her head.

"Go ahead honey," Devon said to Storia looking at his mother trying not to cry.

"...from school with Scott and Tommy let us check out the backyard. Then he asked us if we would help him build a mini skateboard ramp to surprise his niece and nephews. He asked us if we saw the movie *Loot*. When we answered no, he took us to see it. He bought my friend Jeff cleats..."

"Samantha's son, Jeff?" Devon asked.

"Yes...he bought them for football practice and he bought Scott gym shoes and clothes for school. He got my nails done and bought me two necklaces and a ring and all of our tickets to homecoming," Storia said proudly.

"Storia, he has always been (Carlee used air quotes) friendly towards you. How did you get pregnant? Which one is your child's father Jeff or Scott? Thomas was letting you have sex in his house, huh?" Carlee asked rudely.

"SHUT UP!!!! PLEASE Pumpkin," Devon said wringing his hands.

"Tommy told me while we were talking on the phone...," Storia started.

"Talking on the phone," Carlee interrupted.

"Yeah, Carlee, he bought me a phone. Well, we only spoke a few times because I lost the phone somewhere; I can't even remember. Tommy told me he really liked hanging out with my friends and me, but he'd like to just do some nice things for me. He said he really liked seeing my face light up when he gave me things. He told me he would like to show me some things that I could tell my friends about and make them jealous," Storia explained.

"Oh god," Grandma Ellie said holding her head.

"I told him he was the father I never had and he told me he wanted to be my friend and better than a father because he could never leave me like you did daddy. He told me only a fool wouldn't be around for someone as beautiful as me," Storia said looking at her father.

"So how does all of this result in a pregnancy for god's sake," Carlee asked pissed. "Tell us Storia."

"Well, if you must know. I didn't know I was going to get pregnant. Because I – he – I told him - - Tommy told me he wanted to show me how much he loved being around me and he fell to his knees and asked me if he could show me, and he kept asking and saying please so I said yes. So, one day, he got this box from the side of the couch, and he handed it to me. I opened it, and it was the coat and outfit I was looking at with my friends at the mall. After that, he put his mouth on my clothes down there, and he kept doing it. He did it until I had a feeling that came over me that felt so different that I started to move too. Then it stopped, and he asked did I see how love felt and even though I didn't say anything, he said he would show me one more time, but he didn't that day. He said he had to go to his nephew's game, so I left," Storia said as a matter of fact.

"Why didn't you tell somebody what happened Storia?" Carlee asked. Grandma Ellie and Devon looked on devastated.

"Because nothing happened... I didn't take off my clothes," Storia said without realizing.

"You took something off; you're pregnant, dummy," Carlee proclaimed.

"Daddy, Carlee called me a dummy," Storia said sounded like an average 15 year old for a moment.

"Carlee, Pumpkin, don't call names," Devon tried to hold back his tears as he looked at his mother. It was too much for him to handle mentally.

"So did anything else happen dear," Grandma Ellie asked calmly.

"We need to call the police," Carlee said.

"For what? Do you see something out the window, Carlee?" Storia asked.

"Apple, what else happened?" Devon asked.

"Well, I kept going over there with my friends and we got to go everywhere we wanted to go. Then when he dropped everyone off, he would ask me if I had a good time and for a few months it would be like this, us just hanging out. When I turned 15, a few months ago, he threw this big birthday party for me at Nouns & Verbs. It was great. There are so many books in that place. When he was about to drive me home, I told him I had to stop at his house and grab my book bag. So, he took me there. Once we got into the house, I grabbed my book bag and headed for the door. He grabbed my arm, and he told me I was beautiful. He told me he loved me and asked if I wanted him to show me how much. I didn't know what to say when he dropped to his knees and put his mouth there. I mean, I still had on my clothes. But, after that, he said he wanted to show me something else that was the same but different. So, he pulled my pants down, and he put his mouth down there, and then he sat me on the couch and put his mouth down there again. Then he told me to put my hands on his head, and I did, and I had that feeling again. Then he took me home," Storia said telling what happened as though it was nothing.

Drawing complete silence from the room Storia continued to tell her family what happened.

"The next day I went back over to his house before school, and he did it again. By Friday, I had been over there every day. That Friday after school, I went over to his house, and he asked me if I loved him, and I said no, but I told him I really liked the way he made me feel, and he said he would like to feel the same way. So, I said okay, but I really didn't know what he was talking about, you know. I just wanted the feeling. He said that we could feel that way together, so he took me to his room, and he took my clothes off and then his, and he did it again with his mouth. Then he put his downstairs into my mouth, and he said he wanted to put it down there on me. He said it would feel better. So, he did, but it didn't. Then it did. I stayed there, and we kept doing the mouth and the down there thing. Then he took me home and asked if I would come over Monday and when I got out of school, we went to dinner and a movie. Then while we were driving home, he stopped over, and we did the mouth thing. Then he told me he would take care of me once we got to his house."

"ENOUGH are you kidding me?" Devon shouted interrupting Storia as she told this disastrous story without understanding what happened to her.

"No, she is not. This is what happened," Grandma Ellie said wiping the tears from her eyes. "Where does he live sweetheart," Grandma Ellie asked.

"Well, that's the thing, grandma. I wasn't having my period, so I told my friend Scott, and he told me to get money from Tommy. So, I did. When I took the money to Scott, he took me to the pharmacy, and we got a test thing in a box. Scott's boyfriend told me to pee on it, and I did, and it said yes with a smiley face. Then, my friend, Danny told me I was pregnant and that I needed to tell Tommy so he could give me some money so I could get rid of it," Storia explained.

"They didn't tell you to tell your mother or your sister, Storia? You didn't think to tell any of us," Carlee asked.

"No. Tommy told me he would take care of me and he was you know. When I went to his house though, he told me not to come to his house anymore. He told me he wasn't the one who got me pregnant and he called me all sorts of names," Storia said as she burst out in tears. "He told me to forget him and where he lived. I was so upset grandma I just jumped on my bike and took off, and I think that is when the car hit me. That's all I remember," Storia said crying uncontrollably.

"That damn bastard, I'm calling the police," Grandma Ellie said digging through her purse for her phone.

"I'll be back," Carlee said storming out of the room.

"Carlee," Devon called going after her.

"Storia, Baby Cakes... why didn't you tell someone what was going on?" Grandma Ellie asked.

"Well there was no one to tell and grandma, I really liked what he was doing, I wanted him to do it," Storia answered.

"He was too old to be with you Storia," Grandma Ellie explained.

"Grandma he said he would take care of me and he was for a long time," Storia said crying.

"Sweetheart, he took advantage of you. You supplied him a house for his dick for a long time. Your mouth and vagina became where he placed his penis, honey. That is what a dick house is; a mouth and or a vagina, and there are other places, but that is not important. Now that a baby is on board, he is in deep trouble. I'll see to that. It turns out this baby is a blessing in disguise because we would have never known about your daily orgasm fix at the hands of this grown ass man had it not been for this baby," Grandma Ellie explained sarcastically.

"What's an orgasm?" Storia asked.

"It is that feeling you experienced over and over again damn it," Grandma Ellie retorted.

CHAPTER 7

Now that Storia was stable, Devon left the hospital to meet with a real estate agent. He thought about his daughters going to live with his mother, and he didn't like the thought. Devon would have to pick up and move his business to another state. He didn't think his company was strong enough to do that at this time, so his only alternative was to purchase a house for the girls in town. He had looked at several houses. He didn't realize the number of vacant homes there was in the city. The thought of purchasing a home where it appeared people were moving out drew uncertainty for him and renting was even more unreasonable. Devon was encouraged about the investment and looked forward to the house hunt.

Devon explained to the agent what he didn't want again after looking at several homes all possessing the things he said he didn't want. After looking at seven more homes, he hired another real estate agent and fired the one he was working with immediately. Devon received a call from the new agent asking to meet him. The new agent emailed him a list of homes five in total. Devon left the hospital having been told by the doctor that Storia wouldn't be discharged for another two weeks to ensure she could walk and control her new baby weight. The doctor was concerned about Storia's ankle that wasn't healing the way he thought it would. The doctor told Devon Storia had x-rays scheduled for the day and she would go to see Dr. Patterson followed by physical therapy. He suggested Devon not come back until later that evening.

Devon met with the new real estate agent at the showing appointment. He was impressed. The house had many attributes Devon was looking for, but the neighborhood wasn't entirely to his liking. The second house was better than the first, but it was the third home he fell in love with and wanted to make an offer but was convinced by his agent to look at the other two before deciding. Devon went to the fourth house and wasn't impressed as he was now comparing it to the homes he saw before. The fifth house was beautiful but overpriced. He asked the agent to find out if the owner would consider reducing the price on the home. Meanwhile, he placed an offer on the third house. The agent spoke with the seller's agent while on the way to the office with Devon. The agent discovered the seller would consider whatever offer made. Devon didn't want to make an offer at the risk of having two accepted proposals, but he submitted an offer for the fifth house for the same amount as the third. He suspected the owner wouldn't come down far enough and he was right. The owners of the third home accepted another offer, so, Devon was back to the drawing board.

The new agent contacted Devon with another five houses and a condominium this time. Devon was discouraged and wasn't interested in seeing more homes. His agent's assistant, Lucy, who would be joining them on the house hunt, convinced him. Lucy assured Devon he would like the selected homes. Devon agreed to meet them at the first house. When Devon arrived, he could not take his eyes off Lucy. She was tall. She had long dark hair and green eyes. Lucy wore a cute skirt and blazer with one of those girly flirty blouses sheer but covered up the essential parts. Devon wasn't sure why he felt so drawn to her. Lucy opened the door while Devon and the new agent walked the perimeter of the house. Devon liked the backyard but was concerned about the pond. He didn't want the additional expense of maintaining it throughout the year. The inside was okay but dated. As he went room to room, he kept bumping into Lucy as though she were doing it on purpose. The condo would have been the next stop, but he was not interested, so they took that one off of the list. The next house was too close to an area he didn't want to be near so, they were off to the fourth home. As they arrived, the new agent received a call. It was the selling agent for the fifth house from two days ago. The owner wanted to revisit the offer Devon made and wanted to know if Devon was still interested. Devon would negotiate, but he told his agent to make him wait. Devon's new agent told the seller's agent he would consult with his client and let him know.

They went on to the last house on the list. Devon immediately thought it would be right for the girls and his mother if she wanted to move in. He looked around and noticed a lot going on in the house. It had several substantial updates but was priced low. He asked the agent why the house was still on the market because it was as far as he could see a significant looking house but the agent wasn't sure. The agent said it was a short sale and the owners were trying to sell it before it went into foreclosure. Devon wasn't sure what that meant, but he knew he didn't have time to deal with an owner and the mortgage company, so they left the house and went on their way to a home Lucy found to replace the condo. It took longer than Devon expected to get to the final house. He calculated the drive time and was not sure if it would be something he would want to do daily; going back and forth to the office at that distance would put too much wear on Devon and his car, he thought. Devon noticed right away that the landscape was gorgeous. The house was huge. The neighbor's lawns were immaculate, and there was a tree formation all the way down the block. He got out of the car and took in a deep breath through his nose. He stood there and looked to be amazed. Lucy began a random conversation with him, and he didn't know what to say in response, so he just asked her to show him around.

After Lucy showed him the house, Devon was so taken he wanted to make an offer but pursued negotiations with the seller of the other home closer commute wise, so Lucy scheduled a showing. Once they arrived, Devon took pictures of the house as he walked through again on his own. The new agent met him upstairs in one of the bedrooms and apologized for Lucy flirting. Devon confessed that he did not realize she was flirting and assured him there was no need for the apology. The two men carried on through the upstairs of the home as Devon took more pictures with his phone. Though he didn't realize Lucy was flirting, he thought to himself to ask her out because he was attracted to her. Devon thought to wait until they were in a different setting. He did not want to mix the business of him finding a home with the personal aspect of the two dating. Devon wanted to complete the process of finding a home for his girls. He did not want his attraction to Lucy and possibly dating her to interfere.

After looking at the house for the second time, Devon made an offer. He settled on the house pretty far from his regular life. Devon thought the fifth home from the second list had more substance, style, and the price was better than the fifth house from the first group of homes. He did not want to go through the same thing he went through with the other owner again. Two days later after negotiating back and forth, Devon's offer was accepted. He immediately hired an inspector who inspected the house and found a few things Devon deemed a deal breaker if the owner didn't agree to fix. However, Devon contacted his agent and had him inquire about the other house. The other house, fifth on the list, was still available, but there was no need to submit an offer because the owner of the house Devon had an offer on agreed to fix the items from the inspection and they moved forward with the deal. On the day of close, Devon went to the bank to get a cashier's check for the amount he needed at closing. Devon received a call from Lucy, a pleasant but shocking surprise since they hadn't seen or spoken to one another since the showings. She wanted to remind him of the closing as if he would forget something like that Devon thought. The call was about something else, but Devon decided not to pursue it, he instead thanked her for the call, and just as he was about to hang up, Lucy asked him out.

Devon signed the mortgage contract for the house and received the keys. He was super excited and could not wait to share his excitement with the girls. Walking out of the closing, Devon decided to drive to his new home. He was bothered by the drive. The traffic wasn't bad, but it was far from everything that used to be close. Devon placed a call to his office. He spoke to his receptionist about setting up a conference call for his staff. Consumed by the drive, Devon knew he wouldn't go to the office much. It was also at that time he realized that one of the spaces in the new home would house his home office, and he wanted to run it by his staff. He had to decide if he wanted to have his team at his house every day.

A representative for the cleaning company Devon called arrived shortly after Devon. He let them into the house so they could access the cost of cleaning the house. His neighbor greeted him and welcomed him to the neighborhood. Devon spoke to the neighbor until the housekeeper came out to share her assessment. He shook the neighbor's hand and then started talking to the cleaning rep as she was coming out of the home. They agreed on a price and soon after, two representatives from the cleaning company arrived and cleaned the house. Devon informed them he would be leaving for a while and instructed them to pull the door shut if he wasn't back by the time they finished. Devon went to his place and looked around. He wasn't happy about having to move. He thought about all of the things he would need for the girls and his mother if she wanted to stay and then he thought about the baby and Lucy. Devon called Lucy. The two scheduled a day to meet. After the call, Devon thought about his plans to marry. He wasn't sure if marriage with the woman he chose was what he wanted any more. Lucy was on his mind more than he ever wanted. All Devon wanted to do was tell Lucy about the girls and the baby to see her reaction and take it from there. He thought about Lucy in ways he didn't understand. It was too soon, but Devon couldn't stop thinking about her in a domestic capacity. What was weird to him as he had this profound revelation is he never thought about the one that he had asked to marry him. Devon never thought about her having his children and never even seen himself marrying her. He thought it was rather strange to have known Cynthia for so long yet never once looked at her as a wife and mother of his children only to have just met Lucy and could see his whole life in her beautiful green eyes. Devon shrugged his shoulders and thought nothing else about it as he locked the door and made his way back to the hospital.

The next day, Devon went to get Lucy to take her to the new house. He let the cleaning reps in and the contractors, the furniture deliverymen and his company's staff who had come over to see if they could set up one room for Devon's home office. Lucy turned out to be very helpful Devon thought so while he serviced his clients, he left Lucy to do the rest. Devon's meetings were fantastic. He concentrated entirely on each without interruption. He was delighted as he got into the car and put on his seatbelt. Driving, Devon anticipated a call from Lucy with a work-related question but instead enjoyed his long ride back to his house. He did not receive one call from Lucy. There was not one question asking what he liked, what he thought or that she needed his input. Devon was pleased but thought he may be moving too fast with Lucy.

Listening to his messages, Devon learned Storia's discharge date, his mother moving in with him for a while to help with the girls; Lucy was leaving the new house. She would return the next day to let the contractors and staff members in, and unfortunately, Cynthia was on the warpath. Devon contacted Lucy to follow up on the progress. Lucy told him one of the bedrooms was set up, but the contractors were still working in the kitchen and lower level bathroom. He learned that the staff had chosen the room by the sunroom in the back and were setting up things nicely. Lucy told Devon she ordered a desk and chair for his new office and she helped the receptionist get set up so they could communicate now that Devon would no longer be in the office physically. Lucy then asked Devon if he wanted to keep the office space. She explained that she could find a building closer to the new home that could be used to meet his clients instead of meeting with them in his home. Lucy also suggested that he could rent space for a day when he needed to meet with clients to eliminate having to pay a monthly leasing fee for a building that no longer suited his needs. Devon was smitten with Lucy. He decided at that moment that it was time to tell her about Cynthia. He was sure now that he wanted to take what they had, whatever it was, to the next level.

#

Devon went to the hospital to visit Storia. She was in good spirits. He called his mother who had returned to her home state and spoke to her while also carrying on a conversation with Carlee who had not left the hospital since Storia arrived except to go to school. Devon chatted a little longer with his mother who informed him she would be departing on the 8:30p flight and would be there by 10p. She wanted to confirm with him he would be at the airport to pick her up when she landed. Devon assured his mother he would be there but did not guarantee it would be him thinking he could send Carlee. Devon concerned about Carlee talked about her being at the hospital and going to school from there. Carlee told him she tried to go to her mom's house and was met with cursing and attempted physical abuse. She said Bill allowed her to get some of her things while her mom was gone with the twins and gave her money for food and personals. Devon shared with Carlee he bought a home for them and let her know that the house would be ready in time for Storia. She gets to leave tomorrow. Carlee was pleased to hear the news and excitedly told her friends about it as she spoke to them until it was time to go pick up her grandmother.

Devon walked out of the hospital room leaving Carlee there talking to her friends on her cell and Storia napping.

He drove over to the bar and grill to meet Lucy for drinks. Devon was sitting on the outside of the building towards the back in a discrete area purposely. As Lucy walked up, he noticed the wind sweeping her dark hair. Now she had on slacks, a blouse, and heels. As she approached, her perfume had beaten her there. It was light and floral, was very fitting for the day as it was sweet and fresh, and went with the type of day taking place. He greeted her. She leaned in to hug him. He returned the jester. He waited for her to sit down, and then followed. The conversation was great. They talked about everything from business to zoos in different states. It was fascinating what she knew. It wasn't about things and more things. It was about art and theater. Traveling and exploring. The conversation ignited him.

Devon explained his situation to Lucy. She looked disappointed but understanding. Lucy welcomed any talk of the girls, but Cynthia was another story. He told her he liked how she handled his business. She expressed how she wanted more than afternoon cocktails and salad. He revealed that he could see their relationship going much further. She described a picture of them being a power couple. He said this, and then she said that and, they kept talking to one another until Devon's phone rang. It was Carlee letting him know she would need the car to go pick up her grandmother. Devon had forgotten about his mother; he realized he lost himself in the moment of Lucy. He told Lucy he had to go. She let him know without hesitation that she was not interested in being the other woman. He assured her that if or when that time came she would be the only woman. She politely let him know she would not wait around waiting for him to decide. He told her he would not do that to her. They gave one another a friendly peck on both cheeks, Lucy left, and Devon paid the bill then departed.

# # #

Devon walked into the hospital room and handed Carlee the keys then instructed her. He called his mother to let her know Carlee was on her way but had to leave a message. Dr. Budding walked in and let Devon know Storia's discharge date had arrived. In the morning, Storia would head home. Dr. Budding followed - up with Devon about Stora's care once discharged. The first thing Dr. Budding addressed was the cast on Storia's leg. She believed that the pregnancy was causing the prolonged healing process. She expressed the need to keep the cast on though it would be a burden. Dr. Budding said that an occupational therapist would come to the house two days a week, as would a physical therapist. She then explained the difference. She voiced her concerned about Storia's emotional state and suggested that Devon consider having Storia see Dr. Analyn or someone who could help her out of the state of denial Storia seemed to be in and address the relationship with the family as a whole. She stressed that if she got word or inclination that the mother was around, she would not hesitate to contact child protective service and involve them. Dr. Budding told Devon that though the girls would be moving with him, she hadn't made up her mind entirely on if she wouldn't get child protective service involved because she was genuinely disturbed about what happened to Storia and how she is reacting to the whole ordeal. Dr. Budding stressed getting the police involved as well as psychological assistance. Devon agreed.

Carlee returned to the hospital without her grandmother. Devon inquired about her whereabouts and Carlee told him she wanted to go to a hotel. Carlee explained to her dad what her grandmother said about being tired and how she needed rest from the trip preparation and the trip itself. Devon was relieved. He called his mother to let her know about Storia. He also told his mother what the doctor said as Storia continued to sleep and Carlee listened.

CHAPTER 8

After the long drive, Devon, his mother and daughters arrived at the new house. Everyone was in awe of the house pulling into the driveway. Devon's mother expressed how proud she was of Devon for committing to the girls by purchasing a home where the girls could grow up and be safe. Devon agreed as he smiled from ear-to-ear. He could not get over how the beautiful landscape and the house itself. He was even surprised at how he found the home and closing so soon. He had it in him, he thought but was saddened by the fact that it took this incident. He couldn't believe it took his crazed ex-wife, one of his kids tucked away in military school, one daughter attention deprived and one nearly six months pregnant because she too is apparently attention deprived before he made his move in the father department. At that moment, he was disgusted with himself.

"Come on Storia. You're taking all day," Carlee called as she raced out of the car and was already in the house.

"Stop yelling at that girl Carlee, you know she is going to be slow," Grandma Ellie said.

"You could have helped me, Carlee," Storia said trying to maneuver the knee scooter to the porch.

"Come on honey," Devon said as he picked his daughter up and took her up the stairs. "I'll bring in your walker in a minute, but Apple I need you to stay off your ankle," he instructed. "You have to learn to balance your weight until they remove the cast next week."

"Ahh, daddy. I wanna see the rest of the house," Storia said pouting as she sat on the edge of the couch.

"Between your ankle and leg, your leg is healed more than your ankle, so try to stay off of your ankle, honey," Grandma Ellie confirmed Devon's instruction.

"The house is certainly big enough Storia. You'll be able to use the knee scooter. I'll bring it in," Carlee said excitedly.

"Thank you," Storia said swing around on the couch trying to take in all that she could from her view.

Devon brought in Storia's wheelchair followed by Carlee with Storia's knee scooter. Carlee helped Storia into the wheelchair and then whirled her around the house both laughing all the way. Grandma Ellie sat in a chair by the window and smiled as she enjoyed the breeze. She watched Devon as he hugged Carlee and thanked her for showing her sister around the house. Grandma Ellie listened to Devon caution Carlee to be careful whirling Storia around the house. He followed his strict instructions with a kiss on the forehead to Carlee and a warm pat on the head to Storia ruffling her hair. After receiving criticism from both girls for messing up Storia's hair, Carlee took her sister to the backyard.

Devon grabbed the lemonade he and his mother ordered from the restaurant and made his way into the living area. He gave his mother her drink and sat in a chair next to hers. They talked and laughed about some lighter subjects before tackling the real elephant in the room. As they discuss the situation with Devon's ex-wife, Jessi, and the molester, Thomas, there was a knock at the door. Devon was surprised as he looked at his phone for messages about a visitor and then assumed it was a neighbor. He was right. His neighbor introduced herself and her children who stood beside her. Devon invited them into the house and introduced the woman and her children to his mother. She had food she had prepared that day. She explained how she thought to bring it over when she saw the young girl in the wheelchair. Devon expressed his gratitude as he took the prepared meal out of the neighbor's hands. He thanked her and assured that he would have his daughter return her Tupperware. She thanked him, and she and her children went on their way.

Devon went to the back to check in on the girls. Storia was leaning on Carlee with ankle up, wobbling as she attempted to walk in her cast. Storia walked a little, and the Carlee turned her around and walked her back to the wheelchair stressing her concern about Storia overdoing it. Devon returned to the chair where he left his mother still enjoying the breeze coming through the window. Devon sat down. He and his mother continued the conversation. Devon looked at his watch. It was 10 minutes to 10a. Lucy pulled up. Devon tried to harness his smile, but it wasn't working as he rushed to the door to let Lucy in before she used her key.

Devon introduced Lucy to his mother. Lucy was delighted to meet her and felt in her mind that Devon was serious about what he said he wanted their relationship to be. Lucy thought Devon could have called her and canceled her trip to the house since he was there now giving her no real opportunity to see what was going on. Devon went to the back of the house as Lucy and Ellie began a conversation. He wanted Carlee to bring Storia in the house so she could prepare for her appointments. Once Carlee came into the house with Storia, she helped her to the bathroom. When they came out of the restroom, Devon introduced them to Lucy. Lucy was pleased to meet them. She explained that she was helping their father with the transition while he was busy with them. They were happy to hear the things Lucy continued saying as to them it proved that their dad was putting them before the things that made him so busy. After Lucy finished talking to the girls, Devon pulled her to the side and spoke to her. Lucy interrupted and went to her bag and pulled out a pad. She apologized and asked Devon to continue. Devon was impressed. He kept giving Lucy instructions on how he wanted her to handle some of his business while he dealt with the appointments Storia had for the week. He explained how he wouldn't put her in that position and before he could finish the rest, Lucy stressed how she would want to meet the therapist if she were in his shoes and she encouraged Devon to ask plenty of questions about Storia's progress. Devon agreed. Lucy left on her way to complete the many tasks Devon gave her.

As Devon walked into the house, he thought to keep the relationship between him and Lucy professional for now, so he called her. When Lucy answered her phone, Devon explained that though he knew she was helping him, he wanted to talk salary with her. Lucy was offended for a moment but thought about what he was saying and agreed with Devon. She would draw a salary for being his assistant and use the back staff entrance instead of the front door. That kept things honest and professional while they were sorting out what wasn't a full-blown relationship. Lucy hung up the phone respecting Devon for thinking of her in that manner since she was taking time away from prospecting to help him. In the meanwhile, Devon instructed Carlee to go to the school and pick up the assignments Storia was missing, and he encouraged her to do the same so she wouldn't fail. Devon had spoken to the principal who was very understanding and had instructed the teachers to provide as much as they could to the girls to ensure their promotions by the end of the year; especially Carlee who was a senior.

Grandma Ellie hobbled towards the kitchen after she finished talking to the staff members in Devon's office putting files together for his next meeting. She was delighted with how the kitchen turned out. She spoke to the contractor as he was completing the final details of the remodel. Storia strolled into the living area on her knee scooter slowly wobbling all the way. She sat on the couch. Devon came into the living area smiling at her as she was trying to adjust herself to the couch. The therapist arrived as scheduled. She worked with Storia for an hour. Devon looked at his watch; it was almost 1p. He figured in his head Storia would be busy until two, his staff would leave at three, Carlee wouldn't return for a few hours, and his mother was conversing with the contractor. As he watched the therapist work with Storia, he answered emails on his phone, asked the therapist questions, and made calls. Devon had not heard from Lucy. Once the therapist left, he took Storia to the guest room. She said she was tired and wanted to lie down. Storia got in the bed and turned on the television. Devon walked into his office and spoke with his staff. They briefed him, synchronized his phone and gave him the paperwork for his upcoming meetings. Soon after, Devon's team left vowing to return the next day.

The contractor was gone, and Carlee was pulling into the driveway to share how she lost the last hour of her life looking for the house. She complained about how she left her cell charging so she couldn't call, and how disturbed she was by the directions received from some flirty old guys to the house. Carlee was happy to be home finally. She went into the living room and crashed on the couch. Grandma Ellie was in what turned out to be her favorite chair by the window. She requested from Devon a rocking chair for her to sit in along with her lazy boy. He debated with her to no avail at which time he conceded promising the chair by the weekend. Carlee asked about Storia learning that Storia was sleep. Carlee went check in on her anyway.

Carlee grabbed the cards off the counter and went to her sister's temporary room. They talked and played cards for two hours. Carlee then helped Storia out of bed and onto her scooter. She walked alongside Storia's broken side wanting to protect her if she stumbled. Carlee and Storia made it to the living area and sat on the couch. It was huge and could probably seat eight to ten people. Carlee gently picked up Storia's legs and swung them over onto the couch. Carlee asked her father what was for dinner. Grandma interrupted the conversation boasting about the meal she prepared. Carlee went to the kitchen and made a plate for her and her sister. She took a standing tray from the side of the counter and wiped it off. Then, Carlee put the stand in front of Storia. She went back into the kitchen and grabbed their plates. Carlee placed Storia's plate on the tray, and then sat at the bottom of Storia's feet, and they ate what their grandmother prepared. Carlee told Storia about the homework she had, and as they conversed back and forth then, there was a knock at the door.

Devon had just gotten off the phone with Lucy, so he knew it wasn't her and hoped that it wasn't another neighbor. He laughed in his head as he headed to the door thinking about the neighbor who brought over the meal. It was a version of tuna casserole Devon never had before by its looks. The girls and his mother tasted it and almost simultaneously spit it out. Their facial expression was like something seen in a comedy hour. It must have been horrible he laughed. Carlee couldn't wait to take the Tupperware back. The neighbor was surprised to see her Tupperware back so quickly. Carlee explained that she transferred it to another vessel... the garbage. Devon thought about the hilarious situation as he headed to the door.

"Who is it?" Devon said as he approached the door.

Whoever it was, it was inaudible to Devon. He opened the door. It was Cynthia. He unlocked the screen door and opened it for her. How did she know where he lived he thought to himself? Devon thought to himself silently about how inconsiderate he must be for not calling Cynthia since postponing the wedding. Cynthia walked in visibly upset but speaking to everyone as though she wasn't. Grandma Ellie, Carlee, and Storia spoke as they kept eating. Devon introduced Cynthia to his mother and his girls. Cynthia spoke as she zoomed in on Storia's belly sticking out clad in maternity attire. Cynthia, with an awkward smile, asked the girls how they were doing then looked at Devon.

"Can I have a word with you dear?" Cynthia asked with a painted on grin.

"Sure. Let's go to the back," Devon replied rubbing his hands down the sides of his pants.

"This is a beautiful home. The rent must be murder," Cynthia inquired. "Years lease?" she asked.

"Uh no, I bought this beauty. It was priced very well too, and the payments are less than what I was paying in rent at the apartment even with insurance and taxes," Devon bragged not quite catching himself in time.

"So, you purchased this house? You purchased this house without including me, huh?" Cynthia asked with her tongue in cheek trying to stay calm.

"Well, yeah, I had to," Devon replied now kicking himself for gloating.

"You had to, huh? So, you didn't have to call me and tell me about it?" Cynthia asked sarcastically.

"Well, I have been so busy with everything. I haven't had time. You have to cut me a break on this one. No one could have foretold the events that have taken place in the last couple of months," Devon explained.

"No, I understand your daughter was in a car accident. I understand you had to postpone the wedding so that you could see about her, but I don't see why their lives have to interfere with my life and the life I am supposed to have with you," Cynthia said with a straight face.

"Are you kidding me? Those are my daughters," Now Devon was the one trying not to get upset.

"So what, they are your daughters. Why does that mean you purchase a house, move them and apparently your mother into the house, and then you move into the house with them? Why does that mean that, Devon?" Cynthia argued.

"It means that because they could not go back to their mother's house. It means that because my mother doesn't live in this state. It means that because my mother is not their mother and they are not her responsibility. I wasn't going to NOT see my girls due to their living situation. I am their father, and it was up to me to secure their living arrangement not put them on my mother. As their father, I'm supposed to take care of them," Devon replied harshly.

"So, you sacrifice our wedding and our lives together for an arrangement that we could have talked about and come up with a civil solution that would have worked out for all of us?" Cynthia questioned.

"Well, if that is how you see it, yeah," Devon said callously.

Cynthia slapped Devon, cried, and yelled.

"You bastard! I gave up everything for what you said we had!

"I didn't ask you to do that and how was I to know this was going to happen?" Devon said with little compassion.

"Okay it happened but does that mean you throw everything we have away just to cater solely to it?" Cynthia asked. She wanted Devon to acknowledge he hurt her.

"I want you to be a part of my life, but I won't choose between you and my kids, and if you loved me, you wouldn't require that of me. I won't lose them again. Not for you, anyone, or anything," Devon said shaking his head and turning away from Cynthia.

"How dare you waste my time, propose to me, and then try to suggest I'm making you choose. If you want out say it, say so," Cynthia demanded.

"So – Cynthia – so," Devon said looking Cynthia in her eyes without blinking or hesitation.

"What? Just like that?" Cynthia yelled following Devon as he headed for the door.

"Are you are about to do this? Look, my ex-wife bailed on my girls. A man my age repeatedly raped and impregnated my daughter. Since Storia's incident, we, for certain, have deprived Carlee of love, affection, and attention, yet she has taken care of her sister since day zero. If you don't understand why I need to be here for my girls, then you have serious issues beyond anything that is reasonable. Do you understand how fucked up the nature of this situation?" Devon was interrupted.

"Daddy, I wasn't raped," Storia interrupted still in denial about what happened to her.

"It's messing me up inside Cynthia. Do you not understand that? Can you not see past what you want? Those are my daughters. If you had kids with me and something like this god-forbid happened to one of them wouldn't you want me to react just the same?" Devon tried to reason with Cynthia. "Go if you want but if you stay, stay because you love me and want to make a difference in me and my girl's lives and not for your agenda. If your needs are all you care about, let's end it now because I am not going to turn my back on my girls to fulfill them," Devon secretly wanted Cynthia to end their relationship.

"You are an asshole. You think because you've bought this house and moved those misfits in you are grand? Do you think you deserve the father of the year award?" Cynthia yelled.

"Goodbye Cynthia," Devon shook and dropped his head.

"You think you can come into my life, waste my time and energy with your lies, then tell me to suck it up and accept this crap you're shoveling? You think you can just excuse me out of your life like the last two years never happened?" Cynthia screamed hysterically.

"What do you want from me?" Devon yelled then stopped himself.

"I want the house – THIS house! I want the special attention because I'm carrying your child! I want you to escort me as your WIFE to the doctor's office so we can smile and cry over our first sonogram and heartbeat. I want our family to join us for birthdays and Christmas' and other holidays. You promised me this, and now it's goodbye Cynthia? Take it or leave it, Cynthia? Am I not fulfilling your needs, Cynthia? Why am I the one getting the short end of this because your daughter liked getting fuc...?" Carlee suddenly interrupted.

"Now wait a minute Miss Girl! I know you're not about to say what I think you're about to say! I know what you're trying to insinuate and how dare you!" Carlee jumped off the couch and walked over to Cynthia angrily.

"This is what I'm talking about with your girls. Your girls have no respect, and you want me to put up with this?" Cynthia screamed.

"BITCH!!!" Carlee screamed over Devon's shoulder. Devon tried to escort her back to the couch, but Carlee jumped over the sofa, ran over to Cynthia, and they started fighting.

"Stop it! Stop it!" Storia cried as Devon tried to get between them.

"Calm down," Grandma Ellie said pulling Storia over to her chest.

"Break it up! Carlee! Stop!" Devon yelled trying to separate Cynthia and Carlee taking a punch to the nose.

Devon finally gets a small break between the two, and it is enough to push Cynthia back. As he does, Carlee jumps up and hits Cynthia in the eye. Cynthia grabs her eye and bends over then with full force charges Devon to get at Carlee.

Doorbell rings –

While Devon tried to keep Cynthia and Carlee apart, he takes much of the blows meant for the other until he gets hit in the testicles. Devon goes down in pain and Cynthia and Carlee go at each other breaking the glasses and plates that sat on the table that also broke when Carlee pushed Cynthia down on it. Grandma Ellie made her way to the door and asked for the visitor for an announcement before she opened the door. With Storia trying to get up from the couch, Cynthia and Carlee fighting like two people in a ring and Devon rocking back and forth in pain across the floor, Grandma Ellie could not hear so she opened the door. It was the police.

"We've had several calls about a disturbance. What's going on in there?" the officer said flashing his light in on the fight.

Grandma Ellie unlocked the screen door and allowed the officers into the home. The officers rush to the fight and cuff Cynthia and Carlee then help Devon up from the floor. Devon still bent over made his way over to the couch and lay down with his hands between his legs.

"I'll tell you what's going on! I'll tell you what's going on!" Cynthia yelled.

"I want this bitch out of my house!" Carlee screamed.

"This isn't your house you stupid whore!"

"Oh, on the contrary, bitch! It's why you're mad. My father bought this house for my sister and me - NOT you."

"Calm down both of you. Whose house is this?" the officer asked.

"This is my house," Devon answered breathing heavily.

"Do you own it with this woman? What's your name ma'am?" the officer asked trying to figure out what was going on.

"No," Devon responded coughing.

"Cynthia Madison."

"Okay, Ms?" asked the officer.

"Yes," Cynthia answered.

"Okay, Ms. Madison. You cannot be here causing conflict in someone else's home. Now what I observed was mutual combat, but if one of you wants to press charges you can," the officer stated.

"You don't understand," Cynthia said crying. "He asked me to marry him. He promised me we would be together. We made plans then his daughter goes out and gets pregnant by some child molester, and he tells me the plans we made mean dick."

"Your daughter is pregnant by a child molester?" the officer asked looking at Devon.

"Is that all you heard?" Cynthia asked.

"Yes," Devon said frowning in response to the pain he is still feeling.

"Are the police involved?" the police questioned.

"No," Devon answered.

"Is that all you heard?" Cynthia asked again.

"Quiet ma'am," the officer said looking at Cynthia intensely.

"We were waiting for the baby to arrive so we'd have proof," Devon responded embarrassed.

"Is your daughter saying she had a sexual encounter or encounters with this guy?" the officer asked writing on his tablet.

"Well, yes and please don't ask her because she goes into great detail that is beyond disturbing," Devon said looking away from the officer.

That's your proof. What's this person's name?" the officer inquired.

"Thomas Kowalski," Devon answered.

"Is that what your daughter said?" the officer looked over at Storia.

"She calls him Tommy. In a later conversation, she told us his name," Grandma Ellie answered.

"Do you know his address?" the officer questioned.

"Storia - Apple. What's Tommy's address?" Devon asked looking at Cynthia still in handcuffs.

"I don't know daddy. I only know how to get there. Why?" Storia asked from the other room.

"No reason Apple. Could you show me where on our way to the doctor's appointment tomorrow?"

"Sure daddy. Maybe he had a change of heart," Storia said innocently.

"How old is she?" the officer asked puzzled.

"She's 15. She has been 15 for all of six months," Devon said bitterly.

"Whoa. It sounds like this guy screwed around with your daughter's head," the officer said sadly.

"Yeah, in a major way. I want to beat the crap out of the guy, but I just can't afford to go to jail. She needs me," Devon was pissed.

"Okay. Here is my card. I'll search for the name once I get in the car, but once you have his address, contact me," the officer said firmly as he removed the cuffs from Carlee's wrist.

"Okay," Devon said taking the card from the officer's hand.

"Ma'am you're going to have to vacate the premises," the other officer said as the first officer went to look up the name.

"I don't believe this! This situation is such bullshit!" Cynthia argued.

"Ma'am do you have any possessions here?" the second officer asked.

"No!" Carlee, Grandma Ellie, and Devon replied at the same time.

Cynthia rolled her eyes as the officer took her by the arm to her car; onlookers from the neighborhood watched. Cynthia cried.

"What a day," Grandma Ellie said as she watched the officer take the cuffs off Cynthia and watched her get in her car.

"You know Carlee, you have a real potty mouth," Devon fussed.

"Dad, you saw how she was acting," Carlee explained.

"Regardless, Carlee. You have to learn how to curve your temper," Devon said calmly.

"Yes sir," Carlee dragged.

"Storia," Devon called.

"I'll go check on her," Carlee said grabbing her sweater.

"While you're in there, wash your face. It's brutal," Devon said looking at his daughter.

Storia came wobbling in walking on the heel of her cast with the other leg resting on her orthopedic scooter. Devon touched Storia's face as he watched her struggling to make it in from the restroom. Storia headed for her temporary bedroom. He kissed her on the forehead and told her she did a good job. Devon expressed to his mother how he couldn't wait until tomorrow. He would finally have the address. Grandma Ellie made her way to the bedroom adjacent Storia's. Carlee came in from the bathroom having washed her face and helped Storia the rest of the way into the bedroom. Carlee helped Storia into her nightclothes and the bed. When Carlee finished assisting Storia, she peeked into her grandmother's room and said goodnight. Carlee continued on her way through the family room. She kissed her father and went upstairs to her bedroom.

Well rested, the next morning, Carlee stares at the ceiling smiling and rejoicing as she looked around the room. Her dad attempted to make her room delightful. The walls were the color of bubble gum and the furniture like the stuff you see in movies where the princess ends up after going through a life-changing struggle. Carlee rolled to her side and thought about the things she had to do; then she jumped up. "Storia," she said aloud as she ran to her closet and grabbed the first thing on the hanger. Carlee ran with clothes in hand to the bathroom to take a shower. She shook the water from her hair, dressed and ran downstairs to the guest room.

"Storia, are you awake?" Carlee asked as she knocked and opened the door.

"I am now," Storia said in a haze.

"How are you feeling this morning?" Carlee asked concerned.

"I am okay, I guess," Storia answered seeming grumpy.

"Well, let me help you up," Carlee walked from the closet with a dress in her hands. "We have to go to the mall to get some clothes for you. This dress is probably going to be a bit tight," Carlee placed the clothes on the bed and helped Storia up.

"Yeah, my clothes are too small now, dang', Storia hobbled to the bathroom.

"You're going to be fine Stor. We are in this together. I will not leave your side. You believe me don't you?" Carlee shook her head to avoid the tears from falling.

"I do believe you, but I don't want you to spend your life fussing over me. I got myself into this mess. I am ashamed. I don't know what I am going to do with a baby without its father Carlee," Storia had her head down looking up to notice Carlee pulling a plastic garbage bag out of her pocket.

"Sit here Storia. Listen, I know that no one can say anything to you about this Tommy guy, but Storia, he is damn lousy news. Were you thinking about having sex before seeing this guy again that is dad's age? (Storia shook her head) I don't want to upset you, but this shouldn't be happening at all to you, Storie. Try not to worry too much about it. You have us - me, dad, grandma, maybe Bevie, and maybe Soda. We are going to see you through this obstacle," Carlee tried to comfort her little sister without letting on how pissed she was about the overall situation.

# # #

The morning was beautiful. The birds were singing and chirping with one another. Grandma Ellie opened the window to a pleasant breeze, squirrels chasing one another and neighbors across the way heading out of their homes. Devon walked out of the house as Grandma Ellie shut the door behind him. He told Carlee to open the door to the SUV while he picked Storia up, walked her down the stairs to the SUV, and placed her in the seat then he pulled the seatbelt across her chest. Carlee got in the back, and the three started their journey down Johnson Boulevard.

Thirty minutes later, they arrived on Planning Street.

"Daddy, if you turn down this street, it's the only green and white house on the block. It has a cool skateboard ramp from the front to the back; the neighbors hate it," Storia recalled the memory as though it was yesterday.

"This street is called Grey Purse Drive, huh? Write that down Pumpkin," Devon requested of Carlee.

"Already done dad. Where's the house Storia?" Carlee grilled.

"That one right there," Storia pointed.

"11912," Devon called out as he parked in front of the house and got out.

"Got it," Carlee wrote the numbers in front of the street name. "No one's there," Carlee noticed.

"What do you mean?" Storia asked.

"The place is empty honey. See the paper on the windows?" Devon replied as he walked up the stairs and looked into the windows of the vacant home.

"What do you mean?" Storia said anxiously.

"He moved out Apple," Devon said concerned.

"What?" Storia cried out hysterically.

Devon walked back to the SUV, handed the officer's card to Carlee, and asked her to call and leave their information with a phone number and the address for Thomas Kowalski. Carlee complied as Devon went to look in the mailbox. He removed the mail. "Let it be a forwarding address on this letter," Devon thought to himself as he flipped through the mail noticing one with a yellow sticker.

"What you got?" Carlee yelled just hanging up from speaking with the officer.

"Oh, I don't know yet. I have what looks like a credit card statement and another bill of some kind," Devon said opening the credit card statement.

"The police are on the way," Carlee said getting back into the SUV.

"Did you all make him move?" Storia yelled.

"No Storia. No one said anything to him. We didn't know until you just showed us where he lived," Carlee tried to reason with Storia.

"Where is he daddy?" Storia asked yelling out to her father making his way up the stairs to look through the cracks in the window that the brown paper didn't cover. It was empty inside. He could see no furniture or anything that resembled activity, so Devon walked back to the vehicle.

"Where is he daddy?" Storia asked again.

"That's a good question Apple," Devon stuck his face in the driver's side window.

"Hello?" Carlee answered her phone.

Devon comforted Storia as he waited for the police. Once the police arrived, they ask him a few more questions then told him to go home. Devon got into his SUV and looked at Storia who could not take her eyes off the house. Storia asked if the officers would discover what happened to Tommy and Devon replied saying he hoped the police find him soon. Devon drove home; both girls fell asleep on the way. When they arrived at the house, Carlee jumped out with Devon and opened the passenger door. Devon lifted Storia out of the vehicle while Carlee ran on the porch and rang the doorbell. Grandma Ellie opened the door, and they all went into the house. Carlee went to the guest room with Storia, and they fell asleep while Devon sat in the family room with his mother telling her what happened.

Devon was furious at the turn of events. Grandma Ellie spoke soothingly to Devon. She hoped he would calm down, but it didn't help until Devon's phone rang. Grandma Ellie walked towards the kitchen as Devon answered his phone. He looked at his caller ID to see it was Lucy. Grandma Ellie prepared something for lunch and started dinner. She used the time she spent cutting onions to cry. She was devastated but felt the need to be strong for her son and granddaughters. Devon talked to Lucy for hours about everything including her tasks for the next day. Lucy told Devon about the outcomes of the business she handled for him that day. Devon responded as best he could, but Lucy sensed something was wrong and asked him how was his day and if he wanted to talk about it. At first, Devon rejected the offer citing that it would not be fair to her but Lucy insisted, and Devon unloaded all of the problems he withheld initially. Lucy handled it like a pro. She was understanding, encouraging, sweet, sincere, and honest as she responded to Devon. Devon couldn't believe how sensitive and accommodating Lucy was to his needs even as he spoke about Cynthia. She recommended he get some rest. Devon agreed. Lucy told Devon she would stop by in the morning to meet with the staff and brief them on the upcoming changes. Devon voiced his appreciation. The two said their goodnights and ended the call. Devon took a shower then had dinner with his mother.

#

The next day was Storia's appointment. Devon was nervous but optimistic. This date would be the first one about the baby since Storia got out of the hospital. Grandma Ellie cooked an excellent breakfast. Everyone ate, and Carlee rushed to the SUV to open the door for Grandma Ellie and Storia. Grandma Ellie got in first. This time she sat in the front seat. Carlee closed the door then ran on the porch. She took the house keys from her father and locked the door while Devon picked up Storia and walked her to the vehicle helping her with her seatbelt. Carlee checked the doorknob to make sure the door was secured. She locked the screen door, ran off the porch, and jumped into the SUV.

"Hello," Carlee answered her phone as she got into the vehicle without looking to see who was calling. "No. I'm on my way to an appointment. What's going on with you? She said to the caller. "Who told you that?" Carlee was got upset by what she heard. "Oh really?" Carlee asked sarcastically. "My sister is none of your business, and as a friend, I would like it if you told those other rumor spreaders the same," Carlee said glaring out of the window of the SUV. "Well, I don't have anything else to say," Carlee yelled at the caller. "Well you tell Scott I said he might as well come all the way out since he's acting like a bitch!" Carlee shouted hanging up on the caller.

"You know dad. I know you didn't want to uproot us, but I think that you should have. We need new schools. Maybe a new area while we're at it even though I know we just moved in. Florida is always beautiful," Carlee said disgusted by the telephone conversation she had.

"We're not moving to Florida," Devon looked at his mother then into the rearview mirror.

"Well, it's not like you're gonna work shit out with Cynthia after that stunt!" Carlee said with no remorse.

"Carlee, you're grounded!" Devon said firmly.

"For what?" Carlee asked.

"Because I told you and have been telling you to watch your mouth and I'm fed up," Devon said as he looked in the rearview mirror.

"Well, dad you really can't after four or five years step in, and parent like you've been here all along," Carlee said aggravated.

"Don't give me that Carlee. You cannot excuse your behavior by my actions or the actions of your mother. You have to choose right from wrong Carlee. These are my rules: respect the house and each other, school Monday through Friday, no skipping, no cursing, and you complete homework and chores before performing any extracurricular activity. Now, I've called in a housekeeper to help with the house while Storia is in the casts since you have been helping her so faithfully and diligently. If you have a problem with the rules, Carlee, then we should re-evaluate your living arrangement. Consequences for breaking the rules – any of them are grounds for punishment, and that means no phone or internet and no outside activities for a week," Devon explained to Carlee.

"A week dad, come on. It was one word," Carlee said as she tried to negotiate.

"No, it was several words. That one word was the straw that broke the camel's back," Devon rebutted.

"What Camel?" Carlee asked rebelliously.

"Never your mind. You're grounded! One week. Understand?" Devon instructed Carlee.

"Yes dad, Uggggg!!!" Carlee said with frustration.

"Want to make it two?" Devon asked.

"No," Carlee said quickly.

"Then straighten it up, young lady!" Grandma Ellie said getting into the situation.

"Yes ma'am," Carlee said to her grandmother. "Military Madness, dad. I'm 17. I'm too old for a punishment," Carlee added.

"No you're not," Devon debated.

"Dad, yes I am," Carlee continued.

"Why don't we try two?" Grandma suggested.

"No, no, no. I'll take the week," Carlee said reluctantly giving Storia the evil eye for laughing.

CHAPTER 9

Devon received a call from the officer working on his daughter's case. The officer was upset and eager to find Kowalski. He was concerned about some things, which were the reason he was calling, and though he did not want to be rude, the officer had to resolve the things he was concerned about with Devon.

"Did you want to press charges Mr. DeLuca?" the officer asked negatively.

"Damn right I do. Are you kidding? Of course, I want to press charges," Devon replied questioning the question.

"The reason I ask, well, (pause) well, had we not come out for that disturbance you had at your house, we would have never known this awful thing happened to your little girl," the officer tried not to be too disrespectful. "How far along in the pregnancy is your daughter, Mr. DeLuca."

"Listen I understand, but it is embarrassing when your little girl is expressing clearly and naively that this monster did not rape her and that she kept going over to the S.O.B's house for more. She's 36 weeks," Devon stated adjusting his throat as he could hear it cracking with emotions that overwhelmed him.

"Mr. DeLuca, your daughter is human. She is young, but it doesn't mean because she is young, she doesn't have feelings sexually, even though it is wrong. She was responding to the stimulation, not the pervert administering those feelings. These guys practice on many children. Your daughter is not the first one he has done this too, so there is no need for you to be embarrassed. It is about communicating with the child. When you make children aware of these types of people and the fact that they are out here, in more cases than none, they don't fall for the grooming. He played on her emotion because he watched her and knew she was vulnerable. He spotted her weakness, and I don't know how this is going to sound to you, but apparently, he liked her because Mr. DeLuca, the guy we're looking for is a child murderer. He kills his victims after he finishes with them. So, while we will question him about this situation with your daughter, our main focus is busting his ass for these murders," the officer explained.

"He repeatedly raped my daughter. What do you mean by the question? Question him about what? He did it!" Devon said acting as though he did not hear what the officer said.

"Sir, we're always in need of a confession. It takes the strain off having to put your daughter or kids like her on the stand. And, by the way, she is not saying he raped her which becomes a 'she told me she was 18' case and he is possibly out the door," the officer said calmly.

"Are you crazy? This shit started when she was 13. He started mouthing her at 14 and penetrating at 15. He groomed her good. He catered to her and her friends and made them feel comfortable. Then he went in for the conquest," Devon said yelling into the phone.

"I would appreciate a confession over a girl telling the jury she liked the feeling she got from this alleged pedophile. How old did your daughter tell him she was? This guy is a murderer Mr. DeLuca. I'd like to bring him in on the rape charge, ask him some questions, and grab his DNA. I want to nail his ass for the murders so that he can live his life on death row and not just get time for your daughter's rape then he is back on the street for good behavior," the officer said now just as angry as Devon.

"You son of a bitch," Devon said hitting the wall.

"These are the questions I ask myself. I don't need this bastard to walk I need a confession. This guy kills little girls. We don't have enough proof to charge him with murder because he's so smooth, but we have your daughter whom he did not kill. That's a start. The neighbors saw him talking to the young girls, but they never see the young girls with him or at his house. There is never that placement. There is no semen. There are no marks, no hairs, no traces, no trails, just dead little girls. We have a girl who left that house some years ago and told her mother that the man that lives in the green and white house put his finger on her privacy and then couldn't remember the street that the green and white house was on. The little girl doesn't live far from the Grey Purse Drive home. Now I have your daughter allegedly pregnant by this guy who no one has ever seen with women or men, and you want me to take him in, lock him up and start a trial with your daughter saying she went back, she told no one and most of all, Kowalski didn't rape her. She liked the feeling. Yes, he groomed her, but most children groomed don't know that is what is happening. Unfortunately, I've had to work many child abuse cases, but I will say this, children who survive molestation or sexual abuse, when you talk to them, they never like the person touching them inappropriately. It does not matter that they were experiencing a feel-good sensation, they end up confused, but they're never a protector of the abuser. You have kids who do fall into these sex traps because they are getting something out of the situation and that is why they never tell. That makes this case a misdemeanor. He walks with probation and a fine unless I can pin her rape and those murders on him," the officer explained having calmed down.

"Unbe -fucking – livable," Devon said dropping his head and pressing the release button on his phone ending his conversation with the officer.

"Mother!" Devon called.

"Dad, you're grounded! Cursing is breaking the house rules. The officer is right. Thomas groomed Storia for a long time." Carlee replied.

"What? Wait a minute. You hold that thought. Hello," Devon answered his phone.

"Mr. DeLuca, I understand you're upset but listen. We can charge Kowalski with unlawful sex with a minor that resulted in pregnancy, but depending on his attorney and what is worked out in the courts, we're looking at a misdemeanor instead of a felony conviction. We want a felony conviction. We do not want him walking away with a fine and less than a year in the county or worse, probation. We want him to do time in prison, especially if we can't get him for the murders," the officer said trying to reason with Devon.

"She's pregnant by that asshole," Devon repeated. "To make things worse, my oldest daughter just dropped a wonderful statement on me about this guy grooming my daughter."

"What is your oldest daughter saying? As far as your younger girl being pregnant by Kowalski, it needs to be proven, sir. If Kowalski walks in stating he didn't know how old..." the officer said before being interrupted.

"He threw her a damn party for her 15th birthday. Are you flipping kidding me? They all have pictures and videos on their phones and shit of her and him together. Are you effing kidding me, right now? You're shitting me right?" Devon now engulfed with rage.

"Dad! I can hear you, and you're grounded, dad. You're grounded," Carlee said surprised having never heard her father speak in such a way.

"Tell the officer what you were about to tell me," Devon gave Carlee the phone and walked away rubbing his forehead and pushing his hair back before stepping out and slamming the screen door.

"Hello?" Carlee said not knowing where to start.

"What do you know about your sister and Kowalski?" The officer asked.

"Well, he used to date my mom. He was buying my brother and me whatever we wanted at Storia's request. Storia was maybe 8 or 9. I remember him because he would look at her, like, the way men looked at the women in romance movies. My brother never liked him and always caused trouble when he was around. That is the reason why he ended up in boarding school. My mother ignored the things my brother said to her because Kowalski paid most of the bills. My brother started keeping Storia around him all of the time, and that is what made Kowalski move out. Right after that, my mom sent my brother away.

"Did you tell your father this information?" the officer asked.

"No, I only confirmed it was the same guy the other day."

"Can you give your father the phone? Thanks for the information; it was helpful."

"You're welcome. Hold on, I'll get my dad."

Carlee took the phone to her father.

"Yeah," Devon was pissed.

"Mr. DeLuca, if your daughter is, in fact, carrying Kowalski's kid, it's a no-brainer," the officer said not mentioning what Carlee told him or how Kowalski being a murderer was more critical.

"We got him, Joe. Kowalski is held up at the Ink Lady Inn on Crest Aide," the officer's partner said.

"Hey, Mr. DeLuca I have to go. I'll be in touch," the officer ended the conversation.

"Uh daddy – look," Storia said as water rolled down her inner thighs.

"Did you pee on yourself dummy? You should have said you had to use the bathroom. I would have helped you," Carlee said laughing at Storia.

"Daddy, Carlee called me a dummy," Storia licked her tongue out at Carlee.

"Carlee you're on punishment two weeks," Devon said responding to Storia.

"Awww, dad. You should be on punishment too," Carlee replied.

"For your information, I didn't have to use it. I didn't feel like I had to use it anyway," Storia looked down as she turned to hobble to the guest room.

Devon paused for a minute and thought about what Storia said as Carlee used a paper towel to clean up the liquid. Devon called for his mother.

"Apple, honey," Devon called to Storia. "You're gonna have the baby soon honey," Devon said trying not to panic. "Come on let's get you to the hospital," he instructed.

"Wait dad she's wet," Carlee said running into the bedroom to get Storia a change of clothes.

"Carlee, please Pumpkin hurry up. We have to go. Mother," Devon called his mother suddenly realizing she wasn't there.

Devon ran to the SUV and pulled it up to the house. He ran into the house and grabbed a towel, Storia's bag and the bag they made for the baby. He placed the towel on the seat then put the rest of the things in the car. When Devon ran back in the house and saw Carlee and Storia making their way up the hall, he gave Carlee the house keys, picked up Storia, took her out of the door, and placed her on top of the towel in the vehicle. Carlee locked the door and jumped off the porch missing the stairs onto the ground. She jumped into the SUV, and the three sped off.

"How are you feeling honey," Devon asked Storia.

"I feel okay daddy," Storia answered rubbing her belly vigorously.

"Hey, grandma. Storia peed on herself. We're on our way to the hospital," Carlee laughed.

"I didn't piss on myself! Daddy, can you tell Carlee to shut up," Storia shouted.

"Carlee, Pumpkin you're aggravating the situation honey, please not now," Devon said while looking at the speedometer.

"Daddy, it's starting to hurt badly," Storia said rocking from side to side rubbing her belly.

"I know sweetheart. We're almost there. You're about to have the baby honey," Devon said turning the corner sharply.

"Oh shit! Sorry, dad. Oh my god. Oh my god," the turn scared Carlee.

They arrive at the emergency entrance 35 minutes later

"Okay Apple we're there," Devon pulled into the parking space.

(blowing) "Daddy!"

"Get that wheelchair Carlee," Devon helped Storia out of the car.

"Okay," Carlee ran to get a wheelchair.

"Hold it Carlee, honey," Devon assisted Storia into the wheelchair.

"Uggg. Woooo. Oh crap," Storia moaned as she dealt with the pain.

"Good job, Apple." (Walking down the hall) "Excuse me. My daughter is having a baby" (talking to someone in scrubs walking down the hall in the opposite direction) "She's in labor. Where do I go?"

The nurse gave Devon directions. He had to follow the yellow line and register at the desk. Devon walked quickly following the yellow line where he found the counter with a receptionist on the phone. Devon signed his name and then called out to the person standing behind the receptionist.

"Daddy, I feel pressure like I need to push or something. There is a lot of pressure daddy. It is hurting," Storia cried.

The nurse got on the loudspeaker and called triage stat. Then she hurries around the desk, got behind the wheelchair, and rolled Storia down the hall Carlee and Devon in pursuit. Two orderlies rushed in. One held the wheelchair while the other picked up Storia and places her on the bed. Other nurses rushed in and pulled the curtain. They undress Storia and put two gowns on her one facing the front the other facing the back. One nurse placed a monitor around Storia's belly. Another nurse cleansed her vaginal area. Another inserted an IV and heart monitor for Storia, and one took her blood pressure. The last nurse got Dr. Patterson on the phone expressing the urgent nature of the event.

It took nearly ten minutes for Dr. Patterson to arrive at the birthing center. Dr. Patterson instructed one nurse to check Storia to see how much she dilated and Dr. Patterson told one of the other nurses to look at the monitor to see how often Storia was contracting.

"Ahh...woo, woo, woo, woo, blowing isn't working. Ahhh what are you doing?" Storia screamed.

"I know it is a bit uncomfortable. You're just about there," the nurse answered Storia. "Dr. Patterson, she's just about there. She's dilated to 8 cm, and she's experiencing contractions about three minutes apart," the nurse reported.

"It's going to be okay," Devon tried to comfort Storia. "I'll be with you through this process."

"Wow Storia. Your hot pot is about to pop. Hahaha," Carlee said kissing Storia.

"Shut up! Shut up! Shut up!" Storia screamed.

"Okay, let's get her to the birthing room," one nurse said.

The orderlies picked up the bed Storia was on and placed it on a rolling bed. The orderlies, with the birthing team, and Dr. Patterson rushed down the hall, Devon following, Storia screaming at the top of her lungs.

"Hi, Storia. Listen, honey. Don't yell; it won't help. What we're going to do is breath. Okay? Breath honey," Dr. Patterson said calmly demonstrating how she wanted Storia to breathe. Your little bundle is early, huh? That's right honey, breath. Inhale, take in the air through your nose...exhale the air out of your mouth."

"Okay, but my back hurts so badly, it all hurts so much," Storia cried.

"We got the show, Dr. P," the nurse informed.

The orderlies pushed the bed into the birthing room. Dr. Patterson directed Devon into the changing area so that he could suit up and wash his hands. Dr. Patterson scrubbed her hands and stepped into her theater boots as the nurse equipped her with a surgical cap, a mask, visor, and apron that the nurse tied for Dr. Patterson. Dr.

Patterson rushed over to a visually uncomfortable Storia as another nurse held gloves open for Dr. Patterson to insert her hands. The third nurse gave Dr. Patterson the nod; Storia's cervix was fully dilated. The birthing team had everything ready for the pre-term infant. Devon looked on with concern as to him it seemed like everyone from the neonatal unit was in the room. Devon had no idea what a neonatologist was, but he was told that as soon as the baby was delivered, the neonatologist will check the baby's health and if there was something wrong, there were baby specific specialists in the room that would deal with whatever the issue.

"Okay baby girl. You're there. Okay, when I say push, I want you to give me one big push okay?" Dr. Patterson instructed.

"Okay," Storia cried.

"It's okay, Apple. Hold my hand," Devon looked at Storia behind his mask. He tried to keep her calm, but he could not stop the tears from rolling down his face.

"Daddy, don't cry," Storia said blowing hard as she pushed.

"Push Storia, push honey," Dr. Patterson said gently.

Dr. Patterson continued giving Storia instructions. Storia kept pushing, and Devon continued to cry. Meanwhile, Carlee met up with her grandmother, and the two waited in the lobby. Carlee paced back and forth, wringing her hands as she grew more concerned about her sister. She looked around and noticed that the waiting room was fairly busy, so she went to the other side of the room where there was hardly anyone waiting.

"Please, Father forgive my dirty mouth. I'm sorry. I just get so mad sometimes. I'm sorry for fighting with Cynthia too. I'm always furious Father, but I swear I try. I know my sister should not have slept with that jerk but Father her hormones I guess got the best of her. Father forgive her and help her deliver this baby Father. Please. Thank you," Carlee prayed with her eyes shut tight.

"Push Storia. Big push sweetheart," Dr. Patterson said now concerned.

"I can't. I'm tired," Storia said.

"Okay, okay, okay," Dr. Patterson said noticing the cord wrapped around the baby's throat. "Okay honey, just one last push."

Storia drew the strength to push the best she could. As she lay back down, she could hear her baby crying.

"It's a girl," Dr. Patterson said happily.

There was no response from Storia.

"Did you decide what you would name her?" one nurse asked.

Storia didn't respond to the nurse's question.

"Uh no. Not yet," Devon replied looking at Storia.

"We're going to ask you to step out granddad so we can get Storia, and the baby cleaned up. We will get you once we move Storia to recovery. You and the rest of the family can see her before she's moved to her room okay?" the nurse detailed.

"Okay," Devon said looking at Storia who was staring at the wall away from everyone.

The neonatal team took the baby girl who was slightly jaundiced. They cleaned up Storia and put her in a new gown. Storia watched the neonatal team fuss over her baby. They weighed and measured her, took her blood and collected her urine. Then, checked her blood pressure and heart rate, and once the team was done, the nurse placed a diaper on the newborn and put her in a bassinet, and then the nurse covered the baby's eyes and attached a lightbox to the bassinet. Storia turned over after she saw the nurse turn on the fluorescent light to start the young infant's phototherapy.

Devon went into the lobby where he met Carlee and his mother, Ellie. He cried. He told his mother there was something wrong with Storia. Ellie grew concerned at the way Devon was describing the situation, and when she saw Dr. Patterson, she pulled her to the side and asked her what was going on. Dr. Patterson explained that Storia was a little withdrawn and it was probably stemming from the trauma of childbirth at her age. She assured that Storia would be fine though it may take a while. Dr. Patterson gave the family some literature about postpartum depression. She shared with the family stories about how other women have had it and snapped right back and how there were some who took a little longer than anticipated. Dr. Patterson asked that the family be patient and shower Storia with love and attention.

Two hours passed before one nurse came and greeted the family. She told the family Storia had left recovery and was now in her room. The nurse then pulled Dr. Patterson to the side and spoke with her about Storia's condition. Devon overheard the nurse saying Storia had rejected the baby, did not want to allow the baby to latch, and hematology wanted to schedule an appointment for her to monitor her CBC. Devon saw Dr. Patterson nodding her head in agreement and heard the doctor saying to the nurse Storia was too young for what she just experienced. Dr. Patterson turned back to the family said a few more kind words and excused herself. The nurse then took the family to see Storia.

As the nurse walked the family into the room, she spoke to Grandma Ellie about talking to Storia to see if she would consider nursing her baby. The nurse shared with the family that she got no response from Storia when she mentioned the subject then, Carlee told the nurse Storia would breastfeed her daughter but needed a little time. The nurse told Carlee there was a class on breastfeeding offered free that Storia and a guest could attend while Storia was admitted. Carlee noted as she, her father and grandmother walked into Storia's room. Carlee looked over at Storia then walked over to her and rubbed her hair. Storia was still staring at the wall with tears from her left eye falling into her right one; she quietly sobbed to herself. Carlee walked over to the purse she had dropped near where her grandmother was sitting. She grabbed her brush out of it, went back over to Storia, and brushed her hair.

Carlee always thought Storia was more beautiful than she was, but she wasn't mad about it because Storia never treated her like she knew it. As she brushed Storia's long dark locks, she looked at how from the middle of the strand to the end, Storia's hair had a pretty S pattern. The S format went the whole length of her hair even though Storia had been lying on it for the past ten hours. Carlee could only do one side since Storia wasn't moving. Carlee then got an idea, so she walked back over to her bag and grabbed the comb out of it, walked back over to Storia and parted her hair down the back, then brushed it more and braided Storia's hair. Her dad gave her a ponytail holder so she could put it on the end of Storia's braid to keep it from unraveling. Then, Carlee twirled the braid around in a circle and placed it under itself to make it hold.

"See, now you have a braid like Princess Olivia on one side," Carlee said making a Start Stars reference since Storia loved the show. "I'll do the other side when you turn around," Carlee said to her sister kissing her on her cheek.

The nurse rolled the baby in, but Storia did not move. Grandma Ellie was delighted to see the baby and would be the first to hold her. She was glad to see her great-grandchild no matter how she got there. Grandma Ellie smiled from ear-to-ear as she looked at the baby. The baby had big beautiful eyes like her mother. Grandma Ellie wondered if her eyes would change the way Storia's eyes did when she was in different moods. The baby went from Grandma Ellie to Devon both were taken by the baby's features and complexion. The nurse explained how the baby was gaining her natural color as the jaundice treatments were working.

"Hello Storia," Dr. Patterson said walking into the room. Storia didn't respond.

"Did you get a chance to hold your beautiful baby yet?" Dr. Patterson followed.

Storia still did not respond.

"Well come on sweetie. That's okay, you'll get around to it. She looks just like you, ya know? She is absolutely stunning," Dr. Patterson touted. "Let's get you turned around here so I can check you out honey," Dr. Patterson instructed.

Storia slowly turned around while the nurse pulled the curtain. As Dr. Patterson checked Storia out, she spoke to her.

"You'll be with us for three days babe. We're going to make sure everything is coming together down there; you will also have the casts removed as scheduled. I hope that your bones aren't as soft as they were a few weeks ago. I would hate to have to send you home in a fresh new cast. Since you have given birth, your body can start circulating nutrients to your limbs instead of the growing fetus. If you plan to breastfeed or expel milk for your baby, make sure not to consume too much sugar. Okay? While you're here, I want you to see Dr. Henry in hematology so he can keep an eye on your blood stores," Dr. Patterson continued as she took off her gloves. "I know you're not talking now, but you'll be okay," she continued. "The nurses will take care of little bit while you get a few more days of rest okay?" Dr. Patterson didn't expect a response. She pushed the curtain back towards the wall, smiled at the family and wrote in Storia's chart.

As the baby cried, Storia remained unbothered.

"May I have a diaper please," Carlee asked the nurse.

The nurse went to the cabinet, pulled out a diaper and a pre-made bottle, and handed it to Carlee.

"Thank you," Carlee laid the baby in the hospital bassinet and changed her diaper.

"Did you decide on her name Storia?" Dr. Patterson asked not expecting an answer as she placed more information about Storia in her digital file.

"Her name is Hannah," Carlee declared. "Hannah Marie DeLuca."

"Kowalski," Storia said. "Hannah Marie Kowalski.

"Not," Carlee said kissing her niece.

"Are you okay Storia?" Carlee asked.

Storia gave no response.

"Storia?" Devon called.

No reply.

"This is common Mr. DeLuca. We will give her something so she can rest. Don't be too concerned. Like I said and gave you literature about postpartum depression. I believe that is what she is experiencing. We can get Dr. Analyn in here if you like, but sometimes new mothers snap right out of it and then sometimes their hormones don't reset, and there is a little withdrawal that happens," Dr. Patterson said softly.

"Thanks, doc," Devon dropped his head and walked over to his mother.

"She'll be fine son," Grandma Ellie said.

"You're welcome. Again, if you like, I'll send Dr. Analyn over to talk with her," Dr. Patterson walked towards the door.

"We'll see," Devon replied.

"Okay," Dr. Patterson said as the door closed behind her.

"You are such a sweet baby. Just like your mother," Carlee said to her niece.

"I'll take her now. She has to get back under the lights. We only take the babies out to allow them to nurse or feed them and change their diaper," the nurse said smiling.

"Okay," Carlee handed the baby to the nurse. "I'll see you later Hannah Marie."

"Here Carlee, call this number," Devon said handing Carlee the business card to the officer.

"Okay," Carlee said taking the card.

"Apple, you feel like talking?" Devon looked at Storia.

No response.

Devon walked over to his mother and talked to her about what was going on with Storia. They talked back and forth about the situation and figured out what it would take to care for the baby. Devon got on his cell phone to check in with Lucy. Preoccupied with the tasks Devon asked her to complete, she could not talk long, but Lucy was happy to hear about Storia having a safe delivery. Lucy was not pleased when Devon gave her more assignments. Lucy tried to be funny, and let Devon know that he owed her big time of which he conceded; he wasn't in the mood for joking.

CHAPTER 10

"Your honor, it has been determined that Thomas Henry Kowalski fathered the child of Storia Emily Anna DeLuca, a minor under 16 and three-quarters years of age. We asked that you set no bond and he remains in our custody," the prosecuting attorney said as he looked at the judge and the defense attorney.

"Your honor my client is not a flight risk," the defense attorney said.

"Save it, counselor. Your client is being bound over for trial. Bailiff, please remove Mr. Kowalski from my sight," the judge replied.

"Richard you know this is BS. How was he to know she was 15?" the defense attorney asked.

"15 and pregnant is how he left her. For god's sake, are you blind? Haven't you looked at the evidence?" the prosecutor was offended.

"It was a birthday party. Anyone can photoshop a picture of a person into another image."

"What? I am not suggesting that the young lady is completely innocent to be fair, but this is the reason why we have laws. If you listen to the young girl, you automatically know that she is immature. She had many encounters with your client. He groomed her for years. He sucked her in by using her friends and their trust. She trusted him, and he took significant advantage of that."

"So, he helped a bunch of kids."

"He helped a bunch of kids? Every time he did something for those kids, he made her pay with sex and that sex resulted in pregnancy. Apparently, you didn't hear or understand what I said; have you heard the victim's story? Have you heard how she speaks? She's a teenaged child, Marvin. You were given this case late. The attorney before you quit. Ask yourself why that attorney withdrew from this situation. It was certainly not because he lacked skills. If I were you, I wouldn't attach my career to defending someone like this. I know everyone is entitled to a defense, but not for this type of situation. This rape isn't his first, and if we don't stop him, it won't be his last. If I have something to do with it, Thomas won't walk the Earth for a long while."

"The police haven't produced any evidence putting my client at the scene of any of those murdered girls."

"I am not sure why you mentioned the murdered girls. I didn't say anything about the murdered girls who happen to look a lot like my victim; clearly, he has a type."

"Come on Richard, he has a type?"

"It's not unusual to you that all of the dead girls are tall for their age; have light eyes, dark hair, and full lips? That's not strange to you? Hell, I didn't know we had so many brunettes with light eyes in town."

"Honestly, I put no thought into it at all."

"This young girl was lucky, and it probably had a lot to do with her willing having a sexual situation with him whereas the other girls showed signs of captivity and severe abuse."

"Hmm, so it couldn't be a guy having a situation with a girl who lied to him about her age?"

"Not with that birthday party he threw for her. Anything else?"

"Any chance of a deal?"

"With a 99.7% DNA result from the infant belonging to the girl who just turned 16, who actually became a victim of grooming at 9 when he actually lived with the mother, dry humped when she was 13, and raped at 14, not on my watch. You think he deserves to walk amongst other people's children? Marvin, you're a smart man, you just need to do the math."

"Put your so-called victim on the stand and let her talk about how she liked having sex with my client; she came to his house every day Richard."

"Ump, maybe you're not so smart. Yes, she did say and do some incredibly stupid things; she's human, not dead. Kowalski is 17 years older than her. She describes him as someone like her father but who does boyfriend things to her...as Kowalski defined it because he didn't want the girl to look at him as a father. He told her he cared and would take care of her always no matter what. He said that to her. He bought her and her pals things their parents wouldn't buy and often couldn't afford. He took them everywhere they wanted to go, and he paid for anything and everything they wanted. He spared no expense for her 15th birthday party that you say she stole his credit card to have, yet he was there. He's on video paying. He is on video hugging her. He is on video interfering in conversations she was having with young boys her age. Her age, mind you. He practically picked her up at one point to get her away from the same boy he saw her talking to earlier at the party because she was dancing with the boy, you know, the boy that he was angry with for being the girl's age. Don't give me that shit about your client didn't know how old she was. He knew exactly how old she was - he likes them that young. All of the dead girls are just as young. He wanted her to be that young. In fact, he needed her to be that young and to prove it, in the video; the cake had the number one and the number five on it. He was standing right behind her when she blew out the candles. Who are you defending Marvin? He is a pedophile. I'd say he's a pretty dangerous one too!"

"We'll see."

"You'll see." (Prosecutor walks out of the courtroom.)

"Damn!"

The defense attorney walked over to the jail to see Kowalski. He entered the visiting area and waited for Kowalski to arrive.

"When am I getting outta here?" asked Thomas.

"No time soon." The defense attorney answered.

"What do you mean?"

"As I said, no time soon. Do you realize your charges? Do you recognize the evidence the other side has on you?"

"It's all lies."

"They have you on tape paying for her birthday party; her 15th birthday party. There are tapes of you at the mall with her buying shoes, jewelry, and clothes and shit."

"Those things were to help those kids out."

"Look, cut the bullshit. You were sleeping with a 15-year-old girl. Fuck, at your age, you were raping this girl. In this state, she cannot consent until she is at least sixteen and three quarters. I understand you've been dry humping and finger fucking her since she was ALMOST 13. Your DNA matches the kid that kid just had a few months ago. I can't help you. I am requesting off this case. It is my job to protect the constitutional rights of any defendant. I'm saying I cannot represent you in good conscious. I couldn't get the DA to negotiate a plea bargain let alone one that you'd think was fair. You may have a defense and you are entitled to a fair trial. If I can't get off this case, I recommend that you plead guilty to sexual misconduct with a minor in hopes that the court offers some mercy and you don't get the kind of time the prosecutor will likely suggest you get."

"If you quit this case, I will sue your ass for legal malpractice. You give me this shit about what - your morals? What's ethical to you? So what - I had sex with her as much as I could - I did, and then, I let her live. After allowing her the life that was all mine, I begged her to come to my house every day – literally - and I taught her things – all sorts of things she didn't know before me. I tasted her sweet little ass, and she enjoyed every lick and every stick. Oh but so did I, Counselor, umm so did I? Nevertheless, it is your job to defend me. Yeah, she had my bastard, but it is your job to provide defense. Did you know she was 12 when I bought ten boxes of cookies from her? When I met her mother, she was some dizzy bitch who was only interested in money. I got her out of the way by giving her my credit card and dropping her off at the mall. She had one thing that I wanted that was priceless to me. She was almost 10 when I met her. It wasn't until I moved within walking distance of her school that I started talking to her, and she was just about 14 when she started mouthing my cock, and the day she turned 15 is when she started taking it in, but it is your job to defend me. That girl had all of me, more than anyone else did. (Thomas said looking down at his fingernails) You know Counselor. I could go on because the memory of her is all I think about nowadays, but I'll do you a solid and spare you the rest of the juicy details since you don't look like you're doing too well. It wouldn't matter anyway because it is your job to defend me and after all, I am innocent until proven guilty."

"So, do you think that your little confession will prompt me to violate this attorney-client privilege thus having my statement throw out, I get disbarred, and you walk if the cops don't come up with any evidence on you about the murders? I'm not that stupid, but you, I not so sure. I'll do you a solid since you spared me your tale of how you fell in love with a child and decided not to kill her. This isn't about the molestation of that young girl you spent so much time grooming and teaching you disgusting piece of shit, this is about all of the young girls you murdered before you got to this one who bared your child.

"Oh, I know they don't have evidence connecting me to those murders. You know, for the ones I left, it was because the mother was a good fuck...a little loose, but it was the least I could do. Now, get me the hell out of here. My girl is almost to age. I think I want to pick up where I left off," Thomas said smugly.

"You can have had a new attorney and perhaps one who will work feverously on your behalf to get you off with a reduced sentence and maybe because this is your first known offense, it is possible that the judge would knock your sentence down to probation. I mean I'm not sure if you're aware, but what you've done is supplied me with a full pledged confession. It would be well worth being disbarred if I knew for sure my statement wouldn't be thrown out. You can sue me until your dick falls off I AM NOT defending you. You are a cold-hearted, sick, self-absorbed, son of a dumb bitch for not aborting your child-raping ass. Guard!"

"That was a nice, well thought out subpar speech. Especially that whole thing about my mother and all, but you just remember Counselor, attorney-client privilege when you're talking to those other shit-cans."

"Guard!"

"I guess I'll see you on Monday with your strategy?"

The defense attorney gave no reply. As he walked through the jail gates, he heard Kowalski's laughter in the background. He leaned against the wall. He was just in the midst of a mass child murderer and rapist. He tried not to throw up having listened to what he thought was the devil in the flesh. He pulled his phone out of his inner pocket and pressed the contacts key, then dialed the name of the person he was looking to contact.

"You have time to talk?"

"Sure. Where?" asked Marvin's colleague.

"12th and Race in 15."

"Okay. I'll be there."

"Hey! I have a big effing problem."

"What's going on?"

"I'll tell you when I see you."

"Okay. See you in 15."

Marvin ended the call then looked at his phone and turned off the recorder. He hit the rewind button for the recording and pressed play. Marvin listened to Thomas 'Tommy' Kowalski confess, and that made him sick. He ran to the concrete staircase, threw his head behind it, and gave up all he had on his stomach. "It seemed like Kowalski was saying something else but what?" Marvin thought to himself. As Marvin stumbled walking to the parking lot, he got into his car, picked up the water bottle in the cup holder of his car and drank from it as though it were a whiskey bottle. He drove to the attendant and paid then drove to Danacule's on the corner of 12th Street and Race to meet with his colleague, Monica.

Marvin arrived at the place. He went in but realized Monica wasn't there yet, so he went outside to wait for her. Marvin chose a table with an umbrella. He knew how Monica tried to avoid the sun at all cost. He sat at a corner table kind of out of the way of immediate traffic, yet could still see her walking up. He saw Monica crossing the street and called out to her. She stopped and looked and then she saw him. Monica walked over just as the waiter was approaching. Marvin ordered a long island ice tea, Monica a white wine spritzer.

"So, what's going on?" Monica asked.

"I have a client who molested a girl that he eventually impregnated. Initially, he told me he was being set up, and after being presented the evidence, this asshole decided to confess to me that not only did he do it but loved it, and she did too, according to him. I think he may have confessed to some murders as well," Marvin explained.

"Damn. What the Fuck! What are you going to do kid?"

"Well, I have it on tape. I want to quit. I am going to ask the courts approval," Marvin drank his long island like water and then ordered another one.

"You recorded him? Does he know? What are you going to cite for quitting? You can't tell them he confessed to you," Monica informed.

"Difference on how to proceed."

"Is he rejecting your suggestion?"

"There are no suggestions. Richard won't accept less than 15 years no parole, and he wants him placed on the sex offender list for eternity."

"Well, did you tell your client about that deal?"

"That's no deal. 15 years, no parole?"

"It was a child Marvin."

"I know Monica." (Slamming the glass on the table)

"I will leave if this is how you're going to act. I can't talk to you."

"Wait. I'm sorry. I'm just so frustrated about this case. I want this guy to do more time than that. You should have heard how he described his obsession with this girl and how he begged her and taught her things. The way he talked about her was like he was with others and maybe because she responded to him; he was utterly in love with her in some sick way. He speaks as though he has not only been with other girls, but he's taken their lives. You should hear how he talks. I have him saying these things. Would you like to hear? It disgusted me, and when he said she loved it, I wanted to apply brutal force."

"My god, no, no, no, I don't want to hear what he has to say, and you need to erase what he said because you can get into significant trouble having recorded him without his permission. Do it the right way. You could cite personality conflicts." (touching his hand)

"Ump."

"Refer another attorney and move on."

"Yeah, he told me he would sue me."

"Well, you have every right to make the request."

"Hell, I'll risk being sued to get off this case. The premium jump would almost be worth getting the hell away from that guy."

"You'll ask the new attorney to make sure he puts empathizes on requesting a continuance and possibly getting Kowalski out of jail until trial. Do you think he is a flight risk?"

"Hell yeah."

"Yeah, but I'm sure you said the judge wasn't going to allow him to bail out."

"Yeah, that was pre-confession. I think this guy wants to get out now. I think he will try to persuade the girl if he had the chance."

"You think he would pursue a relationship with her?"

"You didn't hear how he sounded. He talked as if he still wanted the victim and his current situation is a mere set back. He said people were talking about him to her, but she knows he loves her even after he said mean things to her."

"Wow! You were having a fully fledged conversation with the spawn of Satan," Monica shook her head as she rubbed Marvin's back.

"I don't deny it. Hey, I said no names."

"I don't know who you're talking about and I am not going to find out. We never had this conversation. On another or side note, you want to get together tonight?"

"Sure, pizza at 7?"

"My house or yours?"

"Why don't we meet in the middle?"

"Interesting."

"Red Tail Inn?

"Beautiful."

"When were you there?"

"Jealous?" Monica smiled.

"With whom did you go to Red Tail Inn?

"Frank, Sam, Ed, and John."

(smiling) "I'm not jealous at all, as long as you got no further than the conference center with those clowns."

"No, I used a room to freshen up. Those meetings were all day."

"I'll see tonight at 7. I'll text you the room number."

"Okay."

Marvin sat at the table for hours thinking about what he wanted to do. He could feel the weight of the long island kicking in and knew it wasn't reasonable for him to drive. He saw a waitress walking by with her purse and called her over. He felt he was in luck because the girl lived a few blocks over. He convinced her to drive him home. He told her it would save her the money she would have to pay the taxi and prevent him from trying to drive home because he didn't want to leave his car. The waitress agreed. They walked and talked as they made their way to the parking lot. Marvin handed the waitress the keys and moved the items he had in the passenger's seat. The waitress started the car and waited for Marvin to get buckled in before she took off. On the ride home, Marvin made his decision to withdraw. Forty minutes later, the waitress pulled into Marvin's driveway. She started talking to him then leaned in to kiss him. Marvin guilty pushed her back and explained he already had women problems and didn't need any more trouble. The waitress unzipped her uniform and told Marvin she wouldn't say anything. Marvin declined, opened the car door, and struggled to get out; he was drunker than he wanted to be and didn't know if he would be able to meet Monica. As Marvin walked up the stairs to his condo, the waitress zipped her uniform and started walking fuming over Marvin's rejection. Marvin entered his condo and called Monica. She agreed to come over to his house. Marvin had Monica that night. He begged her to stay, but after having him one more time, she left like she always does; a ritual Marvin hated.

Marvin woke up to his ringing cell phone. He decided not to answer. Instead, he walked into the kitchen and put on a pot of coffee. He had meant to set the timer so that would brew on its own, but he hadn't found the time. He placed a breakfast burrito in the microwave then walked to his room and pulled out a suit. Marvin took a shower then headed back into the kitchen to eat. He poured the coffee into a thermos, grabbed his briefcase, and headed out the door.

Forty-five minutes later, Marvin arrived at the courthouse. He opened his briefcase and pulled out a form letter requesting to be withdrawn from the Kowalski case. He informed the court of Kowalski's refusal after suggesting a voluntary substitution and cited a profound conflict of interest that not only was against his ethics rules but his moral ones as well. Marvin did not mention his client's confession but made it clear that he would be ethically limited in trying to provide a defense for Kowalski. Marvin felt confident that he would be removed from the case. He had 12 weeks before Kowalski's trial. He knew that would be plenty of time for the new lawyer to apprise him or herself with the details within the file.

A whole week and come and gone and Marvin was well into the evening of Friday. He and Monica planned a weekend away, but Marvin was waiting for the other shoe to drop. This will be his seventh attempt at getting Monica out of town, and she always comes up with some excuse. This time, Marvin spent no money. He was going to take Monica to his summer home for some R&R. Marvin turned himself around in his office chair as he thumped a pencil's eraser against his temple. His secretary chimed in to let him know Judge Matterson was on the line. Marvin's heart began to beat; he was nervous. He picked up the phone. The judge asked Marvin some questions to which Marvin invoked his attorney-client privilege. He did say that he wished that he could tell the police what he was told but was sure he would be disbarred. The judge explained that the client was entitled to representation and was within his right to plead as he wished even if he had committed the crimes in question. The judge explained that he understood the predicament he was in and granted his withdrawal. Marvin thanked the judge and ended the call.

Just as he started into his victory lap, his secretary informed him that Monica was on the line. Marvin's happiness turned grim. He picked up the receiver and pressed the blinking key. Before Monica could start her spill, Marvin suggested they not see each other any longer. Monica pursued a conversation she sensed was no longer available. Marvin held the phone in silence devastated at the turn of events. Before ending the call, he told her that he apparently was sharing her with someone since she is only available for a fuck-n-go. He said to her that he wasn't interested in sharing and was no longer into the type of relationship he found himself in and no longer wanted to participate. He didn't leave room for Monica to say anything. He said goodbye and ended the call. He contacted his secretary over the intercom and asked her to cancel his remaining appointments. He looked at his watch, grabbed his suit jacket and left his office. Marvin took the elevator down ignoring all of Monica's incoming calls. Once he made it to his car, he sat stoically. He started his car and drove down the street to Danacule's hoping the waitress was there; she was.

"Hey Dana," Marvin walked up to the waitress.

"I'm cool, Dee," Dana brushed Marvin off coldly.

"You know you're the only one that calls me that, right?"

"So, it's not that special."

"I know you're mad, but you know I was dealing with someone. If I were dealing with you and a waitress came on to me, would you want me to take her down?"

"Was?"

"Is that all you heard?"

"No, I wouldn't want you to take her down. Are you no longer pursuing that situation?"

"I had to let her go. I wanted more than I guess she was willing to give. You win some, you lose some, you know?"

"Well, I'm sorry. You must have really liked that girl because you have never turned me down before."

"I was trying to make something happen, but I guess it just wasn't in the cards."

"So, you think you're about to rebound with me?"

"No, I literally came over to apologize. I don't need you spitting in my food."

"Wow! That's what you think of me? You think I would do something like that?"

"When women are angry, there is no limit to the shit they do. I just know it's all bad all of the time."

"Sorry, you think I would spit in your food. I am not that nasty."

"You wanna get nasty?"

"What?"

"You were setting your beautiful self out for me last week, uh, ten days ago roughly. You know I would have stretched you out."

"Oh yeah,"

"Yeah."

"What are you suggesting?"

"I am suggesting you come away with me this weekend."

"What's in it for me?"

"What do you want?"

"You."

"Well, I'm going to give you me."

"That is not what I mean." "Spill it. What do you want?"

"I want you for more than a weekend or moment. I want the commitment you were willing to invest in the one who didn't want the commitment."

"I didn't say she didn't want to commit. I said she and I want two different things."

"If she wanted to commit, you would not have broken up with her. So what do you say?"

"Dee-Dee, we aren't who we were in college."

"I didn't say we were. However, we're probably better because we're more mature."

"Are you still possessive?"

"If you mean do I still require all of you, yes."

"I can't handle that."

"Oh, but you can mope around trying to find some pussy to fall into to help your broken heart? Okay, I got the picture. Bye Marvin."

"Dana," Marvin pulled her arm turning her around.

"For the record, I have loved you since the day I met you at that fountain. I've never wanted to hurt you. I'm not ready to argue you with you because I work with women. I'm not ready to be mad all day not talking to you because you're mad about something I said or didn't say. I practice law, so I have to be focused for my client's sake. I can't argue day in and out with you to prove some shit that is really psychological; you either trust me or you don't, but I can't weather the Dana Storm. I need and pay too much money for my clothes and shoes. I don't need your cut, burn or bleach drama. I never had that problem with my ex-girl so, that is the type of relationship I'm looking to have with a young lady. I don't think that is you. I do apologize, but I don't want to unpack your baggage."

Marvin walked out of the restaurant alone. He walked to his car where Monica was waiting.

"I was just calling to let you know I was running late," Monica said with two suitcases in her hands.

Marvin smiled. They drove to his house to drop her car off and left that instant.

CHAPTER 11

"I have an interview at Jades daddy, will you watch Hannah?" Storia asked reluctantly.

"Sure honey. Are you thinking about going back to school?"

"Daddy, I told you I wanted to change schools. Once I'm finished with my homeschool maturity leave, I'll be ready to transfer."

"Do you think you will be able to work, go to school and take care of Hannah?'

"Daddy, I don't want to talk about it. It is sad enough I have to go and speak to Dr. Analyn to talk about it, and by the way, she is such a bore."

"Hey honey pie," (Walking in the house) Grandma Ellie spoke to Storia.

"Hey, Nana. How was your outing?"

"Perfect. Hi Devon. You look tired."

"I've been on night duty."

"Storia, this has become the household's baby. There are plenty of people to help in the daytime from Lucy to staff, to the housekeeper, me, your father, and Carlee in the afternoon to name a few. The least you could do is care for her at night. Don't you think that's fair?"

"Ah, grandma. It's hard."

"Tell us about it Storia."

"I have an interview. I don't want to be late. Can you please mail this letter for me?" Storia asked her dad as she handed him the envelope.

"If I'm able to get out honey. I'm exhausted."

"I'll watch the baby. Lie down," Grandma Ellie offered.

"Thank you, mother. Storia, you're going out. Why don't you drop it in the mail?"

"Because I need a stamp daddy."

Carlee jumped out of her friend's car and ran to the house, up the stairs, and into the home.

"Hello everyone. Where is my niece?" Carlee asked.

"I have to go. See you guys later."

Storia walked out of the house got into her friend's car, thanked her for waiting then they drove off.

"Where's she headed?" Carlee asked.

"Interview," Devon answered.

"Oh great."

"She has a letter. Can you put a stamp on it and take it to the post office?" Devon asked.

"Now?"

"Yes."

"Be a dear darling," Grandma Ellie chimed.

"People don't mail things anymore. It is an age of email and text. Who is this to by the way? Ah, she's writing to Thomas," Carlee revealed.

"What?" Grandma Ellie & Devon said simultaneously.

"It is addressed to Thomas, Carlee repeated."

"Open it. Read what it says," Devon requested.

"How did she find out his address? Grandma Ellie inquired.

"This is the information era grandma. Everything is on the Internet."

"What does it say?" Devon's curiosity made him anxious.

"Let me see. It says..." Carlee read aloud.

Dear Tommy,

Please do not contact me anymore. I am finally free without you. You were the worst thing that happened to me I see. You took my choice, and I see now that you have ruined me. You took away my ability to think and make sound decisions for myself without manipulation. You adorned me with your lies. You shattered me, and now I despise looking at any man – I don't trust them, and it is all because of you.

My daughter's father is a child rapist; word on the street also says you're a murderer. One who preys on and kills underage girls. One who puts his mouth where it doesn't belong? One who carelessly drips seeds with contempt, daring the seed to combine with an innocent egg and flourish; you say things that aren't fair. You never cared, and you never were going to be there for me. You're cold and merely rotten to the core. You kept me coming back for more with my pathetic naivety. More lies, more trouble, more rape, I've discovered. I thought you cared for me. I thought you would love and cherish me, and look at me now a young girl - a teenager, no marriage – defiled and I hate you.

I hate you for the love I can't show my child. I hate you because all the while you were using me I loved you. You are a merciless demon that dwells on this Earth, which is really an oxymoron; I hope your soul rots in hell. Though I am fighting mad, I know one day there will be a man that will make up for the lousy excuse I know God didn't create in you.

I sincerely hate you, and you no longer exist. Don't ever contact me again! Do not write to me about my child and if you ever get out and come looking for me, I swear I will take your life or dry trying.

Storia DeLuca

"I'm going to send this right away," Carlee said. She went to the desk to get a new envelope.

"Maybe you better not," Devon coward.

"Dad, I'm sending this letter, cut it out. Storia's letter is excellent," Carlee said as she copied the address from the old envelope.

"Make sure you put fuck you from the family on there before you mail it," Grandma Ellie said without hesitating.

"How about you mail nothing?" Devon rubbed across his forehead.

"Oh, dad. It is about time Storia ripped him a new one. I thought she would never get over giving Hannah his last name, but the thought of Hannah having the last name of the man who through deception and rape is the reason why she's here is tragic, and I guess now Storia is starting to see that. I will mail the letter she wrote. It is the least I can do."

"Stop bringing it up, Carlee," Devon yelled.

"Well, it's true," Carlee reasoned as she responded to the knock on the door.

"Now who is that? Is he trying to sell something?" Grandma Ellie questioned.

"Oh, no granny," Carlee answered as she opened the door. He is my friend Kory. He's taking me roller skating. Come on in Kory."

"Thank you," Kory walked into the house.

"I see you have Eloise syndrome," Grandma Ellie said slyly.

"Mom, please don't start!" Devon grimed.

"Dad, this is Kory. He goes to my school. He is delivering this year's valedictory speech. He is also preparing for the Service Trot this weekend. He plays basketball and football. The coach loves him so much he wanted him to play baseball too, but Kory turned him down and ran track instead. That's how we met," Carlee spoke proudly of Kory's abilities.

"So, Kory. Do you work?" Grandma Ellie asked.

"Anyway, Kory, this is my dad."

"That was rude what you did..." Kory whispered to Carlee. "Nice to meet you, Mr. DeLuca. Is it DeLuca?"

"Please don't start mom," Devon said under his breath. "So, Wow! That's extensive. You should have my daughter write your resume," Devon shook Kory's hand "Nice to meet you as well, and yes, it is DeLuca."

"Carlee's mom cursed me out for calling her Mrs. DeLuca, so I wasn't sure."

"Well, I apologize for her behavior. She can be a bit over the top. It's terrific to meet you, Kory. Have a seat."

"Thank you, sir, and no need to apologize. You're not the cause of her behavior. My grandma says people act the way they choose to act. People may influence a decision we make but ultimately, it's what we decide. It's our choice."

"Your grandmother is wise."

"Speaking of grandmothers being wise. What did you say to my grandbaby?" Grandma Ellie looked boldly at Kory.

"Well ma'am, I told her she was rude. I apologize if I was also rude to whisper. I didn't want to embarrass her and to answer your question; I don't have a job. I am leaving after I graduate so I can get settled where I'm going to attend college. I applied for an after-school position before, but my mother does not want me to work because I have to watch my siblings while she works. She works the mid-afternoon shift and sometimes she doesn't get home until 2 or 3 in the morning."

"What about your dad?" Grandma Ellie questioned.

"My father died after sustaining injuries fighting overseas. He was in the military. I prefer not say which branch in case you were going to ask. He made it through surgery to tell us he loved us and that we were the best thing that ever happened to him in his whole life. That's what I like to think anyway...otherwise he just would have died. He told us he didn't want to stay because his injuries were a lifetime of care. His quality of life would have been demeaning, well, for lack of better term. My grandma said he lost his will to live and chose to move on to rest. I miss my dad. We did everything together."

"How many siblings do you have?"

"Five."

"5? Wow! Do you watch them on your own?"

"Yes, ma'am. My parents wanted a girl, but obviously, that wasn't in the cards. After me, my mom had my twin brothers, who are nine, then she had my other brother who is seven, she had another boy, he is four, and my father told her before he left for overseas that the one she was carrying was the last prize. She is now two. My mom is pregnant, and the doctor said it's a girl too."

"When did your father die?'

"About six months now. My mom thought he was home for good then he said he had another tour so..."

Nina R. Ricci

"Well, you're holding up very well," Devon stated.

"Yeah, I prefer not to talk about it."

"So, what do you want with my granddaughter?"

"Ma!"

"Well, nothing. I'm leaving right after graduation which is in a matter of months. We started talking because we're reading the same book and we couldn't run the other day because it was raining. So, while we waited, we read the book to each other and talked about it. Then she asked me about some of the moves in the book, it's about this roller skating couple, and I told her about the rink on John Stone Blvd, and we decided to go to see if we could make some of the moves."

"What else does the couple do that you all will be practicing?"

"Well, ma'am. I don't want to assume what you mean, so I will simply say, I'm not talking to your granddaughter or taking her out to have sex with her. It was and is a friendly gesture. I have a lot planned and I don't want sex to ruin it. I don't want to practice anything; I only want to be friends and not friends with benefits."

"Are you gay?"

Devon facepalmed, drops his head, and then side-eyed his mother and walked off.

"No."

"You prefer black girls?"

"Are you trying to persuade some sexual encounter? No, I have no preference I'd like to wait."

"I'm not encouraging, but it sounds like you think my granddaughter wouldn't be the best choice for you."

"Huh? How did we get here?" Carlee lifted her hands and shrugged her shoulders.

"Well, your grandmother..." Kory was interrupted.

"It was rhetorical," Carlee smiled.

"It sounded sarcastic, but if you say it was rhetorical, I guess I can't argue."

"What are you going to school for Kory?" Devon chuckled.

"Engineering."

"Yeah, that fits."

"I'm not anal if that's what you're suggesting Mr. DeLuca."

"Hey, I didn't say that at all." (giggling)

"Maybe I should go."

"No! Please. Let me grab my jacket," Carlee hurried to the closet.

"Wait - for what?" Grandma Ellie asked.

"Wow! Are you still thinking about that? Marriage Grandma DeLuca, I am and want to wait for marriage. Once God sends my wife, after I get out of school, enter into my career, buy a house and save some money not at all in that order, but I will marry then."

"Are you a religious nut or Jesus freak? Which one?" Everyone gave Grandma Ellie a dirty look for the question.

"I'm neither. My grandmother showed me in the Bible the things that need to be done to be blessed. The Bible makes suggestions on the way to live. It is up to the individual."

"So, you obey the Bible?"

"Yes. I'm not perfect, but I do my best. I avoid all that is avoidable."

"How old are you?"

"I turned 18 yesterday."

"Well happy belated birthday Kory. Did you get that nice car as a gift?" Devon asked as he looked out of the window.

"Thank you for the birthday wishes Mr. DeLuca. Ahhh no. I got that car for my 16th birthday. I couldn't drive it because I couldn't afford the upkeep at the time, so it has been sitting in my parent's garage."

"Jesus, for two years?" Devon was surprised at Kory's discipline.

"Yes, sir. I would go out and start it up, and my mother drove it around the corner once a week, but it had been under a tarp in the garage."

"Well you don't have a job so how do you pay now?" Grandma Ellie was back to her line of questioning.

"With my inheritance, I received when my father died. I get a living allowance every month."

"Okay, I'm ready. Sorry, it took so long. Storia called. She got the job. She's going through orientation. Hear me, dad?" Carlee walked to the door.

"Yes, Pumpkin. Be safe out there."

"Okay."

"Nice meeting you Mr. DeLuca," Kory said as he walked toward Devon to shake his hand. "You too, Grandma DeLuca. Take care," Kory waved as he walked to the door.

"Same here Kory," Devon smiled.

"Yes, sir."

"Carlee, can I see you a moment? Just a quick moment," Grandma Ellie requested.

"I'll be waiting by the car," Kory walked out of the door.

"Okay," Carlee watched Kory walk out the door. She walked over to her grandmother.

"Let me tell you. That boy is a catch. If you are your darling little self and not the annoying person you're capable of being, you just might have a chance. I'm telling you, he's going places. That boy is going somewhere prominent. If I were you, I'd make my time with him memorable."

"Grandma, we're young. We have plenty of time to figure things out."

"Not for long. I am telling you some girl is going to come along and sweep that boy up. You want a man that is going to care for you and your children Carlee. You can ignore me if you want, but take a moment and look around here and tell me if you've seen or heard anyone who speaks the way that young man speaks. There is no one that I've seen yet that is suitable for you or Storia. Well, maybe there's a young man for Storia."

"Wow, yeah, I gotta go grandma. Love you," Carlee walked towards the door. "Love you, dad."

"10 o'clock Carlee," Devon instructed.

"Yes, dad."

"Can you believe that kid?" Devon turned to his mother.

"Talk to your daughter son. That boy is going places. Can you imagine Carlee watching five kids soon to be six?"

"I can't imagine her quoting anything you say."

Nina R. Ricci

CHAPTER 12

Storia spent most of her time in Jades in the break room watching hosting videos. She was given a complimentary drink. She was told that she could order whatever she wanted if she needed something to eat. Storia turned up the volume in her headphones as she realized it was loud in the diner and she couldn't hear. She got up as the video was playing in the background and peeked out the door to see what was going on in the dining area. From her angle, she really could see nothing, so she stepped out of the room. Her new boss, Jimmy Franklin saw her and invited her over to where he was standing. He spoke to her about the traffic and asked her if she had questions so far. Storia answered no. She explained she had become bored with the videos and just wanted to be on the floor observing what happens on any particular day. Her new boss expressed his appreciation for her initiative and praised her desire to get in and take the position head-on. He advised her to watch the other waitresses and hosts, so she sat on the bar stool and watched the other staff.

Storia wasn't sure if she liked the way the greeters were greeting or the how the waitresses were serving the guest. She thought to herself how she would be once she worked in the position. As she shifted from bar stool to bar stool, she noticed that she was getting stares and deep glances. She looked up in the mirror behind the bar to see if there was something on her face or in her hair. She stopped her boss walking by and asked him if there was something on her face or in her hair or teeth. He answered her and asked her why she was concerned. Storia explained how she was moving from one place to another and noticed people staring at her so just wondered if something was wrong. Storia's boss told her to look in the mirror. He then asked her to follow him. Storia got off the bar stool and followed her boss as he walked towards the break room. He invited her into the break room. Storia thought okay it's the break room so what. Storia's boss asked her to look in the mirror that was on the wall. The mirror was long and looking into it one could see their whole body.

Storia's boss was very friendly and handsome. He was tall and had thick wavy hair. His eyes were deep and almond shaped. They were brown, and his lashes were long and to die for she thought. She could see the dark circles coming in around his eyes as though he wasn't getting enough rest. He was fatherly Storia noticed and the things he said to her that she felt as though he may have said the same thing to his daughters. He told her to take a long look in the mirror and come to terms with how beautiful she was and how that beauty causes people to want to stop and stare. Her boss told her she was a different kind of fascinating because it was pure and honest. He told her not to go beyond lip-gloss and mascara. He said to her that her natural beauty was raw and attracting. She spent the next twenty minutes trying to see what her boss was talking about when it came to her beauty. She hated her hair that day. She wished she had washed it. Though it didn't smell, it just wasn't doing what she wanted it to do. She also thought she looked tired. She had been tossing and turning since having Hannah. Then she stopped herself. She looked in the mirror. She walked up to the mirror staring at it thinking she could see what looked like a pleasant light. As she got closer to the mirror, she touched the reflection of her face. She reached to the mirror that showed a representation of her hair. She looked at her eyes, her nose, and her lips and then at that moment, she could see her father in her. She was in awe wondering how she missed the girl she was looking at in the mirror. Storia was in what she thought she knew as love. She turned swinging her hair, and she felt different. "Let them look," she thought.

Storia walked out of the break room door with such a presence about herself. She was feeling confident or arrogant; she couldn't decide. She walked up to her boss and asked him if she could practice her position on the floor. Her boss looked at her and stared. Storia saw how he looked and knew he saw what she did. She gave a half smile and looked around at the patrons. Her boss went over to the girl serving as the host and told her to take a break. He directed the host to relieve one of the other waitresses when she came off her break. Then he called one of the other staff members and told her to keep an eye on Storia because he would let her try out her position as host. The other staff member happily agreed and took a seat at the host's station. The boss brought Storia over to her area and introduced her to the other staff member. He told Storia if she had questions, she could ask the other staff member.

Storia approved and walked over to the stand where people were waiting to sit. Storia walked into the dining area to look at the seating arrangement. She thought the seating arrangement of the dining room was confusing, but she made no fuss. She wondered if it would be possible for the waitresses to tell her what sections were available so she wouldn't have to walk back and forth pass people seated to see what was going on with seating arrangements. She saw that several areas were open, so she walked over to greet the guest.

"Hi. I'm your host, Storia. Welcome to Jade. Are you dining with us or will you order take out?"

"We're eating here. We need seating for six," the customer requested.

"Okay. I can seat you now and bring your group as they arrive if you like."

"No. I'll wait."

"Okay. You can have a seat. Just let me know once your party arrives."

"Okay. Let me ask you something."

"Yes."

"Umm, (clears throat) where's the bathroom?"

"Oh. (smiling) Go straight ahead then make a left."

"Thanks."

"You're welcome."

"You're doing a great job Storia," Jimmy smiled.

"Well, thank you," Storia responded as she continued to greet the customers. "Hi. Are you dining in or take out?"

"Take out," another customer answered.

"Okay. Follow the bar around the corner until you get to the counter. Your order can be made or picked up there."

"Thank you."

"You're welcome," Storia smiled.

"Excuse me," the first customer interrupted.

"Yes. Has your party arrived?"

"No, they haven't arrived. Question."

"Okay – shoot."

"Do you still like older men?"

"Excuse me?" Taken aback, Storia could not believe his question.

"Well, I'm older and looking."

"You have me, confused sir. Once your party arrives let me know, and I'll seat you. Excuse me, sir," Storia walked pass the customer. "Hi. May I help you?"

"Take out," customer 3 said.

"Sure. Follow the bar around the corner until you get to the counter. Your order can be made or picked up there," Storia cleared her throat and was no longer smiling.

"So, of course, you've gotten a little older, and you've filled out quite a bit in ALL THE RIGHT PLACES. I'm excited just talking about it. I'd love to show you some things. I could teach you ANYTHING you want to learn. My money is as long as my tongue. We could make this happen, and you could have anything you want without having to work in this place. I bet your tingling down there just thinking about the possibility," the first customer continued to annoy Storia.

"I don't think so, and I'm going to have to ask you to leave me alone, please," Storia walked away feeling uncomfortable with her head tilted to the side. She was trying not to cause a scene.

"I'll leave you alone for now," the customer said as he followed Storia. "I don't want to create a situation. Let me say this...," the customer grabbed Storia's arm and turned her around. "You are a gorgeous girl. You could command whatever you wanted. I'd love to relax all over you. I'd be at your beckon call. I swear. Think about it, and if you decide, I'm the owner of those businesses down the street in the strip. I'm always there. My name is Paul. Come and see me anytime, any day. Okay?"

"NO! PLEASE - GO AWAY!" Storia spoke with her teeth clenched. She looked out of the corner of her eye to see if anyone else heard her.

"Storia, is there something wrong?" Jimmy asked.

"No, Jimmy. I was saying my party stood me up and she was expressing her sorrow about it," Paul said to Storia's boss.

"Oh okay," Jimmy looked suspicious. "Yeah, she's been smiling now all of a sudden. I wouldn't think that would be something to be so upset about but teenagers now days are so dramatic," Jimmy said as he looked for Storia who had gone to the back.

"Yeah, I have a couple of girls of my own her age, so I know what you mean," Paul lied.

"Well, maybe your party will catch up with you later, and we'll see you some other time."

"Hey Jimmy, Storia is taking a break," the waitress informed.

"Well, it seems she was more upset than I thought," Jimmy looked at Paul angrily.

"I'll call for reservations once I speak with my group," Paul said as he walked towards the door.

"Yeah, you do that. Have a great evening." Jimmy threw the towel in his hand down on the bar and walked to the break room.

"I don't think I'll be able to do this. I can't work here," Storia cried.

"Why not?" the waitress asked as Jimmy eavesdropped on their conversation.

"Because people know me. They know what happened to me."

"What people? What did you do?"

"Oh, nothing. Forget it." Storia got up to walk out.

Storia stomped out of the restaurant with her boss following.

"Storia, Storia," Jimmy called.

"Please Mr. Franklin, please leave me alone," Storia said clearly rattled.

"Wait a minute," Jimmy ran to catch up with Storia who was walking fast. "Hey listen. I don't know what that customer said to you, but you were doing great for your first day. You can't let people upset you," Jimmy stood back with his hands on her shoulders. "What I want you to do is come back and take some time, get something to eat and if you're feeling up to it, come back on the floor.

We need you, and I would like you to stay. If not, clock out and go home BUT, but Storia, come back tomorrow okay? I'll make sure nothing like whatever you experienced tonight happens again."

"Okay," Storia walked back towards the restaurant.

"Okay. Good. Wonderful. Which one are you going to do?"

"I'm going to take some time and get myself together. I'll grab something to eat maybe watch the rest of the orientation videos and then get back on the floor."

"That a girl. Okay."

Storia's boss looked at the ground not to give his feelings away to Storia. He escorted her back into the restaurant, and the staff and some customers clapped. Storia walked to the break room and dropped her head between her legs. She held her head down for a while thinking about what Paul said. She was sickened by the thought and wasn't attracted to him, but she was in turmoil about the possibility. Storia noticed her hair touching the floor. She gasped and went into her purse to grab her brush; she stood in the mirror thinking about Paul's reddish-orange hair. She thought about his green eyes and the freckles that crossed his nose. His lips were thin, his hands were stubby, and he was short. All the qualities he possessed, she did not like. He wasn't that attractive either she thought in conflict with herself about why she was even thinking about him. She brushed her hair then walked back over to her purse and pulled out her lip-gloss, walked back over to the mirror and rolled the balm across her lips, and then she adjusted her clothing, put her purse in the locker, walked back onto the floor, and continued working.

Five hours later and now off work, Storia clocked out. She received a pat on the back from her co-workers and a kind smile from her boss. She smiled and thanked everyone for their encouragement. Her friend texted her to let her know she was outside. Storia texted her back to let her know she was on her way out. Storia grabbed her purse and her schedule and walked out of the break room. She told everyone she would see them tomorrow and walked out the door. As Storia headed to the car, her friend was driving; Paul appeared from behind the sign.

"What are you doing here?" Storia was disgusted.

"Well, the high school students who work for me get off between 8 and nine, so I figured it would be the same for you," Paul replied.

"Who is this guy?" Storia's friend asked.

"He is the customer who came up to me and said name my price. I believe he lived next door to Tommy. I don't know; I use to see him a lot over that way."

"So you do remember me?" Paul smiled.

"Well, my name is Georgia." Paul shifted his eyes to her briefly before looking back at Storia. "If I can name my price, you can talk to me."

"What?" Storia glanced over at Georgia shocked.

"What, what?" Georgia had no shame.

"What are you saying that's what?"

"I'm saying if he's paying. You fill in the rest."

"What are you saying? Are you insane?" Storia whispered.

"I'm saying let's get this money. We both can do it."

"No, we both can't do it, I don't want to."

"Hey listen. I'm going to get going. There are too many people coming around." Paul walked away.

"Come on Storia. It's nothing. It doesn't take that long, and before you know it, you're at the mall. We'll make him use a condom." Georgia all but begged.

"Condoms are not a cure-all... I take it that you've done this before?" Storia was appalled.

"I've had sex with high school boys who say they like you or they love you. They get the sex and then they don't want anything else to do with you," Georgia explained.

"High School boys do that? Wow, so it never ends huh? A much older person said he loved me, we had sex all of the time. I got pregnant then he wanted nothing to do with me."

"Well, that's what I'm saying. We should be the ones calling the shots, not them."

"Well, I guess that's true. We control the situation instead of falling into the love trap and being filled with lies."

"This way, we're here for one thing and one thing only."

"Sex?"

"No silly. Money. Yes, we're going to have sex, but it will be for the money. Now, which way did that pervert go?"

Storia laughed as she got into the car.

"He went down that way. He's on foot, but before we partake in this prostitution gig, I need to get this straight with you, I'll sit on his face, but I'm not having sex that involves penis penetration with him at all - ever. Understood?"

"Are you serious?"

"Yes. I will walk out."

"Okay, okay."

Georgia slowly drove through the parking lot looking for Paul. Storia returned text messages with her sister and goofed around on the internet on her phone. Georgia found Paul walking down a dark dirt road. She turned down the street and got on the side of the street that would put Paul on her side of the car. Storia kept her head down the whole time Georgia talked to Paul. Paul continued looking over at Storia hoping she would look at him. She didn't even peek his way. Georgia asked Paul if he could afford the two. Paul asked if she (Storia) would be involved. Georgia assured him she would. Paul let Georgia know without hesitation he was only interested in Storia as far as providing for but he would take her for a ride for the hell of it. Georgia tried to act as if the statement didn't bother her because she needed the money. Georgia noticed Storia wasn't interested at all so Georgia interrupted her and asked her if she would tell Paul she would be involved. Storia looked at Georgia and reminded her of what she agreed to do. Storia looked at Paul and asked if he had $1,000. Paul looked at her and could see she was dead serious.

Georgia was shocked. She could not believe Storia said that much. She was thinking $70 - $80. What was most shocking is when she heard Paul say yeah. He said yes she thought. Storia added that what she quoted was for her and had nothing to do with Georgia's fee. Georgia was stunned. Paul expressed that he had the money but did not have it on him. Storia told Paul to take Georgia's number, and when he had it, he could call and let her know. Georgia softly told Paul to make that $1100. Paul expressed that he was after Storia, so she thought to make it light. She thought she would have to split $80, but to have $100 to herself was awesome she thought. Georgia thought Storia went overboard with the price and was sure Paul would not call back. Georgia started on her journey of taking Storia home fuming all the way. Georgia and Storia got into an argument about the price Storia quoted to Paul. Storia told Georgia if she didn't like the rate she quoted that was her problem because she didn't want to be with Paul anyway. Shocked and dismayed, Georgia told Storia to get off her high horse, and then her phone rang. It was Paul. He had the money. Georgia was dazed. He had the money she thought to herself. Georgia asked Paul his location, he told her, and she made a U-turn. Georgia told Storia. Storia reiterated that she would not have sexual intercourse with him. Georgia informed her he wasn't paying that kind of money for her presence. Storia told her not to be so sure. Storia told Georgia she was only interested in seeing what his mouth could do. She said to Georgia that she would give her $200 to do the rest. Georgia gladly agreed, and the two met with Paul. Storia stuck her hand out for the money. Paul quickly placed it in her hand and then went to hold her. Georgia stepped in and touched Paul. She told him to allow Storia to put her earnings in her purse. Georgia noticed he couldn't take his eyes off of Storia. Georgia sat Paul down on the pull out couch in the back of Paul's office. Storia teased around waiting for Georgia. Together the girls performed, and though Paul didn't get who he wanted, he thought at least he had Storia in the room. He knew he would have to work on getting rid of her friend, but it was too late. He had reached his climax, and the girls were gone.

CHAPTER 13

"When is the last time you spoke to Storia? She got off work at nine. It's 11," Devon asked with concern in his voice.

"I sent her a text earlier, dad. She said Georgia was bringing her home. I'll give her a call," Carlee said as she placed a call to Storia.

Carlee allowed the phone to ring until it went to voicemail.

"Dad, she's not picking up."

"That's okay Pumpkin. Storia is outside sitting in the car," Devon said relieved.

Storia and Georgia were in the car laughing. Storia wasn't impressed as she listened to Georgia go on and on about Paul and how things felt to her. Storia didn't care. In her mind, she was thinking about how she made $800 in less than 15 minutes not counting the drive. Storia figured it would be good working with Georgia for a little while since she was so comfortable with sleeping with strangers. Storia tried to keep up with what Georgia was saying, but she just was not interested. Storia thought of herself as on a level way above Georgia. Storia looked at

Georgia. She picked away at everything about her from her lousy tan, her haircut that is wrong for her face, her hair color that is wrong for her complexion and her clothes that are too tight and tacky. Georgia was a prostitute Storia confessed, and now she was one too. Storia declared to herself that she would not be a grimy looking whore but a glamorous one. Georgia could continue to be the streetwalker accepting pennies to fuck, but she was a high-class call girl, and she would be on Heidi's level except, she wouldn't turn into a madam and wouldn't go to jail. Storia quickly returned to reality. She would prostitute as much as she could since she was living with her father and most of all, her grandmother.

"Good score kid. See you tomorrow?" Georgia said gleefully.

"Yeah. I'll see you tomorrow. Did you see all of the money Paul had in that safe? Do you think he left it open for our view?" Storia asked as she stuck her head in the passenger side window. She was putting plans in motion in her mind.

"You know what? I was busy trying to control that bulge that he wanted to unleash on you. I didn't notice, and you apparently didn't see that beyond creepy look he was giving you the whole time. I mean even when I was giving it my all, I thought, he couldn't and wouldn't take his eyes off you."

"I told you what he used to do. The guy is sick. That is why I didn't want to get anything started with him. He's not good at all either now that I think about it, I don't care how much money he had I won't be dealing with him again."

"Yeah, but we could do it a couple of more times and double the amount each time."

"I don't know Georgia, I'm not feeling seconds." Storia looked towards her house.

"Well, I do. Did you hear how Paul begged you while you were plopping down on his face? That was ridiculous but hilarious. Why were you moaning? Was he biting you?"

"No. It's just that after it's happening for a minute with Paul's tongue, there is this feeling, you know, the orgasm that comes over me that is so strong, but he messed it up by opening his mouth and sucking. On top of that, he was doing it too hard. I could feel the sensation and then wow it was gone. I would have to work his face again to get it back, but I was over the situation."

"So, you don't like sex with men?" Georgia asked giggling.

"Well, that is not what I said. Yes, I do like having sex with men if you're talking about them putting their mouth on me. I've only had sex penis wise with one person, and I didn't care for it too much. I have not had sex with girls...so, there is that. I've only had any kind of sex with Tommy. Between his mouth and dick, as you so elegantly put it, I preferred his tongue otherwise the whole act was horrible."

"So, how do you get the feeling? Orgasm?" Georgia asked curiously.

"You've never been in the act of sex then feel something completely different than what you were feeling at first?"

"No, I never had that. Did you see how Paul was trying to make us touch each other?"

"Truthfully, I liked that part," Storia laughed.

"Me too. (giggling) I just wanted to see what you were going to say."

"You're funny."

"Do you think you can show me that feeling one day? Not with the mouth but like with the dick?"

"Well, didn't you notice? I don't have one."

"I know, I know, you're so silly. I have one."

"You're a guy?" Storia asked confused.

"Girl, don't you know anything?"

"What? You said you had one."

"I have a rubber one."

"What?"

"Ask your dad if you can come over to my house and I'll show you."

"I guess my grandma was right; you do learn something new every day... and, ahh, news flash. Haven't you heard? I have a baby."

"You don't want that kid. You never have her. That is your sister's kid, your father's kid, even your grandmother's kid. Who are you fooling?"

"That's terrible. Why would you say something so awful, Georgia?"

"Storia you've been my best friend for a while. I love you like you're better than my sister. I would never tell anyone what happened tonight and I'm expecting you not to tell anyone either. DON'T TELL ANYONE!"

"Are you kidding? How do I begin to bring up what happened tonight in a conversation? Who am I going to tell that I whored myself out with Georgia to some old ass man?"

"I'm just saying. Tommy was a pedophile. You're a good girl. When that messed up crap was happening to you, it was happening to me too, but my mom was in on the whole thing. My mom would always talk about men like Tommy, but she would sleep with them. Then they would threaten to leave her unless they could have one of us and so on nightly bases, it was either my sister or me that was always up for grabs. Storia if I hear this back, I will know that it came from you because you are the only one that I've ever shared this with do you understand?"

"Yes. I wouldn't tell anyone your mother did that."

"My mother needs a man in her life. She will do whatever it takes to make sure they stay. If she had to have a baby girl to keep a man she would."

"Georgia, don't say that."

"All I am saying is there are a lot of Tommy's around here. Girls, our age can make some money. Girls like my sister can make more."

"Isn't your sister on drugs though?"

"Yeah, she couldn't handle it. That is how she copes. She is sick now. She can hardly function without booze, drugs, or both. Once she gets high, there is no stopping her," Georgia laughed.

"I don't think that is very funny Gia."

"You haven't called me that in ages."

"My Nana said it is too much to remember everyone's name. I am starting to agree," Storia smiled.

"Paul is a perverted pedophile who has reduced us to str..."

"Dick houses?" Storia interrupted.

"Dick house, (giggling) but with that said Storia, why be broke? Why let these guys have the only thing they seem to care about for free? Why walk away wet and broke and then broken when they don't call? My mom is pregnant again. That is why I said what I said. She doesn't have us to fall back on, so the skank is about to pop one out by who knows who."

"Whoa. Why do you think your mom doesn't know who got her pregnant?"

"All I know is every day for the last five months, there have been at least seven guys going in and coming out of her bedroom. Three of them came on to me, and when I turned them down, she slapped me and told me to get out and come back when I was ready to help with the rent. She called me a jealous bitch when I had sex with the one she sent into my room then put me out and said I didn't want her to have anything. She is such a fucking loser. My grandmother went to welfare to report what was happening and my mother cussed her out and took my sister and me back. I haven't seen any of her men since, but I hear them at night. I have to lock my door otherwise when they are supposedly on their way to the bathroom; they try to creep in my or my sister's room."

"Why don't you get a place of your own? I couldn't imagine this happening to me. I would move. Speaking of which, I am not coming to your house with all of that going on with your mom and her friends."

"I guess you have a point. I'll just have to come over here. I don't make enough to pay rent and buy food and stuff. Taking care of this car is a lot. I just put this old wooden chair under the doorknob."

"Huh?"

"Yeah. The two legs on the floor make it hard to push the door open."

"Wow, Georgia. I never knew that about you or your mom. I'm very sorry this happened to you."

"Storia, I gotta get some money so I can get a place of my own. If not, I'll continue getting raped for free or for the benefit of my mother?"

"What's the difference between them and Paul?"

"They don't have any money, and I don't want to do anything with any of them. Besides, all of those men have had my mom. Paul is charming, and he has money."

"Are you kidding me?"

"No Storia. I'm not kidding at all. You can stay in this godforsaken town, but I'm not. I have to get out of here. This place is too small for me. I know Tommy hurt you. I know you liked him a lot, and he was great in the beginning, but the truth is, Tommy was awesome so he could have sex with you. He was stupid for not wearing a rubber, but I heard he liked you a lot and probably just didn't care about the consequences. He probably never meant to get you pregnant; at the same time, he must have wanted you to get pregnant because he didn't use precaution. I guess it's just a vicious cycle. I also hear there is nothing like virgin sex. Accept that reality. He did what he did, and you have the result of it. You're angry because it couldn't be a secret or rumor to be dispelled because you have the living proof in your kid. It's not her fault though."

"I know. I feel sorry for my child."

"Give her away."

"I can't do that."

"She is the evidence of what happened between you and Tommy, Storia. Maybe you wouldn't be so depressed if she wasn't around. Think about it. You're taking care of a baby that you had by a man whose house you went to sell cookies. He set you up Storia. He tricked you. He lied to you. He made you whatever feeling you're going to show me, but you weren't supposed to be exposed to this sensation by him. But, you could use that experience. Hell, as much sex as I've had, I still don't know about orgasms, but he's an old man who does know, he has sex experience, we don't know anything about sex on his level. He knew how to get you there and make you have this sensation. He knew what to say to keep you coming back, and in the end, Thomas repeatedly raped you. Then when you got pregnant, he called you a whore and had the nerve to tell you he could never love a whore, your baby wasn't his and then threatened to kill you. That is a lot to have to remember every time you look at that kid. Storia, just put her up for adoption. That way you don't have to see the guilt and shame in her eyes every time you look at her."

"Why did you have to bring all of that up? It's really late, I have to go." Storia cried.

"I didn't mean anything by it I was just saying I would imagine your life being better if you didn't have to look at the result of what happened to you."

Storia wiped her face and got out of the car. Georgia apologized, but Storia didn't respond. She walked into the house and spoke to no one.

"Storia honey what wrong?" Devon asked.

Storia didn't respond. She ran up the stairs to her room and slammed the door.

"I guess we're on baby duty tonight," Grandma Ellie shook her head as she looked at Devon.

"Something is going on with her ma. I can feel it."

"Yeah, it's the baby."

"I think it's something else, but why do you say that?"

"Well, no matter what you say or think Devon, she kept going back."

"Ma."

"She liked him. She wanted what he was doing to her and for her. She doesn't have that anymore. The baby gets the attention. She doesn't go anywhere or to any new places like he used to take her. She hasn't had anything purchased for her since the maturity clothes and then all the extra attention and gifts and the sex."

"Ma!"

"Oh come on Devon. I know she was 14, but it's not numb down there. You heard her. I mean I'm just thinking of how..."

"Mom. I just can't listen to you talk about my now 16-year-old daughter this way," Devon interrupted.

"I think I would have gone there with my suitcase and moved in at my age."

"Ma!!!"

"I'm thinking about me, dear, not Storia. Me. You know honey. I need to get out more."

"Oh brother, I'm going to bed."

"Goodnight."

"Goodnight mom."

Devon headed into his room and called Lucy. They talked until they fell asleep on each other. Grandma Ellie continued to sit in her favorite chair dozing off then waking herself up when her head got too heavy. The house was quiet. Grandma Ellie stood up and stretched. She looked over at the grandfather clock. It was 3:30 in the morning. Grandma Ellie laid out on the sectional when suddenly the sound of Hannah crying overtook the peace that filled the house. Grandma Ellie could hear Carlee walking to Hannah's bedroom.

"Well, well, well. Hannah, Hannah, Hannah (singing) Hi," Carlee walked up to the crib to a crying Hannah. "Awww. What's the matter with Hannie Poo-Poo? Come on. Let auntie know what's on your mind," Carlee put her ear by Hannah's mouth as Hannah cried. "Oh, you're upset I'm not your mom," Carlee picked up Hannah. "Well, me too. Hopefully, I'll be a good substitute even though generally, subs are crappy. That's just my opinion based on my experience," Carlee said to Hannah. "There's nothing like the real thing, huh?"Carlee cradled Hannah. "Okay honey, sweetie as grandma would say. While your bottle is warming, let's check those puffy panties. Oh, the puffy panties are wet. Oh – O Let's get a little powder down there girl," Carlee changed Hannah's diaper as she started to cry again. "Oh, I know. Here's your bottle. It's all nice and warm. Here you go."

Carlee fed Hannah, burped her, and continued talking to her as she rocked in the rocker.

"Aren't you big for four months old? Yes, you are. Yes, you are. What's that?" Carlee said asking as if Hannah is talking to her. Where's your mom? Well, she's probably sleeping. She has school, and she has to work tomorrow, you know?" Carlee said as she continued to talk to Hannah. "Granny will take you to the doctor. My dad, your granddad will meet with a client, and I will go to school and hopefully be asked out again by Kory, huh?" Carlee spoke to Hannah as she placed Hannah on her shoulder and continued to rock. "Yeah. I like Kory a lot but not because of what grandma said. He seems very cool. He told me last time we were hanging out too much and he just wanted to be friends. What do you think about that?" Carlee asked Hannah as she looked at her; Hannah was just about sleep. "He doesn't hug or kiss and barely wants to touch the same items I touch let along my hand," Carlee confessed as she continued to rock Hannah. "What you say?" Carlee asked as if Hannah asked another question. "Well, I know he believes in the Bible," Carlee said as if she was answering an actual question.

Carlee looked at Hannah. She was sleep. Carlee kissed Hannah and put her in her crib. She stood by her bed for a moment and watched Hannah making sure that she was sleeping. Carlee confirmed that Hannah was sleep, turned around and walked towards the door. Once she got to the door, she reached for the light, in walked Storia.

"Oh, now you come in," Carlee was snarky.

"Come here Carlee, let me ask you something. I don't want to disturb her."

"Okay," Carlee walked out of Hannah's room and down the hall. "What's up?"

"I want to give Hannah up for adoption."

"You what? Storia I know you have an issue with her but think about this. Are you sure this is what you want to do?" Carlee asked sadly.

"I don't want to be around her Carlee. I hate her," Storia cried as she made the cruel confession.

"You don't hate her you hate the association she has that's all. Storia, it's going to take some time."

"Do you know how it feels to hear you up with her, dad, and Nana up with her every time she cries and not me? I feel like the worse person in the world," Storia muttered.

"We love you Storia, and we love Hannah. We understand. I know I am hard on you and I don't know why. I think I am mad that you can't just get over this, but the thing is, this has never happened to me, so how can I say with ease get over it. I'm sorry. I don't want you to give her up Storia."

"It's not fair Carlee. What I am doing is not fair."

"Storia if you think about it, you were so hurt after the accident you had no choice but to carry her. It wasn't like you could leave the hospital and have that procedure that would have taken care of all of this. You had so many injuries when that car struck you. I think it is incredible that Hannah is not screwed up with all of the meds and radiation. So do you want to give her up because you were taken advantage of by that creep?"

"I wasn't Carlee. I wanted him to do it."

"Storia, you wanted him to make you feel the way he was making you feel by your admission. It was a feeling.

What did you know about all of what he did to you before he did it?" Carlee watched Storia drop her head.

"I knew nothing, that's what."

"You should never have had that feeling with him Storia. Of course, you kept going back. Give a kid a bag of candy, and his hand will be in it until someone takes it from him or he eats all of the candy. In your case, you got pregnant. You're still stuck on him and how he just wanted the sex. If it were Max providing this pleasure Storia, you would have kept going back to him, and he's your age. You went back for the orgasm Storia, not him. He is wrong because he knew you were a child and he still pursued you. He is in jail because he raped you Storia. You were a minor. Hell, technically, you still are you know? You were not old enough to consent to what he did to you even if you agreed. He is in jail because he purposed and set out to sleep with a minor. He should have gotten more than 15 years for how he has ruined your thought process. That's what he did Storia. Not you."

"Have you ever had sex before Carlee?"

"No. Not yet. Why?"

"I was going to ask you about the feeling."

"What feeling?"

"There is a feeling that happens during sex. It is kind of after the pain once the finger or penis goes in there. Grandma said it is an orgasm."

"Oh god, I cannot believe you're saying this to me."

"I'm sorry. Forget it."

"No. I am angry all over again. Damn it. Yeah, it is called an orgasm. It is a sensation that comes over you after enough friction builds. Why?"

"How do you know about it?"

"Well, and this is between you and me. I have been reading about it because I want to experience it soon. Why are you asking me so much about the subject?"

"Wow, you're going to experience it soon with who? I just need to know how to show someone else how to achieve one."

"Yeah...wait a minute, what?"

"Hopefully, with someone your age. Maybe it won't hurt so much."

"Well, it is going to hurt because it will be the first time. Technically, besides reading about it, I know nothing about it, but grandma says that it is what every woman should be shooting for an orgasm when she lays with a man. She said if the woman is happy down there, she sleeps well and functions better throughout the day. Don't try to veer from the subject. What do you mean show someone? "

"Don't worry about it. You said you didn't know. Do you believe grandma?" Storia giggled and shook her head.

"I don't know. I guess. I mean grandma says some pretty over the top things, ya know. You should have heard how she grilled Kory. I have to wait and see."

"Why do you have to wait?"

"I am going to tell you another secret, and I know since you never said anything about Thomas; you're not going to say anything about this, right?"

"Okay, right. I won't."

"I want Kory to be my first."

"The black Kory or Cory Madison or is it, Matherson? I can never remember his last name."

"What is with you and grandma?"

"What do you mean?"

"Your black problem."

"I don't have a black problem. I actually like Kory. I'm just surprised. I didn't think you wouldn't want to go that route because of what keeps happening to Aunt Eloise."

"Yeah, I'm not sure I do want to go through that cause grandma was rude to him, but every time I'm around him, I get to feeling like I want to kiss him and touch him and let him touch me."

"Well, what happens that you don't?"

"He doesn't believe in that. He said it is a commandment that you can't have sex with someone you're not married to or to a person you don't want to marry; something, I can't remember exactly."

"Well yeah, but I thought that WAS for married people? There were no weddings like what happens now. When you lay with a man or woman in that day, the person became the spouse in the eyes of God. The Bible says that Scripture will remain the same, always. That means for those who live according to Scripture, even in this day and age, will not lay with a person if he or she is not looking to make the person the spouse."

"How do you know Storia?"

"How do I know? Because I read it silly. First off, there are only ten of them. You can read them in no time if you are interested. All of the men in Scripture had a wife, wives, or concubines."

"Wow. What else does it say?"

"Here's something."

"What?"

"Read it! It's the Bible Carlee. It has many historical events in it, and by the way, gee whiz, you do some work. That's it."

"Well aren't you Miss Smarty Pants. Anyway, back to something that matters. I like him, and I'm hoping to be the first for him."

"Well, I know one thing, if he believes in the Bible and he lives by it, you better understand that it is more important to him than you. If you want him to like you, I suggest you start going to church with him, and you better get very familiar with the Bible because that's the only way you're going to get his attention."

"That's stupid Storia."

"It may be, but the only way you're getting into his pants is if God says to him you're his wife."

"What the hell? That's absurd."

"Not really. It is not unreasonable at all. Kory is choosing to live a chaste life, no worries."

"We'll see."

"We'll see you get kicked to the curb if you do something outside of what he believes."

"How do you know about him Storia?"

"He tutors during the time I have lab and all the girls who approach him flirt with him. He always talks to them about loving God and themselves so that the man God sends can love them. Those girls look way better than you."

"Gee thanks."

"Well, some of them anyway."

"Wow, you're too kind."

"The other day he asked them if they had plans after high school. All of them giggled, and he stared briefly then walked away so, he will not be interested in you."

"The hits just keep coming, huh? Have you ever tried to come on to Kory, Storia? Tell the truth."

"No. I'm not interested in him, and I have never been. He has spoken to me on three different occasions; once to say hello, he asked me how I was doing, and after we had a tempered conversation about the church, he said, "God bless you" before he walked away. So you figure it out."

"Why was he talking to you about the church?"

"Carlee, he always finds some reason to talk to me about God and the church.

"Ump, that is not strange to you?"

"Well, let me see... a handsome guy who could get whoever he wanted, whenever he wanted, spending his time talking about God roughly 90 percent of the time when he could be talking to who he wants to take down first...no, that is not strange at all."

"I swear I don't know you anymore Storia."

"I am just stating the facts; that boy is yummy."

CHAPTER 14

Storia left her last class. She went to her locker and grabbed her sweater then turned on her phone. She went over to the bench and sat down. She looked at the messages coming in on her phone. She stared at them concerned about the unknown phone numbers. She pressed the voicemail key and waited for the automated voice then entered her password. She listened to the 26 messages she had and noticed that most were Georgia. Many were of Georgia saying the same thing, so she went through them deleting after she listened. There was a call from Carlee. She listened to the voice message then called her, and they spoke for a moment. She threw her book bag over her arm and walked down the hall. She ran into Kory, and they spoke briefly about God. He invited her to church; then they talked a little longer, after which Storia continued down the stairs. Storia walked out of the door and looked at her watch. She sat on a massive boulder in front of the school speaking to people she knew as they walked by the stone. Storia looked at her phone to see who was calling.

"Hello," Storia answered.

"Hey, Storia. I'm almost there. Is it on for tonight?" Georgia asked anxiously.

"Nope, I got two more days on the rag. Talk to me then."

"How about some new guys?"

"I don't know about that. I have to see who it is first. How do these men look?"

"Rich."

"I'm not doing this with you, and I'm certainly not doing everyone you do, Gia. I want to choose."

"Just make sure they will spread the wealth."

(laughing) "See you shortly."

"Same place?"

"Yeap, that's where I'll be."

Storia waited for Georgia to pull up.

"Hey, Storia. Where have you been?" Storia's old friend, Scott asked.

"I'm talking to you now just to tell you I am not talking to you Scott. That is all."

"Awww, come on Storia. I apologized a million times."

Storia walked away ignoring everything Scott said.

"Storia – Storia," Kory called.

"Yeah, who's calling me?" Storia yelled as she continued to walk towards Georgia's car.

"Here I am."

"Oh, hey again."

"Hey."

"What's up?"

"Your sister called me and left me a message. I have been trying to call her, but my calls to her are going straight to voicemail so, can you give her a message for me?"

"Sure."

"Cool. Tell your sister to be ready by six. I'll be there to pick her up."

"Oh. Okay."

"Storia," called Georgia.

"You never answered, are you coming?" Kory asked.

"Forgive me, I have a lot going on, coming where?" Storia inquired.

"To church. I asked you in the hall. You never answered."

"Umm – yeap, you sure did. Anyway, I don't get to see Carlee until I get home. I have to work tonight. I just spoke to her not too long ago. I'll give her your message when I speak to her again. To answer the question I thought I already answered when I said I have to work tonight in the hall...No Kory. I cannot take you up on your invite because I have to work tonight."

"I suppose I did hear you say that... I apologize," Kory smiled as Storia pushed her hair behind her ear. He caught himself and stopped himself from staring.

"Yeah, that's okay. I'll make sure to give Carlee your message for tonight."

"Okay, thanks."

"You're welcome."

Storia ran over and got in the car. Georgia started the car and headed to Storia's job.

"Wow. That was long. Was that guy pricing the services?"

"Pricing? As if. He is so hot though. If I didn't respect his love for God, I would take full advantage of my turn with him, but he is one of Carlee's friends. He just wanted me to deliver a message to her for him."

"You are right about him being cute, and I bet he is hung," Georgia giggled.

"Hung, what does that mean?"

"Girl, you don't know anything. Rumor has it that most black guys have big dicks."

"The proper term is penis; most of them have a big penis. Why can't you just say penis? But do they really?"

"I don't know I have never been with a black guy, I mean I wouldn't mind," Georgia laughed.

"Wow. I think I would be shaken. It already hurts."

"It just hurt because it was your first time. After a few times, it's really nothing."

"So if it is so big, does it fit?"

"It probably fits alright. Nice and smug," the girls laugh loudly. "So, I met this guy named Roger...," Georgia began.

"Where did you meet him?

"I met him at the mall. He bought a bunch of stuff."

"How do you know?"

"I followed him."

"Oh, Georgia."

"He was sitting on the bench talking on the phone, so I sat next to him. He looked at me, and I said hello. We started talking."

"And now you want to sleep with him?"

"Yeah, he has a combination of a whole lot of good-looking actor face going on, a nice body, and best of all, money."

"I don't know about this Gia."

Just as Georgia pulled up into the parking lot

"Well, just meet him. Here he is now." Roger pulled up beside Georgia's car.

"What?" Storia was confused.

"Hi!" Georgia batted her eyes.

"Hello," Roger said. He stared at Storia and waited for her to speak.

"This is my best friend, Storia."

"Hi," Storia spoke dryly.

"Your name is unique. Good to meet you," Roger stared intently.

"Whatcha into tonight?" Georgia asked sensing the awkwardness.

"Hopefully, one or both of you, but what do you have in mind?" Roger stared at Storia. He wanted her to answer.

"I'm sorry I'm off for the next few days. By the way, why are you staring at me?" Storia asked rudely.

"Oops, was I staring? I'm really, sorry. You're very nice looking. I didn't mean to stare. If I made you feel uncomfortable, I'm really, sorry. Hey, look I have to get out of here. If you want to meet up later, you know where to reach me." Roger drove away.

"Well, that was weird and so was he. Drive around the corner, and I'll walk the rest of the way. That way you don't have to turn around."

"Okay. Storia, you gotta loosen up. We can make a lot of money," Georgia said as she drove around the corner.

"Georgia, me and you see things much differently. See ya," Storia got out of Georgia's car.

"See ya," Georgia didn't want Storia to notice how upset she was about Roger.

Storia walked into her job and over to the time clock. She went over to the mirror took her brush out of her purse then brushed her hair. She fussed with the curls as they fell gently upon her back then put the brush back and grabs her lip gloss and a piece of gum. She tosses the gum in her mouth and put on the lip-gloss. After applying the lip-gloss, she put it in her uniform pocket and took perfume out of her purse. She dabbed a tad on her neck and wrist then put it in her locker with her bag closed and placed her lock back on the door. Storia walked over to the bathroom. Once she finished taking care of her lady business, she washed and dried her hands then looked in the mirror and adjusted her clothes then stepped out onto the restaurant floor. As soon as Storia turned the corner out of the break room, she walked a couple of feet to her station, and Paul walked into the restaurant.

"Hello pretty lady," Paul said with his hands in his pocket.

"What are you doing here?" Storia said rudely.

"I was thinking about that night. I can't get to you without your friend unless I come here," Paul said. He attempted to flirt with Storia, but she rejected him.

"You're here because you can't get to me? I don't understand," Storia said trying to walk around the table.

"I want to see you and you only," Paul confessed.

"Well, as you can see I'm working. I can't talk to you about personal issues now," Storia acted like she didn't hear what he said.

"Is it okay to come back once you're off?" Paul asked politely. Now Storia's boss, Jimmy was looking her way.

"Ummm, no. I have a way home," Storia said walking towards her station.

"I want to do more than take you home," Paul walked alongside her. "You smell wonderful."

(Stuttering) "P---au---l, I um, listen...about that night," Storia didn't know what to say.

"I can't forget you. The taste you left in my mouth. Well, let me put it like this, the taste is still there. I'm salivating," Paul looked like he had stepped back into that night.

"You really should go," Storia looked away from Paul.

"I'll be back at 9," Paul declared.

Paul left the restaurant, and Storia continued to serve the customers waiting for a seat. As the time for her to get off work neared, Storia stepped closer to the bar. As she stood in one spot, she spoke to the people passing her on their way to their seats. Shortly after she said hello to the patrons, a man started talking to her. She didn't know how to respond to what he was saying, but she acknowledged him. He had dark, stark features. His haircut reminded her of how men in the military have their hair cut, and he seemed tall. Since he was sitting down, she couldn't tell. His eyes were grim and deep - blue – but like contacts and not his regular eye color. Storia was conflicted because he really didn't look like the contact wearing kind, and then he spoke, and his voice was delightful to hear repeatedly.

"Excuse me, I'm talking to you," the guy said as he looked at Storia.

"Yes, I know. May I help you?" Storia had to snap out of the trace she was in briefly.

"You and your friend do parties?" the guy asked.

"I don't understand. Do parties?"

"I am throwing a bachelor's party for a friend of mine. I'm looking for some entertainment."

"What makes you think I entertain?"

"Well, your friend is all but advertising on television."

"Okay, maybe I'm missing something. Advertising?"

"Last week I saw you getting in her car. Hell, I even saw your friend negotiating with the owners of the businesses down the road and tonight, he all but had you on one of those Jade fancy platters with a biscuit and gravy. I can imagine how the conversation went as I watched you having this talk with him in this mirror. I wanted to save you from him so that I could have the same discussion with you, but I didn't because by eavesdropping on the conversation, I see that your friend is the mastermind behind this venture. The thing is you're the one everyone wants. A man would give anything for time with you."

"In all that you said, you disappoint me. I thought that you were smart. You look smart. Let me allow you to hear it from the horse's mouth since you didn't seem to get it with all of your watching and listening. I am not my friend, and I do not operate like my friend. My friend takes me home. I am not sure what she is quote advertising unquote, but I guarantee it is not for anything to do with me. No one advertises shit for me. She doesn't set appointments on my schedule, and I am not a cheap trick. If you want to be with me, you're going to have to pay and did I fuckin' mention that I am not cheap. You got me, cowboy?" Storia looked into his eyes almost forgetting she was being watched. At that moment, she didn't care. She was beyond angry.

"Well, well, well. There is someone in there I would love to get to know. At first, I thought you were going to be a little tongue-tied, but I see you know what you want. I like that. Name your price, but your friend has been around several blocks, and she reeks of it even though she's young – and inexperienced, I'll pass on her."

"What?"

"Well, what I know is everyone knows you two have been friends for a long time and I know that she knows that everyone wants you. You know why, because when she is out there doing all of this (air quotes) advertising, we, meaning men around town, ask her about you. I know I did. I got the tongue lashing of my life on how she is so tired of people asking her about you, but I guess since she is so faithful with dropping you off and picking you up, she must see the light. Hell, because of you, and her promise to bring you along, business has been picking up for her. Sweetheart, no one in this town, would pay for particular activities they've had for free. She told me and many others that you wanted to get down, but not without her. She said to me that you enjoy being with older men. That statement has had me intrigued for days now. I want you to myself at that bachelor's party. Your friend, I could care for the rest. My name is Carlos by the way. If this is something you want to get into, I defiantly will be around." (Carlos got off of the bar stool and placed a tip on the bar for Storia along with a card with his number on it) "The party is in three weeks." (Carlos walked towards the door.)

Storia could not believe what she heard. She didn't know what to be first, pissed or very pissed. She stormed around the bar and through the break room to the time clock where she clocked out. She walked over to her locker, opened it and grabbed her purse. She looked at the card Carlos gave her then slipped it into her bag. Storia walked over to the mirror and wiped the inner corner of her eyes, adjusted her clothes and walked out the break room door.

"Storia, can I have a word with you?" Jimmy asked.

Storia noticed that he wasn't as friendly as usual. She walked over to the bar.

"You know Storia; I like you. I think you're doing well here and the customers seem to like you – especially the male customers. I've witnessed two separate conversations with two different individuals that you looked like you didn't appreciate being a part of in any way. Do you know how to drive?" Jimmy asked.

"Yes sir, but I don't have a driver's license. My father said that I would have to be able to take care of the car. Well, I can't afford the insurance right now," Storia wondered where her boss was going with the question.

"I see. Well, listen and I'm not trying to offend you Storia, but I have to say this. You need to go to the DMV and get your driver's license. Can you go and take the test tomorrow? I will give you the money," Storia thought her boss sounded concerned.

"What?" Storia tried to understand what her boss was saying.

"I have a daughter who is 13 and one who is 18. You fall in between the two. My daughters have good friends, and they have very unsavory friends. My 18-year-old has a new car. The older model she has is not what she wants, but there is nothing owed on it, and there is nothing wrong with it; it's just an older model. I want to give you that car. I will keep insurance on it until you can afford it or maybe six to eight months until you perhaps find a new way home. The girl who picks you up is not a good person. She is using you Storia, or she wants to use you. I see her around and Storia seriously, she gets around. Here take this. Go to the DMV from school tomorrow. Take the test," Jimmy handed Storia money for her license.

"I can't take your money, Mr. Franklin," Storia said pushing his hand with the money away.

"I insist Storia. This bar and restaurant is my business, not a place for underaged girls to pick up older men," Jimmy said sternly. Storia felt the sting of the statement.

"Hey Jimmy, we have a problem over here," a waitress called.

(Jimmy got up from the bar stool) "Get YOUR life in order Storia. You're nothing like that girl you call your friend, but if you continue to keep company with her, that opinion will change," Jimmy walked around the bar to see what was going on in the dining area.

Storia sat on the bar stool for a moment collecting her thoughts about everything that was said to her that day. She picked the money up from the bar and placed it in her purse. She walked towards the front when she heard a commotion.

"Hey! I asked you a question. Is Storia here?" Georgia said yelling at the waitress.

"Yeah she's here," Jimmy said coming from the bar area. "Why don't you go on? I'll make sure she gets home."

"Oh, Jimmy is going to make sure Storia gets home, huh? What else is James Franklin going to make sure Storia gets?" Georgia was yelling at the top of her lungs.

"Well I'm also hoping to get her disconnected from you," Jimmy said sincerely of his employee. Storia looked on from the back listening.

"Oh, are you the association police?" Georgia asked Jimmy angrily.

"You're no good for that kid Georgia. This shit that you're doing is a scheme that benefits you and you alone. Storia is much better than you are character-wise. She is a much smarter girl who has potential to do whatever she wants; she doesn't need you tarnishing the reputation she is trying to rebuild," Jimmy said looking at Georgia in disgust.

"What are you talking about?" Georgia asked innocently.

"I'm talking about you whoring around and using that girl to get more business for yourself. Do you think those men want you? They are begging you for her. You are getting paid because you are bringing her as though you're some fucking whore pimp. They don't want you," Jimmy said plainly.

"She's not your daughter, Jimmy. What I do is none of your business and the same for Storia's affairs," Georgia shouted.

"I'm making it my business, Georgia. No one wants you. You know why? No one wants you because many have had you already thanks to your whore mother. That will not happen to Storia," Jimmy said passionately.

"Screw you, Jimmy. What do you think your precious daughter is better than me? Oh, I see, you think no one is tampering with her because you're a devoted dad? You think you got to her in time. You think Natalie is pure; you would like to think that, huh? Keep telling yourself that shit," Georgia said now really upset.

"Georgia, go home," Jimmy said trying to be polite.

"Hey, Georgia, I apologize for the wait. I was in the bathroom taking care of my lady business. What's going on?" Storia asked acting as she heard nothing said.

"Oh, nothing. You and I were just leaving," Georgia said shaken.

"I'll see you tomorrow Mr. Franklin after I take care of that thing we talked about," Storia looked at her boss. She just wanted to get Georgia out of the restaurant.

"Mandy can drop you off Storia. She is going your way Storia," Jimmy said as a last resort.

"Oh that's okay," Storia gave her boss a look she thought he as a father would understand. "Gia is already here. She'll take me home."

"Yeah, Mr. Franklin, I'll take her home," Georgia said storming out of the restaurant.

"Remember what I told you Storia," Jimmy pushed the chair under the table so hard it fell over.

"I will Mr. Frankin," Storia yelled. She pushed Georgia out of the door.

Jimmy took his phone out of his pocket and contacted his cousin, Ian. He wrestled with this idea but called him anyway. As he spoke to Ian, he could hear in Ian's voice that he was not very pleased with what he heard. Jimmy begged Ian not to do anything other than keep Storia safe. Jimmy thought that by saying that, it would be enough to keep Ian honest. Ian had no qualms about protecting Storia. Ian felt he would do whatever he had to do to safeguard Storia until it was his time with her.

CHAPTER 15

"So where we headed?" Carlee asked excitedly.

"Did you like my church?" Kory asked not wanting to answer Carlee's question.

"Yeah, it was actually really cool," Carlee replied.

"What do you plan on doing when you get out of school? Is anyone pounding down your door begging you to come to their school?" Kory asked looking at Carlee as he waited for the light to turn green.

"Well," Carlee said remembering the conversation she had with her sister now realizing Storia was right. "I'm going to the local university. My sister is going through something right now, and my niece needs me, so I'm going to take care of her," Carlee said with passion.

"Yeah, I do notice you have her all of the time," Kory said pulling off the red light.

"Yeah," Carlee smiled.

"Well, I commend you. That's noble. I mean I know Hannah is your niece, but she's your niece," Kory said reasonably.

"As I said, my sister is having a hard time with the whole situation she went through with the pregnancy and getting pregnant in the first place. From the time Hannah came into this world, my sister has been distant," Carlee confess sorrowfully.

"Hannah is such a beautiful name. Did you know that Hannah is one of our biblical ancestors?" Kory asked excitedly.

"No, I didn't know that," Carlee said. "Who was she?"

"Well, she was a woman who I think has favor with God because her heart was so pure. She was married to Elkanah who was married to another. Some say it was because Hannah couldn't have children. The two women lived with him. The other wife had many children by Elkanah, but Hannah, the one he loved more, struggled with fertility. They would go every year to give their sacrifice, and Hannah was unhappy because she couldn't bear children. Well, when they went to the temple, Hannah prayed and prayed and prayed. Her feelings hurt and nothing made her happy. So she told the Father-God that if He allowed her to become pregnant, she would sacrifice that child by bringing that child back to the temple and allowing him to serve there. Well, she finally got pregnant, and she kept her word. She had Samuel, the prophet. After she did that, she had five more children. Isn't that blessed?" Kory said telling the story as if he were there.

"Wow. That is an awesome story. I guess I should teach Hannah about the Hannah of the Bible," Carlee said looking at Kory as though he was a star.

"Yeah, you should. On a sadder note though, my cousin was raped, and that resulted in a pregnancy. She knew the guy though," Kory explained.

"Was he an older man?" Carlee asked thinking it may have been the same situation.

"No, my cousin actually went out on a date with this guy. He walked her to the door and as soon as she opened the door, he pushed her in on the floor in the doorway. He beat her up pretty badly. When her parents got home, they thought someone broke into the house. They didn't even recognize their child she was beaten so badly," Kory said shaking his head.

"Wow," Carlee placed her hand over her mouth.

"Yeah. It was pretty messed up. My cousin was in the hospital for a week," Kory continued.

"Man. So she found out she was pregnant when?" Carlee asked.

"I don't know. It was later - like a couple of months after, but when my cousin found out, she, against what everybody in the family wanted, had the procedure," Kory said sadly.

"Yeah my mom wanted my sister to terminate the pregnancy, but my father and granny didn't want my sister to do that, and besides, she was pretty far into the pregnancy when we found out," Carlee explained.

"Wow, that's messed up. Well, I asked you about your plans because I liked you and wanted to get an idea of where your head was about your future. You get me, and you understand where I'm coming from when I say I want to wait until marriage and I just want to be friends. There's no pressure with you," Kory sounded at ease.

"Well, umm...it's probably a relief to not have to think if I will let you kiss, touch, or fool around with me huh?" Carlee asked feeling that exact thing.

"Yeah, it is a relief," Kory said arriving at the park. "You know girls have to know their worth. Anyway, I'm glad you're not aggressive and needy," Kory continued.

"That's a turn off to you?" Carlee asked now thinking she didn't know her worth.

"Heck yeah. A young lady should be just that – a lady. She is growing into her confidence. She understands her place in society and knows or is figuring out what she wants to offer the world. She may not be that comfortable in her skin, but she is connected to God and is being guided wisely. You know? Has your father ever told you that? My father told me that," Kory walked alongside Carlee through the grass.

"No. My dad never said anything like that to me. You're probably the only guy in this town who feels the way you do. You have this philosophy," Carlee couldn't help but think Storia called this one.

"No, I'm not. My father, brothers, two of my cousins and several of my uncles feel the same. It's not easy. Yeah, my hormones test me some days. I mean some girls dress like strippers or low-class streetwalkers and they prance all of that flesh around. Guys like me who try not to look get hit with this all day every day it is pretty irresistible especially if the girl is just giving it out. You just have to persevere. Don't get me wrong, young women can wear whatever they want it is up to young men to practice restraint. It just makes it difficult when everything is exposed and in our eye gates. When I think about everyone I know who includes sex in their relationship outside of marriage at my age, he is a father – a deadbeat one a lot of cases or in some instance has had an STD or two. Then after they've had every kind of sex there is to have, their prowess is elevated and next thing you know they are bringing objects and other people into a relationship that is only supposed to be this something special between the two and completely defiles this act that is also supposed to be sacred. If kids my age are buck wild and fancy-free, having sex all over the place then what do we have to look forward to when we grow up?" Kory asked. Carlee thought all he needed was a soapbox.

"Well, besides what happened to my sister, I never thought about it until you. To be honest, I never thought about it until you," Carlee noticed Kory slowing down. "You are the first person I ever thought about wanting to give myself to. I didn't know your views on the subject until talking to you and getting to know you," Carlee looked at Kory. She noticed he didn't like what he heard.

"Let's go back this way," Kory pointed back towards the car.

"You are so nice and kind and giving," Carlee said noticing Kory opening the car door, so she got in. "My father likes you and surprising my grandmother loves you. I wanted to go to church with you because I wanted to get to know your way of life, but I realize now, I can't make you chose me based on what I think you like," Carlee confessed noticing Kory was driving pretty fast and in complete silence. "I have to be who I am and hope that you like me as much as I like you. I know you're going away and truthfully, it is killing me because I don't want to lose the incredible feeling I have when I'm around you. I don't want to imagine not talking to you, and I know once you're with someone else, that someone won't want you talking to me. I know because I wouldn't. You're a good guy," Carlee could see she was almost to her house. "I wish you all the success God has stored up in this world for you," she concluded.

"Thank you," Kory said now waiting for Carlee to get out of the car.

"No...really. I think it's best if we go on to prepare for life's plan. I can't take being around you knowing that in a matter of months you'll be gone," Carlee said now starting to feel the sting of what she was doing.

"Carlee, you don't know how things will work out in or with life, but you have to know that everything that happens does for a reason or due to a consequence. I appreciate you for being honest with me and in turn, I will do the same. I cannot say that when we are together, I don't want to touch your face or hold your hand. I can't say I don't want to kiss you, but I can't allow those feelings to take me to a place physically I know I am not ready for mentally. I'm not ready to have a relationship that involves physical, sexual activities. I'm too busy trying to develop a relationship with God so I can be the man I need to be for my wife. Understand this; if I can think of you to sleep with you but not enough to marry you, I'm not in Divine order. Your father takes care of you right?" Kory asked looking at Carlee to make sure she understood what he is saying.

"Yes," Carlee answered quickly.

"He provides everything you need right now. When you leave his house, it's supposed to be with your husband who is supposed to pick up where your father left off. If you decide to leave the house before you start to court, God the Father is supposed to take care of you until your husband comes. This is the way of God. Do you understand?" Kory asked.

"No one thinks like that Kory," Carlee said frustrated.

"That is why you're supposed to lead and do it on your own despite what someone else does or doesn't do. That's the problem, Carlee. Everyone has fallen away from what's supposed to be taking place, and that is why in part society is in the condition it is in today," Kory said putting his hands together.

"You are way before your time Kory... the things you say to me are profound. Hey! I'll see you around," Carlee said getting out of the car.

"Yeah, you will, for just a little while longer," Kory responded.

Carlee got out of the car. She walked towards the stairs and started crying along the way. She had so many thoughts going through her mind, and the only thing she could think is how she would not see him the way she wanted to see him. She wouldn't be on the passenger side riding to some place that was a surprise. She had to open her big mouth she said to herself. She walked into the house, head down, dragging her book bag, ignoring the calls coming in on her phone.

"What's wrong, Pumpkin?" Devon asked

"I - - told - - Kory - - I didn't - - want to see him anymore," Carlee tried to explain through the outburst of tears, now crying uncontrollably and inaudibly.

"YOU DID WHAT?" Grandma Ellie yelled making her way to the living room.

"Oh honey," Devon said trying to console Carlee. "I'm sorry to hear that."

"Dad. He's too perfect. He would never choose me," Carlee said sounding defeated.

"Sweetheart, Kory isn't perfect. He is just trying hard to practice what he learned, what he knows, and what he believes. Kory is right not to want to get involved in sexual activities because for men, honey; it becomes a distraction. Once he starts, it becomes his focus, and he can't just stop. It's better to wait; otherwise, for men, it becomes a tale of chasing tail. Besides honey, you're too young to be thinking about this," Devon explained still holding Carlee.

"But dad, I love him," Carlee said barely audible.

"Honey you have to understand...Kory's lifestyle is much more structured. It is how he lives. You can't start living this lifestyle and think he will fall for you. Honey, I've loved you since you were born. I tried to be there for you, your brother and Storia, but your mother opposed me a lot, and I got tired of fighting. I apologize. Maybe if I was there, I could have shown you that I loved you and taught you the importance of loving yourself. That is what gets and keeps the guy. Don't feel compelled to trap a guy into liking you by becoming someone you're not. Be comfortable enough to be yourself. Show the individual who you are and let he or she get to know whom you are as a person. Allow the individual to like and fall in love with the real you. Okay?" Devon kissed Carlee on the forehead and allowed her to sit on the couch.

"Okay (sniff) dad. Okay," Carlee said as she wiped her tears.

"I hope you didn't blow it, honey," Grandma Ellie said sitting in her favorite chair by the window.

"Ma. Don't say that," Devon said hoping his mother wouldn't start in on Carlee.

"I mean you're right dear, but she may have blown it. She could have just remained friends with him and spoke to him every now and again; you know every once in a while just to keep him thinking of her. Oh well," Grandma Ellie said as though she was the one who broke up with Kory.

"Where's Storia?" Carlee asked wiping her nose.

"She hasn't made it in yet. She's on her way. She said her boss wanted to talk to her," Devon said standing by the door.

"Did she get fired?" Carlee asked.

"She didn't say. She sounded well enough," Devon answered.

"You never can tell with Storia," Grandma Ellie replied looking out of the window.

"How long has Hannah been sleeping?" Carlee continued with her questioning.

"About thirty minutes," Grandma Ellie answered.

"Speaking of my darling sister," Carlee said watching the headlights pull up in the driveway.

"You feel better?" Devon asked sounding relieved himself.

"Yeah, thanks, dad. I just felt this heaviness when I thought about him going away, and some panic like I couldn't be without him," Carlee said speaking of Kory.

"Separation anxiety?" Grandma Ellie said shaking her head.

"What's that?" Carlee asked frowning.

"Hello everyone," Storia said walking in the door.

"Oh my god. Ma," Devon said responding to his mother's off diagnoses. "Hey Apple," Devon said kissing Storia's forehead.

"What's what?" Storia said having heard the end of the conversation as she was coming into the door.

"You're late," Grandma Ellie said to Storia looking at Devon.

"Here we go," Devon looked at his mother from the corner of his eye quickly shaking his head and moving his hand across his throat.

"Separation anxiety," Carlee said repeating her grandmother.

"Who has that?" Storia asked puzzled. "Hannah?"

"No one honey. Never mind," Devon said laughing.

"Grammy says I have that. What is it?" Carlee asked looking at Storia.

"You and Kory don't see each other anymore?" Storia asked looking at Carlee with a straight face.

"I broke it off," Carlee answered.

"That's smart," Storia stated.

"Storia," Devon yelled from another room having heard her response.

"It's true daddy. Kory is the real deal. Carlee was pretending. It would have never worked. I can see why you're so upset. He is something special however separation anxiety I thought was something little children experience when they are doing something outside of the parent," Storia explained. "I guess it would be rather fitting if you have it," Storia said laughing.

"So what are you saying," Carlee was getting mad at Storia.

"Ump. Don't play. Kory is a breath of fresh air. With him, there is no pressure, hostility, malice, or drama just a good time. Hopefully, you learned something during the time you spent with him," Storia said to Carlee. "Daddy, I need to speak with you please."

"Sure honey just a moment," Devon ended his call with Lucy and went into the family room to hear what Storia had to say.

"Well, umm, I was at work, and as I was getting off my shift, my boss had a talk with me about Georgia. He told me he would give me a car if I got my license and he even gave me the money to go make it happen," Storia told her father.

"Okay, am I missing something?" Devon asked.

"Well, Mr. Franklin was nice about it. He told me about his daughter and was concerned about me being seen and being friends with Georgia. I heard them going postal on each other, and I think something happened between Georgia and Natalie. I also heard Georgia saying some things that I just didn't like so no more friendship with her, but I don't want to be in a Tommy Trap with Mr. Franklin either," Storia said.

"Nothing happened except that bitch slept with some boy Natalie liked, then Natalie slept with the guy to get him to stay, but Natalie wasn't quite as nasty as Georgia, so you pretty much should know what happened next. Then the poor girl started dating a guy from another town, and Georgia slept with that guy too. To top things off, Georgia "made-up" with Natalie, went to her house crying about how she was such a bitch for what she did. Natalie forgave her for some dumb ass reason, they started hanging out, and it went downhill from there. Natalie began to hang with Georgia's sister and got on drugs. It took her a couple of years to kick the habit," Carlee explained. "I doubt Mr. Franklin is trying to sleep with you. He had some real shit happening at his house surrounding that Georgia bitch."

"Why didn't you tell me this?" Storia asked baffled.

"Well, Storia, she seems to like you, and she had never been evil like that towards you. Besides, she's older, and I never thought once she got past the little girl stage you all would be hanging out. I mean, she just started coming back around after the thing with Tommy," Carlee reasoned.

"Yeah, you don't think that's weird or a coincidence?" Storia said aloud while thinking about the situation to herself.

"At first I did but Storia, you're smart. I mean you're brilliant. I figured sooner or later if the bitch would just be herself, you would figure it out cause no one can hide who they are deep down inside," Carlee expressed.

"You are right about that Carlee. You're 100% correct about that, but it would have saved me some time you know. How's Hannah?" Storia asked on an entirely different mission in her mind that would show Georgia.

"Wow Storia, I'm surprised you're asking about her,' Carlee said sarcastically.

"I know, but how is she?" Storia asked ignoring Carlee's sarcasm.

"She is getting big. She seems happy and she sort of looks like dad and grandma. When are you going to see for yourself?" Carlee asked as she searched through her book bag.

"I'm just not ready, Carlee. You know I appreciate how you, daddy and Nana have been taking care of her though," Storia said clearing her throat.

"So you do care for her?" Carlee asked as she stopped rummaging through her book bag and dumping the content on the couch.

"I have something there, I feel it. I'm just not sure what it is," Storia confessed as she watched Carlee.

"I know you seem like you're struggling, but you can mold her where she is nothing like him. She doesn't look like him, and she doesn't have to act like him," Carlee suggested.

"Right now it just feels like it hurts. My mind has been raging, and sometimes I feel like I'm out of control. I don't even know how or who Tommy is as a person since everything he did and said to me was to take what he could from me," Storia said answering Carlee's suggestion.

"Well, what do you wanna do about it?" Carlee asked looking at Storia.

"I am not sure when it comes to Hannah. I know I want to finish school then get out of this god-forsaken city once and for all," Storia said bitterly.

"I know what you mean Storia, but it's not enough money in this town to get out – only enough to survive.

"You just have to tap into the right profession," Storia said tapping her fingers on the side of the lazy boy.

"Well, then I'd say you have a problem because your I.Q. is higher than what you're able to do in this town. Heck, at the hourly rate in this town, it will be a few years before you're able to save enough to get out of here," Carlee said looking through the junk she poured on the couch.

"You think so, huh?" Storia continued to watch Carlee. "What are you looking for?"

"I met a guy. He gave me his number because at the time my phone was dead. Now I can't find his number. When you leave are you taking Hannah with you?" Carlee asked shuffling through the pages of her books in her book bag.

"I hope I will be able to take her, I do. So you've given up on Kory, huh? This new guy, what's his name?" Storia asked smiling about the idea.

"I'm not worried about it now. I think its Evan. I can't remember. I guess I haven't given up on the idea of Kory and me. It seemed perfect, he and I. Anyway, would you like for me to go with you?" Carlee asked as she put the stuff back in her book bag.

"I couldn't ask nor would I ask you to do that. You have a life you should try to pursue," Storia said.

"Storia, Hannah has become my life," Carlee said convincingly.

"Well, I'm getting out of this town, and if you want to go you're welcome, but you will have to be able to hold your own," Storia said getting up from the lazy boy.

"Hold my own for my niece and me?" Carlee asked.

"No. I will make sure Hannah is taken care of, and it won't be what the government is handing out. No man can truly live like that. You all have done a phenomenal job with Hannah; I mean that, and I appreciate it too. I know it is hard. I hear her at night and in the wee hours of the morning and there is something in me that would like to see about her, but I just can't," Storia said looking out of the window.

"If you think so highly of her why don't you want to parent her?" Carlee asked upset by Storia's comment.

"Have you not heard anything I've said? I have many things I have to deal with in my mind as it pertains to Tommy and me. That affects me greatly when it comes to her and if you don't understand that then frankly that is your problem. I care about Hannah, but as far as I am concerned, it wouldn't be a disservice to place her in a home. She can get adopted where she will have a mother and father who love her. You're not going to make me feel guilty about why I don't do this or that. If you don't want to do it, you know you don't have to, but you will not make me feel bad about what you think you're doing and how it's so great and how what I'm doing is so wrong and bad. You're a trip. Daddy and Nana are the ones who take care of her the most and the best Carlee. Don't start feeling yourself," Storia said growing testy of Carlee's tone.

"I'm not going to sit here and try to figure out why you resent Hannah because some dirty pervert repeatedly raped you, you need to come to your senses," Carlee said not knowing why she made that comment.

"I can see that you're stuck on stupid in the worse way. You clearly don't understand, and I won't waste another ounce of my breath trying to explain because it is pointless. You keep telling yourself whatever you think you need to tell yourself to make you the better person or aunt; I don't care. Understand this though; I have an ultimate say as to what happens with my daughter. I don't care how many nights you wake up and attend to her, she is my daughter, and at the end of the day, things will happen the way I want them to happen no matter your opinion," Storia walked towards the stairs angrily.

"No, I don't understand, but I know I love my niece," Carlee didn't want to say anything else since she figured out where Storia was going with what she said.

"Goodnight," Storia said walking up the stairs.

"Goodnight Storia. I love you," Carlee said as she watched Storia stomp up the stairs. Storia didn't say she loved her back.

Carlee walked the living area thinking about what she said to Storia. She thought she might have gone too far. She walked into the kitchen to get some water wondering why she was so mad at Storia. It wasn't like she didn't know what happened to Storia and how she came to be in the situation she thought to herself. Carlee drank some of the water and placed the glass on the table. She sat there thinking about her life without her sister or her niece. Carlee didn't like the way she felt. She poured out the water and left the glass in the sink. Carlee turned off the lights in the kitchen, and living area then walked up the stairs. She stopped at Storia's door as she got to the top of the stairs. She knocked, but Storia didn't answer. She could see the light pouring out the bottom of the door, so she knew Storia was still awake. Carlee assessed Storia to be highly upset with her. Carlee stood at Storia's door for a couple of minutes then walked to her room and lay on the bed until she fell asleep.

Storia sat at her desk writing, calculating, printing, and posting information on her corkboard. She picked up the driver's training book and read about the rules of driving. She heard Hannah cry. Storia tried to continue reading when she realized after a while that Carlee was not coming to Hannah's aid. Storia placed the book on the desk and swerved around in her chair. She put her feet in her slippers, stood up from the chair and walked over to the door. She listened quietly. She slowly opened the door noticing the cries were getting louder. Storia walked over to her desk and grabbed her book then walked down the hall to Hannah's room.

Storia walked into Hannah's nursery and could see Hannah in the shadow of the night light laying in the crib crying at the top of her lungs. Storia walked over to the mini-fridge and took out a bottle as Hannah cried in the crib. She grabs the bowl on the microwave and went to the bathroom to fill the container with water, then walked back to Hannah's room and placed the bowl of water in the microwave for a minute. When the microwave went off, Storia took the bowl out of the microwave and set the bottle in it. While she waited for the bottle to warm, she walked over to Hannah's crib and stuck her finger in the side of Hannah's diaper. She continued to ignore Hannah's crying as she walked over to the diaper stall and took a diaper out. Storia grabbed the wipes then walked back over to Hannah and changed her diaper. Storia took Hannah's old diaper over to the diaper disposal then took a wet wipe and wiped her hands as she walked over to get the bottle. She shook the bottle up and down squirting milk on her wrist to check the temperature.

Storia did not want to pick Hannah up, so she turned her over to the side and propped Hannah with a pillow and placed the bottle in Hannah's mouth. She noticed Hannah holding the bottle as she lay on her side drinking. Storia took the driver's book out of her robe pocket, sat in the rocker, and started reading where she left off. When Storia looked over at Hannah, Storia noticed Hannah drunk her milk. Storia marked the page in her driver's book, stood up, placed the book in her robe pocket, walked over to Hannah, and patted her on her back. Hannah let off a few burps as Storia continued patting her back. Storia removed the pillow and decided to put a sleeper on Hannah because her legs were cold. She went over to Hannah's dresser and noticed Hannah had little in the way of clothing. She thought, in her mind, that was a problem. Hannah had a yellow sleeper that turned out to be too small for her, and the only thing she had was the thin blanket from the hospital. Storia stormed out of Hannah's room and walked to her own. She looked in her dresser drawer got a sweater and took it to Hannah's room. Storia put the article on the bottom half of Hannah's body. Storia was fuming as she walked back to her room. She pulled out her schedule and corrected her previous calculations as she talked to herself complaining about Hannah not having any clothes. She spoke to herself as she fell asleep.

CHAPTER 16

Storia woke up and went to her closet. She picked out something to wear, grabbed underwear and socks and went to the bathroom. She looked at herself in the mirror as she brushed her teeth thinking about what she had planned to do. She squirted her facial product in her hands and washed her face then she brushed her hair up into a ponytail and jumped in the shower. Storia got out of the shower upset. She wasn't sure why she was mad, but she didn't understand why Hannah had no clothing. She patted her hair with the towel and then wrapped the towel around her body and walked down to Hannah's room and peeked in; Hannah was sleep. Storia stepped down to her room and put her favorite scented lotion on her body. She put her clothes on then grabbed jewelry and shoes to complete her look. Storia grabbed her book bag and went downstairs. She took something from the fridge and walked out of the door.

#

Carlee woke up and went to the bathroom. She washed up and brushed her teeth. She walked over to Hannah's room and picked Hannah up from the crib. She walked over to Hannah's dresser to get booties, a pair of shorts and an undershirt. She liked the ones that snapped she thought. Carlee walked Hannah to the bathroom, put her in the bathtub, and washed her. Then Carlee dressed Hannah and placed some of Storia's hair lotion in Hannah's hair. She took Hannah downstairs and put her in the high chair then gave Hannah some fruity rings. Carlee poured orange juice for herself and grabbed a piece of carrot cake Grandma Ellie made. Carlee sat at the bar in the kitchen and watched Hannah eat the fruit rings. She gave Hannah a bottle then went to the door and put on her shoes. Carlee went into the front closet, took Hannah's stroller out, and took it outside. She walked back into the house picked up Hannah then took her outside and placed her in the stroller. As she walked back on the porch, her dad was in the doorway handing her Hannah's diaper bag. Carlee told her father she was going to the park.

#

Devon walked over to his ringing phone sitting on the island in the kitchen and answered, it was Lucy. He and Lucy spoke to one another planning to see each other that night. Devon was excited about them going out. He complained to her about her complaining to him citing he was overworking her. Lucy did not agree as she explained she would never complain because she loved her role in the company. Devon and Lucy laughed as they continued talking with one another. Grandma Ellie interrupted Devon by calling him. He ended the call with Lucy and went to see what was going on with his mother. Grandma

Ellie wanted Devon to get the door; she couldn't get up because her knees were bothering her. It was Kory.

"Hey, Kory. How are you?" Devon asked smiling surprised at how happy he was to see Kory.

"I'm good, Mr. DeLuca. How are things going with you?" Kory asked politely.

"Good, really, good. What can I do for you young man?" Devon asked as he opened the door to welcome Kory into the home.

"Is Carlee around?" Kory asked. He walked into the house.

"No. I'm sorry. She took the baby to the park," Devon said.

"Oh. Okay. Well, could you tell your daughter I just stopped by to see how things were going and to say hello?" Kory noticed Devon looked disappointed.

"Uh, okay Kory. I don't think that's a good idea," Devon said sadly.

"I understand Mr. DeLuca, sorry for disturbing you," Kory said as he opened the door, walked out to the porch and down the stairs.

"Hey Kory, you weren't disturbing me at all," Devon said as Kory stopped to hear what Devon was saying. "I'm just sorry she isn't here. It was great seeing you,"

Devon watched Kory get into his car and drive off. Devon locked the screen door and headed into the kitchen. He took his phone out of his pocket and called Lucy again.

"So he does like her, huh?" Grandma said happily, struggling to make it into the living area.

"It seems like it, but I don't know. I mean, I'm not sure. You know how Carlee feels about him, I just don't want her to get her hopes up," Devon watched his mother move slowly to her favorite chair.

"You're not going to tell her he stopped by are you?"

"Ma, you know how she feels about him," Devon answered.

"That's why you should tell her and let her decide," Grandma Ellie suggested.

"Ma, I just don't want to," Devon said.

"You don't want what dad?" Carlee said coming in the door with Hannah.

"Hey Pumpkin. Hey Hanny," Devon kissed Hannah on the cheek. "How was the park?"

"Dad, the park was fine. What's going on?" Carlee asked as she sat Hannah's bag on the table.

"Well, Pumpkin. Kory stopped by," Devon smiled.

"That's what happened?" Carlee asked puzzled.

"Yeah, I didn't want to tell you because I know how you feel about him," Devon said grabbing Carlee's hands.

"How I felt dad? Kory was so last week," Carlee said lying.

"Okay. Well, glad to know," Devon responded with hesitation.

"Come on Hannah," Carlee said taking Hannah from her stroller. "Let's go take a nap. Have you spoken to Storia?" Carlee asked. She waited for a response from her dad or grandmother.

"No honey. Not yet," Devon answered. Grandma Ellie shook her head vigorously.

"You know she took care of Hannah about three this morning?" Carlee wanted to see what her father would say. She got complete silence from her father. "Dad," she called.

"I heard you Pumpkin. I don't know what you want me to say about that. Isn't that a good thing?" Devon did not want to aggravate Carlee.

"Yes. Yes, it is a good thing," Carlee kissed Hannah softly.

"I wasn't going to bring it up, but Storia cried for about 45 minutes afterward. I mean she went to her room and goofed around for a minute, then she must have got in the bed and starting crying," Carlee added.

"Oh wow. Why do you think Storia went to see about Hannah if she was just going to cry about it?" Devon asked Carlee.

"Because no one else responded and she is compassionate. Make no mistake; she does care about that little girl. Don't blow your relationship with Storia trying to be a hardass about what she is not doing. She needs time. Hell, I would have given her up. I would not, and I repeat I would not have kept the child I obtained through rape. Carlee, clearly you don't understand. I, for one, am surprised she hasn't flipped. Storia has gone through a lot, and you must know by now that seeing and or hearing Hannah every day is a bit too much, in my opinion. It was a good start. Don't you agree? Why can't you rejoice in that?" Grandma Ellie looked at Carlee with contempt.

"I'll talk to her when she gets home," Devon replied.

"What time does she get off now? She gets home later, and later it seems," Grandma Ellie stated with concern.

"Good question. I thought Storia was supposed to work part-time hours since she is still in school," Devon voiced with the same concern. "She gets here around midnight if not later every night."

"She's on schedule every day, is she?" Grandma Ellie asked.

"Seems like it," Devon replied.

"Who is that who runs that restaurant?" Grandma Ellie asked as she looked out the window at the woman walking her dog.

"James from Lawton. You remember his family, right? They called him Lil' Jimmy."

"Yeah, the Franklin's I wanna say," Grandma Ellie said making her way to the door.

"Yeah, that's it. The only one I remember well is Leah," Devon said going towards the door to see what his mother was doing.

"Yes, she was a beautiful girl. The young lady I wanted you to marry," Grandma Ellie said to Devon. "Hey lady! Our flippin' lawn is not your dog's toilet. Get that crap up!" Grandma Ellie screamed.

"Oh mom, please don't start," Devon said speaking of Leah.

"I'm not saying anything. Anything else, anyway," Grandma Ellie said as she made her way back to her favorite chair.

"That trip to the park did her some good. She is out like a light," Carlee said coming into the living area.

"Good. I wonder how long Hannah will sleep." Devon asked rhetorically.

"She seems to be sleeping longer probably because Storia has been putting cereal in with the milk," Carlee concluded.

"Ma, is that good?" Devon asked.

"Well, it doesn't hurt, but she should be sitting her in her highchair because you have to make the hole in the nipple bigger for the cereal to come out. You have to monitor her while she's drinking from those types of bottles to make sure she doesn't choke. How often is she getting one of those bottles?" Grandma Ellie asked.

"I think twice. I noticed it while we were at the park. She usually gets one at night too," Carlee answered.

"How can you tell the ones with cereal in them?" Devon asked.

"The ones with cereal are marked, dad. Storia has them organized fairly well if you're paying attention," Carlee said.

"I did notice bottles in the fridges, but I usually make Hannah's bottle fresh. Like yesterday, I gave her Cere-ohs while I made her bottle. That was fun," Grandma Ellie said laughing.

"I can tell Cere-ohs were well into the living room. How many did you give her cause it seems like there was about a cup on a floor?" Devon asked.

"She pushed the bowl off the sitter," Grandma Ellie giggled.

"Why didn't you get them up mom?" Devon asked.

"I got distracted," Grandma Ellie, replied.

"I'm going to let that go since it's up now," Devon walked towards the door.

"Good decision son," Grandma Ellie noticed Carlee seemed in deep in thought.

"Oh mom," Devon said facepalming.

Devon walked into the living room and picked up the mail from the coffee table. As he walked through the house thumbing through the envelopes, he looked at the clock in the hallway and thought about Storia. Devon went into the family room and picked up his phone. He noticed there were no calls or texts, and then scrolled through his emails and responded to a few as he sat at his desk. Devon opened the drawer and removed his letter opener then opened the mail one time without looking at whom the letters were from or to whom the letters were addressed. He turned the letters around, removed the content from them, and read the information. There were a few notices, a thank you postcard from Bob about the deal they put together, a commission check, and best of all, a letter from his sister, Eloise. It had a few pictures, two tickets to an upcoming game and an 8x11 sheet of paper with I love you written on the very top. Devon smiled then pulled out his phone and sent his sister a text letting her know that he received her note. Devon, tired of texting, called his sister and talked to her and her husband for 20 minutes. Once he ended the call, he reviewed the bills that were a part of the mail he received. He pulled his checkbook out of the drawer and wrote a check for the utilities and the cell phone. He delayed paying the credit card bill and construction invoices until he was able to give more time to the charges and statement. The last item was a letter addressed to Carlee from the local university. As he was about to pull the information from the envelope, Devon heard a car door shut. He got up and walked into the living area then looked at the clock. It was 12:12 a.m.

"Storia," Devon called.

"Yes, daddy. Daddy, I'm tired. I have to take a shower. I'll come back once I finish. I promise. Okay, daddy?" Storia ran up the stairs.

"Okay, Apple. I wanna see you," Devon replied.

"Okay," Storia called down from the top of the steps.

Storia went into her room. She threw her purse on her bed then walked over to her dresser and grabbed a set of pajamas. She took a towel and washcloth out of her closet and went into the bathroom. She brushed her teeth and got into the shower. Storia stood in the water and adjusted the temperature. She grabbed her body wash and poured it on her loofah then washed her body and hair. As Storia stepped under the water, she could faintly hear Hannah crying. She rinsed the soap out of her hair and rung it with her hands. Storia stuck her head out of the shower, but she didn't hear Hannah, so she continued washing. Storia rinsed the soap off her body, turned the water off, and got out of the shower. After putting on body oil, she patted herself dry then put on her nightclothes and robe.

Storia walked down the hall and placed her towels in the laundry basket. As Storia walked pass Hannah's room, she could hear Carlee talking to Hannah. She peeked in the door.

"Are you coming to check on Hannah?" Carlee asked.

"Well, actually I was how is she doing?" Storia answered then asked.

"She was stinky, and I figured probably hungry. I am going to give her the cereal milk. I will sit here with her to make sure everything goes well," Carlee said as she picked Hannah up out of bed.

"That's cool," Storia said smiling at Hannah looking at her.

"Yeah. Why are you coming in so late?" Carlee asked as she gave Hannah her bottle.

"Handling some business," Storia responded.

"I thought you were off at 9?" Carlee looked at Storia suspiciously.

"I am but I told you, I want out of this town," Storia sounded irritated by Carlee's questions.

"So you stay late?" Carlee continued.

"No and please stop asking me so many questions," Storia demanded.

"Why? Are you going to lie to me if I ask you another?" Carlee asked snippily.

"No. I don't have to lie. I'm just going to ignore you as though you've asked nothing," Storia was clearly agitated.

"So, how much have you made so far?" Carlee asked.

"Obviously, you have issues. Since Hannah's fine, I'm going to bed. Goodnight," Storia walked towards the door.

"Are you underground stripping?" Carlee asked as she watched Storia head for the door unbothered by Carlee's question.

"Thanks for taking care of Hannah. I love you, Carlee. Goodnight," Storia walked out of the door and down the hall.

"I love you, Storia, my dear beautiful sister and I will find out what you're up to that has you out so late at night. Goodnight. Isn't that right Hanny Poo? We're going to find out what your mommy is doing?"

Storia went to her room and locked the door. She picked up her clothes from the bed and walked them over to the hamper. Before she threw the clothes in the basket, she stuck her hand in the pocket and pulled out a wad of cash from both pockets. She dropped the clothes in the hamper, walked over, and dropped the money on the bed. She sat on the edge of the bed and grabbed her purse. She walked over to the mirror with her bag and sat her purse on the dresser. She looked at herself, pulled the skin in the corner of her eyes then picked up a cotton ball, dipped it in the eye makeup remover and rubbed her eyes removing the remaining makeup. She pumped moisturizer into her hands, rubbed her hands together, and placed the moisturizer on her face. As she applied the moisturizer, she wiped the tears as they fell down her face. She quickly wiped the last tear and grabbed her purse. She removed the money inside and walked over to her bed.

Storia stacked the money by denomination. She placed the ones first, the fives, tens, the twenties, fifties and the hundred dollar bills she had in her hand. She forgot the tips she had in her hosting uniform, so she walked over and took the money out of the pocket then hung it on the back of the door. Storia walked back over to the bed and placed those bills on top of the money already lying on the bed. Leaving the singles and fives, she picked up and counted the rest. She wrote the amount down folded the cash, bound it with a rubber band, walked over to her closet. She dropped to her knees and reached up to a camel color blazer she had hanging up. She reached into the inner pocket and removed a small key. She kneeled on all fours to reach the little cash box deep in the back of her closet, opened it, and put the money she had on top of the money already in the box. A knock at the door frightened Storia. It was her father. Storia asked her father to wait then she rushed and locked the box, pushed the rows of shoes back, took the key and placed it in the upper pocket of a blue jean vest she had hanging in the back. She walked out of the closet and closed the door.

"Storia," Devon called.

"Daddy, give me a moment. I was busy doing something," Storia replied as she made sure nothing was exposed that her father would see.

Storia grabbed the rest of the money off the bed, folded it, and grabbed a ponytail holder off her dresser. She wrapped the ponytail holder around the cash and then placed the money in her purse. She walked quickly over to the door and opened it.

"What were you doing, honey?" Devon asked.

"Daddy, I was doing girl stuff," Storia said as she grabbed the big brush she had sitting on the bed and brushed her partially dry hair. "What's up daddy?"

"Well honey, I'm worried about you," Devon said standing in the middle of the floor with his hands in his pocket.

"Why?" Storia asked as she twisted her hair.

"Because – well, you've been pretty distant lately. You're working or should I say you're leaving the house every day now and getting home late. Honey, you're only 16. Your work schedule shouldn't be so heavy," Devon said concerned.

"Daddy, I'm almost 17, and I have things that I would like to do," Storia rolled her hair into a ball on top of her head.

"What's that on your corkboard?" Devon asked as he stared.

"Those are my plans and some things I'm working towards," Storia said as her heart began pounding.

"A house, huh?" Devon said as he thought about Storia leaving.

"Yes, daddy a house, I can't live here or in this town forever," Storia tried not to let on that she was nervous.

"Are you taking Hannah with you?" Devon asked curious to know what Storia would say hoping she would answer no.

"Of course, daddy, after all, she is MY daughter," Storia said as though Devon should have known.

"You don't treat her as such, so it's funny you include her," Devon said stiffly.

(Sigh) "I am not about to fight with you, daddy. She is my daughter and when I leave, she leaves," Storia said responding to what she perceived as attitude from her father.

"Well honey, I don't think so," Devon said now wanting to debate.

"Daddy, is this what you wanted? My daughter is not an option. As a matter of fact... daddy, NO! Actually, I am not going to do this with you. Please excuse yourself from my room. I am about to lie down. I do love you daddy, but you don't know me the way you think you do. Good night," Storia said sternly.

"Actually, no I will not excuse myself, Storia, I don't want you working anymore," Devon said firmly.

"Daddy, we can talk about this some other time. I have school in the morning," Storia said with her back to her father.

"Did you hear me Storia? I want you home. Since you have a daughter, when you get out of school, you need to come home and care for her," Devon said thinking he was putting his foot down.

"You know what? Maybe I'll find a place of my own and leave altogether. What I don't need is you trying to be a parent to me. You or mom has been stellar. You did a noble thing taking Carlee and me in especially since I had my daughter, but daddy; please don't act like you've been in my life the whole time. You are my daddy, and the whole thing is nice and all, but you missed the years where you needed to get to know me enough to tell me what to do now. My grades are great, I have a job and baby expenses," Storia tried not to yell, but she was losing control of her vocal range.

"Don't worry about Hannah's expenses," Devon said trying to control what he was feeling after Storia's comment.

"Don't worry about Hannah's expenses and she doesn't have any sleepers? Don't worry about her expenses and she doesn't have a blanket that didn't come from the hospital? Don't worry about her expenses and she doesn't have a pair of shoes that are not tight on her feet? How is that teaching me to be responsible? She'll be walking soon, and she doesn't have a nice pair of soft bottoms so that she can walk. She doesn't have a walker or a playpen. I know you being in my room right now is about something else, but I just don't have the time to address it, daddy. I'm tired, and I have school. Goodnight!" Storia was upset.

"Okay, but we will talk about this later," the tone of Devon's voice was serious but weak.

"Goodnight," Storia ignored Devon's attempt to hug her.

"Goodnight," Devon watched Storia roll over on her bed.

Devon walked out of Storia's room. He closed the door and walked down the stairs. He could see his mother sitting in her favorite chair. He walked over and sat on the couch. The two put their heads together about Storia. Devon told his mother he wanted to have Storia followed. His mother agreed, and the two decided to contact someone they've known a while. Storia kicked the cover off her body. She got up and took her robe off. She lay sideways on the bed and pulled her appointment book from under her bed. Storia looked at the plans posted on the corkboard she had on the wall then she placed a checkmark on the side of names she had in the book, then she transferred that information onto dates the following week. She found another hiding space for her appointment book; then pulled out her journal. She looked at her alarm clock. It was later than she thought. She locked and pushed the journal under her side table. She pushed it to the back and looked to see if it could be seen standing over the table. It was in the right spot she thought. She opened her Bible. As she lay on her back, she closed her eyes and tears began to fall out the sides of her eyes.

"Father, I know you know my heart, yet I have had many now. This is my confession. I have allowed the sex organ of many to enter my mouth and have lain with one unscrupulously. He is not my husband, and I don't want him to be Father, I am ashamed. I need your forgiveness, but I cannot ask of it now; I don't have intentions of stopping what I am doing right now. My life is without meaning in my opinion. I know you would disagree. I am young in years growing older in my mind by the day, and my heart weeps every time I commit this horrid crime against my body. My knowledge of your forgiveness is the peace that I have knowing you are with me. The tears I cry are in vain, but these words in my heart remain. Bow down your ear oh lord hear me. I am poor and needy. Preserve my life, for, in my heart; I am holy. You are my God. Save your servant who trusts you. I give my life and my soul to you. Please hear me, Father, though I am a sinner I need you in my life. Please, Father..." Storia continued praying as she fell asleep with the Bible laying open across her chest on Psalm 86.

#

Carlee spent most of her time between classes looking for Kory. The other time she spent beating herself up for not calling him after her father told her he had stopped by the house. After walking over to the last place she knew him to hang out, she ran to the office to get a pass so she would be able to get into her class. She walked into the office greeted by the assistant principal. He asked her why she was late, she lied, received the pass and just as she was about to push the door to go out, Mr. Hunklebee, the school principal, called her name. Carlee harkened to his call where he proceeded to give Carlee a message for her to give to Storia. Carlee was surprised but took the envelope and told Mr. Hunklebee she would make sure Storia received the content. Mr. Hunklebee then asked Carlee for Storia's phone number. Carlee became suspicious of Mr. Hunklebee. She wanted to know why he needed her direct phone number. Mr. Hunklebee told Carlee it was for his daughter and to make Carlee feel at ease; he asked Carlee to take his daughter's contact information to give to Storia. Mr. Hunklebee wanted Carlee to tell Storia to give his daughter a call. Mr. Hunklebee would further explain to Carlee that his daughter was away at boarding school and just wanted to stay in touch with Storia. Carlee seemed to be okay with the explanation. She took his daughter's number and told him she would make sure she gave Storia the contact info.

Carlee walked away from Mr. Hunklebee feeling as though she was out of the loop, entirely, but she didn't know what circuit exactly. She wondered why he didn't give the envelope and number to Storia himself. She looked at the envelope. It was just a long mailing envelope, but it was thick as if it contained a lot of folded paper. She held it up to the sun, but she could not see through it. Carlee grew more curious as she realized it was a secured envelope, so she shook it, but it didn't shift, and it made no noise. Carlee thought to open the envelope, but she did not have the means to replace it, so she just held on to it as she made her way to her class. Carlee thought to herself that there was no need to open the envelope. Storia would share the contents with her anyway.

Carlee walked into the class and looked around to see from whom she could get notes. She handed the teacher the pass and walked down the row. No sooner than Carlee took to sit down, she was called upon to answer a question posed to the class. She let off a loud sigh, turned around and asked for the page. After receiving the page number, she glanced at the page then asked the teacher to repeat the question. The teacher asked the question again, and Carlee gave her answer.

"Your sister wouldn't have taken so long," the teacher said sarcastically.

"What? Oh? Are you comparing me to my sister? That's professional, thank you so much. You asked a question when I wasn't here; you call on me to answer a question for which I didn't hear then you compare me to my little sister when I ask you for reference information? What a joke!" Carlee said with an attitude as she looked at the students laughing.

"Watch your tone with me, young lady," the teacher said.

"You clown me about my sister, and I have to watch my tone? You have it twisted. Any more questions?" Carlee asked indignantly. She received no reply from the teacher. "I didn't think so," Carlee added.

Carlee sat down and worked on the class assignment. She looked at the board and jotted down the homework assignments then she asked her classmates if there were any notes. Two of her classmates gave her notes they had, so she took out her phone and took pictures thanking her classmates.

"I'll take that phone," the teacher said standing near Carlee's desk.

"No, you won't. I was just taking pictures of the notes because I don't have time to write them all down. What is your problem?" Carlee asked sharply as the teacher walked back towards her desk.

"Your sister is her problem," a classmate whispered.

"You know, Miss DeLuca, I think it is time for you to pay a little visit to the principal's office," the teacher said as she arrived at her desk and wrote out a detention notice for Carlee.

"Okay," Carlee said as she took a picture of the last few notes.

"Give me your number, and I'll call you and give you the assignment information for tomorrow," the classmate whispered.

Carlee wrote her number down on the classmate's notebook then got up from her desk and walked towards the door. Then the bell rang. Carlee walked out the door with the detention notice. She sat on the bench in the hallway and put the detention slip in her bag. Carlee looked through the pictures of the notes and sent them to her email. As she sat on the bench forwarding the photos, her teacher walked over to her and expressed her disappointment with Carlee's behavior. Carlee expressed to the teacher how much it didn't matter to her since she already had detention. Carlee told the teacher she felt attacked for no reason. The teacher apologized and asked her for the detention notice. The teacher let Carlee know that she was upset about something else and her arriving late to her class with a rude, unpleasant demeanor disrupting the class as she took her seat only made her more upset. Carlee handed her teacher the detention slip, looked at her phone, and excused herself telling her teacher she had to get moving before she ended up late for her next class. Her teacher understood and let Carlee go. Carlee noticed her teacher wasn't wearing her wedding ring and quickly asked her about it since her teacher always made a big deal about the ring. Her teacher told her she didn't want to lie or talk about it. Carlee looked at her strangely then power walked down the hall and stairs. She made it down the stair, where her class was two doors away. All of her trying to get to her class on time went out of the window when she saw Kory.

Carlee immediately felt faint. Butterflies rushed to her stomach, and she could feel her heart beating fast. She was frozen. She couldn't take her eyes off of him. Carlee's teacher came out into the hall, and after seeing Carlee told her, she had a few more minutes. Carlee didn't respond as she continued staring as Kory walked by looking at her too. Carlee dropped her head, turned her body slightly and watched Kory as he continued down the hall looking back periodically at Carlee. Carlee's teacher placed her hand on Carlee's waist and pulled her in the class citing young love.

"Honey you won't catch a respectable guy staring so rudely," Carlee's teacher, Mrs. Green said.

"Mrs. Green, he is just so dreamy, I can't help it, at all," Carlee said in a haze.

"Okay honey. Have a seat and let's get focused on the assignment. Do you have your homework assignment? You can turn it in now if you like," Mrs. Green said as she stood near Carlee trying to get her refocused.

Carlee handed Mrs. Green her homework assignment. She went in and out of focus on her class assignment and hardly participated thinking and daydreaming about Kory. She attempted at the pop quiz and was sure she failed. As she exchanged the exam with at least three other students, she pulled a red pen from her bag and waited for the teacher's aide to give the answers aloud so she could check the quiz. She daydreamed in that instance. He kissed her, and she blushed in her daydream. She was brought to reality by the person whose exam she had asking if he had the answer right. Carlee responded curtly. She shouted at her classmate for interrupting her; then she asked the aide to repeat the answers citing her classmate distracted her. Once the answers were given, Carlee signed her name at the bottom and passed the quiz to the front. She wrote the homework assignment down and sat frustrated having had her daydream interrupted.

Carlee slowly put her paperwork in her bag, and then the bell rang. Before she got up from her desk, she thought she should wait to see if Kory would come back pass. She got up from her chair and walked to the door. She adjusted her clothing and walked out. She saw a few people she knew and walked over to them hoping Kory would walk by and interrupt her conversation. She tried not to seem like she was searching for him by gazing down the hall, but she couldn't help herself. She finally made up her mind she wouldn't look, and she didn't. He never came. She talked a little longer and noticed the hall was clearing. She told her friends she would speak to them later and she headed down the stairs. As Carlee walked down the stairs, a friend asked her if she wanted to go to lunch. Carlee wasn't sure because she tried to catch up with Storia, but she agreed to go. Storia headed out into the parking lot with her friend, having just gotten out of class. Once they arrived in the parking lot, her friend took off with her boyfriend leaving Storia to figure out what she would do for lunch. Storia was disappointed hoping to ride with her friend to get fast food but made her way to the lunchroom.

Carlee walked to the parking lot looking at text messages on her phone. She went to the sidewalk and walked towards the back door of the school. Carlee turned around, went back to the school, and stopped at her locker. She threw in her book bag. She put her earbuds in her ears and with her head down searching for music. She walked towards the lunchroom moping still searching for some entertainment. Suddenly, someone bumped into her seemingly purposely. She quickly looked up, and it was him.

"OMG!" Carlee thought to herself nervously.

"You really should look where you're going," Kory said agitatedly.

"Did you see me?" Carlee said softly.

"Do you think that's the point?"

"Well, yeah," Carlee said noticing his demeanor.

"Really?"

"Yes," Carlee said softer than before.

"Do you think you're the only one walking the hall?" Kory said meanly.

"No, I don't, but if you see that I'm not paying attention, do you still walk towards me because you have the right away?" Carlee said not understanding why Kory was so mean to her.

"Yeah, well, I kinda do. The next step for you would be that wall. I bumped into you to get your attention and to say to you pay attention," Kory said strangely.

"Really? That's why you bumped into me? You honestly think I would have walked into the wall? If you want to say something to me, say it. Don't make stuff up just to speak to me," Carlee was lost in Kory's eyes even after he spoke to her bitterly.

"I can't speculate. The only thing I know is I was walking up the hall in the right direction, and you weren't. If you were paying attention, you would have seen that you were on the pathway to walk into that wall. Since I see your facial expression, I guess you're upset about this situation. I apologize. Take it easy," Kory said as he started walking down the hallway realizing he was a jerk.

Carlee panicked. She could not believe after all the thinking she was doing about him it came down to debating about walking up the hallway. She closed her eyes and turned around.

"Kory," Carlee called.

Kory continued walking then slowly turned around, but he said nothing. Carlee ran to him. When she reached him, she looked at him.

"Are you mad?" Carlee asked.

"Not at..." Kory couldn't get the rest of his sentence out.

Carlee kissed Kory. She had in her mind he would push her away so for the second she would feel his lips she took full advantage and just in that second, Kory pushed Carlee away.

"What are you doing, Carlee?" Kory asked looking at her surprised but angry.

Carlee touched her lips not caring what he had to say.

"I'm sorry you didn't want me to do that, but I'm not sorry I kissed you. I feel like I love you, and I don't know how to stop. I'm trying. I don't want to hear any more scripture. I know I was wrong because it is something you don't believe, but if I never see or talk to you again at least, I kissed your lips and touched your face. They were as soft as I could have ever imagined and you smell better than I wished," Carlee said.

Carlee seemingly floated away beaming from ear to ear. She was on a cloud higher than anything she had ever felt. She sent a text to Storia. She had to tell someone.

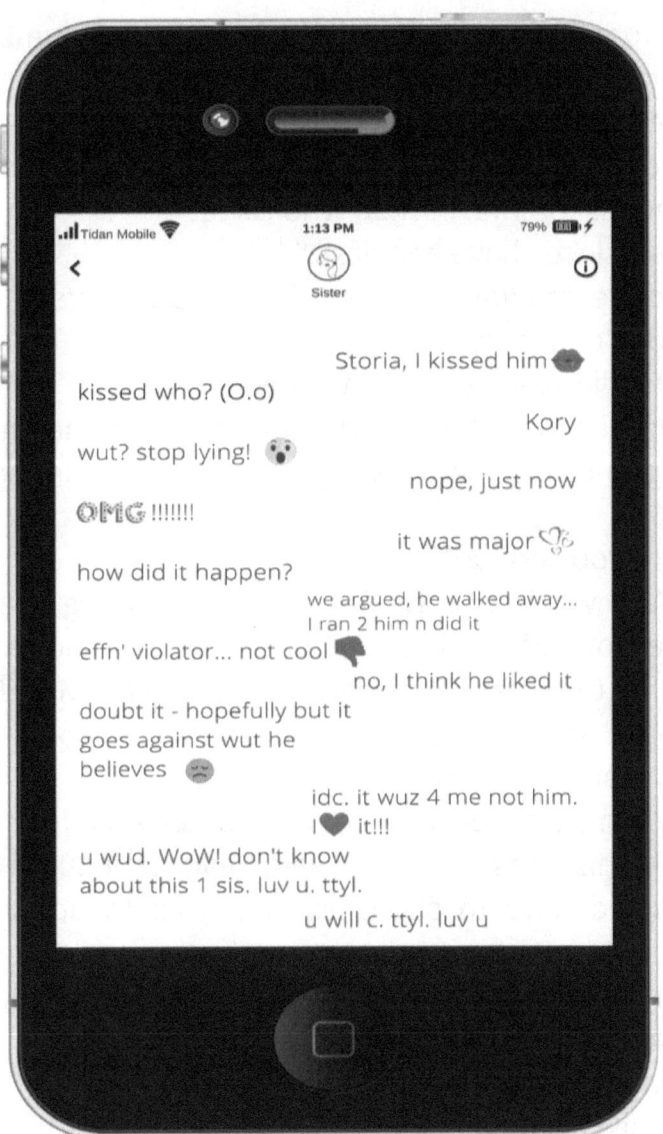

Carlee took a selfie and sent it to Storia. She was so happy with herself she could hardly contain herself.

"Yes Carlee," Storia said annoyed that Carlee called her.

"I forgot to tell you, I have a phone number and envelope from Hunklebee, and completely off topic, Mrs. Parker spazzed on me because of you."

"I don't want either...give that crap back to him, today Carlee. As for Mrs. Parker, who cares?"

"I do since I have her class."

"You're graduating soon, Carlee. Do yourself a favor and don't sweat it."

"She didn't have on her wedding ring."

"No surprise there. Mrs. Parker caught her husband trying to talk me into having relations with him and their son."

"Are you serious?"

"Why would I lie to you about something like that? I walked out of the building, and their son Jac called me over to their car. The whole time I think Mrs. Parker's husband and son want to kidnap me."

"You are crazy," Carlee giggled.

"When I walk over there, Mr. Parker asked if I wanted to take his son's virginity. I said yeah for $3,000. He said he would have to show his son what to do, so I said $7,500. Mr. Parker said okay, and when I repeated what he agreed to pay me $7,500 for, Mrs. Parker threw her ring at him, and that is all that I know."

"Damn Storia, what the fuck?"

"That's what happened."

"No wonders she's pissed."

"Oh well."

"Storia, tell the woman you were just kidding."

"I'm not telling her any such thing. I have to go. I've used my time talking to you. Not cool. Bye Carlee."

Carlee used the remaining time on her lunch in the lunchroom listening to music. She went to the principle to give him the envelope he had given her earlier, but he wouldn't take it. He told Carlee to place the envelope in Storia's hands and tell her no expectations. Carlee had a raised eyebrow moment, but she kept it and put it back in her bag. She asked Mr. Hunklebee if he still wanted Storia to call his daughter and he looked at her confused as if he didn't know what she was talking about, and then suddenly, he, air quotes, remembered. Carlee was over the whole situation by that time. She went to the rest of her classes. At the end of the school day, she went to her locker then raced out the door to bum a ride still on a cloud. She got a ride from one of her friends.

When Carlee arrived at her house, she danced from the car to the house. She dropped her book bag on the couch and picked up Hannah who was in her brand new walker. She danced around the room with Hannah then took her upstairs and changed her diaper. In the process, she noticed Hannah had several new items in her closet, so she dressed Hannah in one of the new outfits. She grabbed a bottle out of the mini-fridge and put it in Hannah's diaper bag, took Hannah and went downstairs. Carlee pulled Hannah's stroller out of the closet and put Hannah's diaper bag in the back, then Hannah in the stroller.

Carlee rolled the stroller out the door and onto the porch. She carried the stroller down the stairs then strolled with Hannah down the street. Carlee walked to the store, which was a little further than what she usually walks when she takes Hannah to the park. To her amazement, she saw Storia with a guy. She stood still hoping Storia didn't look her way. She watched the man walk Storia to the passenger side of his car and open the door for her. She watched Storia get in the car and then she watched him bend over and kiss Storia then close the door. She noticed Storia's attention on him. She watched him get in the car, and the two drove off. Carlee didn't know how to feel. She sent a text message to Storia.

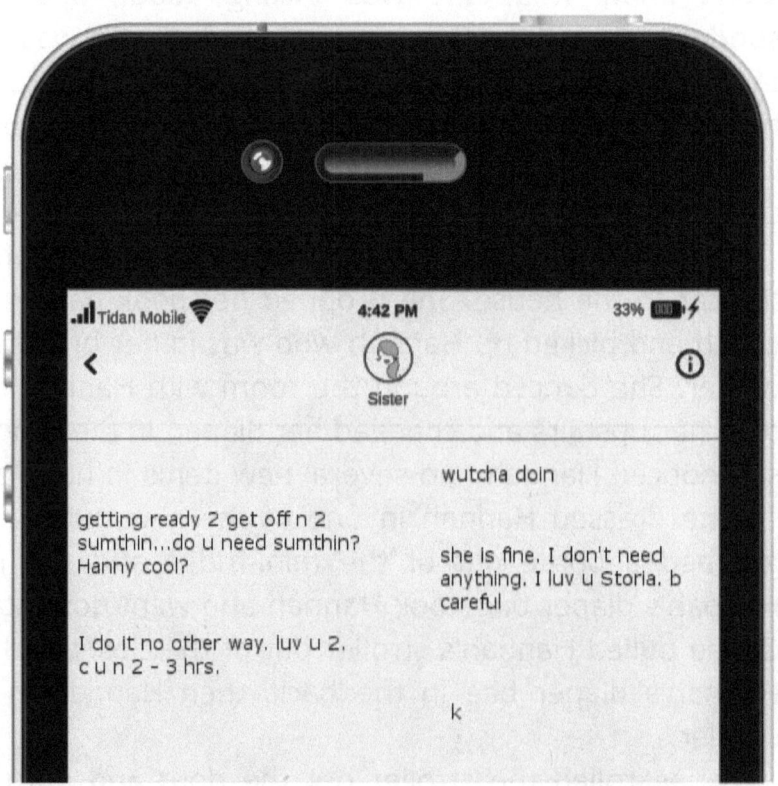

Carlee was stunned. She didn't know what to feel or how to think. She looked at her phone. It was 5:15. She rushed home. She walked in the door trying to avoid everyone and went straight to Hannah's room. She looked in Hannah's drawer and noticed the drawers filled with clothing. She took out a sleeper, put it on Hannah then put Hannah in her crib, and went to her room. She lay on the bed and looked at the ceiling with the envelope she got from her principle in her hand. She thought about everything Storia went through with the rape, the car incident, and the pregnancy. She thought if she should tell what she saw. "What did I see? Was he about 40?" Carlee said to herself. "Did Storia forget that she was only 16?" Carlee continued. She lay sideways on her bed for what seemed like forever to her and then she looked at her phone. It was 5:40. "Dog!" Carlee said aloud.

Carlee jumped up and went over to her closet. She pulled out some slacks and a blouse then she looked at the blazers she had, and none fit for the outfit she picked. She walked down to Storia's room and looked in her closet. In Storia's closet, she saw boxes upon boxes. She looked at a care card and saw a tag on the bag with a $2,200 price tag. She dropped the bag. Then she looked in the next box; it was shoes, costly ones. There were dozens of items. She felt like she was in heaven, but was shocked and angry simultaneously. She saw clothes and shoes and more clothes and shoes for Hannah. She saw coats and dresses; it looked like a department store in Storia's closet. Everything was in this closet from expensive bottles of perfume and jewelry, hats, and scarves, pants, slacks, dresses, the works. It was unbelievable as Carlee stood in Storia's closet. Carlee grabbed a blazer that matched her outfit and made sure she put everything back the way it was. She grabbed the blazer quickly and noticed that once she took the blazer off the hanger, it felt heavy. She looked at the blazer then looked in the inner pocket. There were several prepaid credit cards. Some had fallen out of the pocket along the bed and floor.

Carlee heard someone coming up the stairs. She hurried up and grabbed the cards along with the ones in her jacket. She looked around to find a place to put the cards. She went back into the closet and pulled the boxes out. She took boxes one after another until she got to the bottom. She opened it. She kneeled in amazement. Carlee stared in shock; 100 and 50 dollar bills were stacked loosely in the box. The top hardly kept the money down. There were more cards and earrings in the back in a small tote. She threw the cards in the box, placed the cover on it and stacked the other shoeboxes on top, then slid the boxes back. She stood still on her arms and knees shaking her head back and forth. She backed out of the closet backward, and once she got out of the closet, she raised up placing her hands on her thighs and looking once more into the closet. She slowly closed the door and stood up bending over now hands on her knees; tears fell from her eyes. Carlee was devastated. She put the blazer on and ran to her room. She slid her feet into her dress mules and grabbed the envelope she got from the principal. Carlee took the envelope and went back to Storia's room. She placed it on the shelf in Storia's closet, closed the door, and walked out of Storia's room closing the door after her. She ran downstairs and grabbed the car keys off the hook quickly before her father saw her. She drove north for about ten minutes then made a right. As she sat at the light, she texted Kory to let him know plans changed and she was on her way to the church, and there was no need for him to pick her up. Once the light turned green, she continued straight and turned right made another right, and then a left turn. She arrived at Kory's church. It wasn't quite seven, but she knew she was late. She turned her phone off and quietly crept into the church and had a seat.

Carlee sat in a complete daze not realizing that everyone was staring at her. She cried quietly. A lady from the church asked her if she was all right. Carlee shook her head, and when the church lady asked if she wanted to talk about it, Carlee answered no. The church lady tried to persuade Carlee to speak about it citing it would make her feel better. Carlee told the church lady she was there because she needed somewhere to go where she could think. Carlee said she didn't need the attention she was just trying to process something that she had figured out. Carlee cried uncontrollably. Outdone in her mind, Carlee felt helpless. The church lady sat beside her and held Carlee as she cried. The church lady gave Carlee some tissue and walked Carlee out of the sanctuary. She took her to another room where she watched the service on the monitor. The church lady sat Carlee down then sat next to her. Carlee wiped the tears from her eyes and nose. Carlee apologized and grabbed more tissue. The church lady asked Carlee if she was ready to talk. Carlee told her she didn't want to go over it just yet but wanted to put things together in her head. The church lady stopped asking, and once Carlee calmed down, she went into the sanctuary and listened to the rest of the service. Carlee was still dazed out as she sat in the service digging in her purse looking for an offering. She didn't notice Kory looking at her.

CHAPTER 17

Storia got out of the car and walked towards her house. She was trying to convince Ian she would be fine walking the rest of the way home. Ian wasn't willing to let her out of his sight especially after speaking to his cousin and Storia's father and grandmother.

"You know I can drop you at your door," Ian said smiling at Storia as he drove slowly alongside her walking.

"I'll be fine Ian, I'm not far," Storia said.

"I want to talk to you about something. When can that happen?" Ian asked hoping she would get back in the car.

"Can we talk next time?" Storia asked batting her eyes.

"Not really. You see, you really shouldn't be out like this, you don't get what is happening," Ian said. "I don't want you doing what you're doing.

"We can't be exclusive Ian. I don't want to be exclusive with you right now," Storia said having heard Ian say the exact same thing he was saying.

"I'm not suggesting that we be exclusive, well, I was, but I'm not right now. I mean, I do want to give you better than what you are allowing yourself. Besides, I am waiting for the appropriate time unlike the rest," Ian said sharply.

"What is that supposed to mean Ian?" Storia noticed she was almost home.

"Don't you like being around me?" Ian asked with no signs of letting her walk the rest of the way home on her own.

"Yes, you're different," Storia said as she thought on Ian overall.

"Then what's the problem? Is it money?"

"Well, it is," Storia answered honestly.

"I'll give you whatever you need," Ian said seriously.

"Ian, I don't think you can," Storia said as she looked at him with raised eyebrows.

"Try me. How much?" Ian said kind of upset.

"A lot," Storia answered without being specific.

"What's a lot?" Ian asked wanting Storia to be specific.

"It doesn't matter. I don't want to get into that with you because frankly, it's really none of your business," Storia said as she stopped walking.

"Oh?" Ian said now very angry but not wanting it to show.

"I want to get out of this city and probably state. I want to go somewhere where no one knows me, or what I've done. I want to go to college, maybe have a roommate or something, get a real job, and find my way," Storia explained.

"You could do all of that with me. I would love to help you do all of that."

"Well, let me be the judge of that. Goodnight Ian," Storia smiled. "I don't want or need my father to see you," Storia stood still waiting for Ian to drive off.

"Okay," Ian conceded.

"Call me, or I'll call you," Storia suggested.

"Okay. Goodnight, beautiful," Ian said as he drove away.

"Goodnight," Storia walked the rest of the way to her house shaking her head as she thought about Ian.

Ian drove off and called his cousin, Jimmy. He told him about the date and listened to his cousin mention the men Storia was seeing. Ian told his cousin he would take care of the men and asked him to keep Storia on schedule as much as possible. Jimmy agreed, and they disconnected the call. Ian called Storia to make sure she got to her house; she was still walking, so he talked to her until she told him she was in the house. Ian didn't believe her. Storia's father and grandmother greeted her when she walked into the house. When Ian heard her relatives, he told her he would talk to her soon. Storia asked him to call her in a few hours, and Ian agreed. Storia spoke to her father and grandmother and apologized for being on the phone when she walked into the house. Storia told her father she didn't quit her job, but she asked for shorter hours and fewer days. Devon wasn't too concerned since he heard from the person he had tailing Storia and knew that she was with Jimmy's cousin who is a DEA Agent. He merely said, "Good," and nothing else.

Storia steered clear of her father. She didn't want him to give her the usual forehead kiss. She went to her room and grabbed her PJs and underwear then she went to the bathroom and jumped in the shower. She got out of the shower and put oil on her skin. She brushed her hair and her teeth then took a handful of leave in conditioner and a little gel and placed it in her hair. She wrapped it around into a top bun and put bobby pins in it to hold. She flushed the toilet, washed and dried her hands and walked towards her room. She stuck her head in Hannah's door. Hannah was awake and playing with something in her bed. She went in. She talked to Hannah. She walked over to the mini-fridge and took out a bottle. As she did that, Hannah stood up in her crib holding on the bars. Storia placed the bottle on the top of the mini-fridge and took the bowl off the microwave then walked it down to the bathroom and put water in the container. She walked with the bowl back down to Hannah's room then put it in the microwave.

"I know no one else does it like this, but this is the proper and best way," Storia said talking to Hannah. As Storia waited for the microwave to heat the water, she walked over to Hannah and checked her diaper. "I'll change your diaper while I'm here okay?" Storia said to Hannah. "Once you learn how to walk, you'll have to learn to potty," Storia continued.

Before Storia changed Hannah's diaper, she went over to the microwave and took the bowl of hot water out. She placed the bottle in the water, walked back over to Hannah, and changed her diaper. Once she finished, she picked Hannah up. She couldn't believe she was picking her up. She walked Hannah over to the microwave and took the bottle out of the water. She shook the bottle and squeezed some of the content on the back of her hand. It was still cold, so Storia placed the bottle back in the water. She walked Hannah over to the window and pulled up the blind to look out. Hannah touched Storia's face and put her hand on Storia's mouth. Storia looked at her. She stared at Hannah intensely.

"You don't look anything like him after all," Storia said to Hannah. "You kind of look like Auntie Eloise." You have eyes like her anyway," Storia continued looking at her daughter. "You have my, well, dad's nose. Umm, you must have gotten this curly-curly hair from your granddad's side because everyone on my mom's side has straight hair huh?" Storia wasn't expecting an answer. "Let's check on that bottle," Storia walked with Hannah back over to the bowl.

Storia pulled the bottle out of the water. She tested it again, and this time it was warm. Storia gave Hannah the bottle then walked over to the rocker. She sat in the rocker with Hannah. Hannah sat on her lap drinking from the bottle. Storia put her feet on the ottoman and rocked slowly. Hannah finished drinking from the bottle and layback on Storia's chest. Storia felt her hair and played with the curls swirling them around her fingers. Hannah turned sideways with her ear to Storia's chest then Hannah looked up "mama." Storia looked puzzled, wide-eyed, eyes shifting back and forth. She tried to avoid crying, but her eye ducts uncontrollably filled with water. She couldn't deal with it, so she didn't. She just hoped that she didn't repeat it.

Storia was tired. She tried to get up from the rocker but was exhausted. She held Hannah tight as Hannah laid on her chest quietly seeming to be listening to her heartbeat. Storia dozed off trying to mustard up the strength to get up, put Hannah in her bed, and go to her room. It never happened. Storia and Hannah who sat in Storia's arms fell asleep in the rocker as Carlee peeked in the door opening watching their interaction the whole time.

Hours passed. The whole house was quiet. Everyone was sleeping except Carlee. She had been in and out of the crack in the door wondering when Storia would awake and place Hannah in her crib. Carlee started talking to herself, and at first, everything she was saying about Storia and Hannah was positive. Then suddenly, her thought pattern changed. She was feeling a way about Storia being in Hannah's room. She grew upset about Storia holding Hannah, and how the two slept peacefully in the rocking chair. She was mad about Storia being with the older man earlier and pissed about what it all meant. Storia was in the bedroom talking to Hannah and making her laugh while she played with her. She could hear Storia in Hannah's bedroom shuffling through Hannah's dresser and talking about putting Hannah in the bath.

"Who the crap does she think she is anyway," Carlee said in her mind now fuming at the notion that Storia is even considering being the caregiver after all this time. Carlee was livid. "Well, she is Hannah's mother," Carlee said to herself now trying to negotiate and resolve what she was feeling. "So! She's been her mother since she was born. What does that have to do with anything?" Carlee was seemingly in a debate with herself. She couldn't believe she was having it out and with herself to boot. "What is the matter with me?" Carlee said trying to reason with herself. "Well, am I supposed to answer the questions I'm asking myself?" Carlee thought. "Oh, this whole thing is driving me crazy. I will just go talk to her," Carlee said to herself. She knocked on Hannah's door.

"Yes," Storia said in response to the knock.

"Good morning," Carlee said pushing the door open.

"Hey, big sis, are you coming to get Hannah?" Storia asked.

"Well, I was, but I see you have her and her clothes that she seems to have a lot of by the way," Carlee said not knowing how she was feeling.

"I was going to bathe her, but if you have a routine with her I don't want to interrupt," Storia said nicely ignoring the comment about the clothes.

"I kinda do but if you want to bathe her, you can, it's no big deal. I'm just surprised, that's all," Carlee said. She was trying to describe what she was feeling about the situation to herself.

"You're surprised because I want to give her a bath or is it something else Carlee because your tone is interesting?" Storia looked at Carlee piercing.

"So, you want to give her a bath after almost nine months?" Carlee said trying not to go there but feeling like she couldn't help herself.

"No Carlee. I want to bathe her because she needs a bath and by the way, I'm finally over myself if you don't mind, though, I think it's too late since it seems you do, but whatever. Is it okay with you that I want to be a mother to my daughter?" Storia said ready for the fight.

"I don't know if it is okay or not Storia I mean what kind of mother does that?" Carlee said in a judgmental tone.

"Oh you're funny today, and now I know what mom means when she says to you what I'm about to say...I am not going to entertain your foolishness, Carlee. It is not my problem if you're feeling some kind of way because I came home last night and took care of my daughter for the first time in nine months, oh well. It is also not my concern if you're mad because while you were out strolling my daughter, you saw me getting in a car with one of my guy friends, oh well. It won't be the last time," Storia said carelessly.

"It won't be the last time I'll see you doing that?" Carlee said mad that Storia was showing no emotion.

"No! I can't say if you'll see me or not. If you do, you do, and while you're trying to be all holier than Thou, the next time you take something from me that you didn't ask me for, it will be the last thing you do. I love you, Carlee. I do, but I'm looking at things out of a different set of glasses. You don't run me, and I could care less about how you feel because I am mothering my child. She is not yours no matter what you do for her, and she will always be mine no matter what I don't do for her. You have no right to judge me or throw in my face what I am or am not doing as if you're doing so much. You need to stop looking at things through rose-colored glasses and get the heck off my back while you're there," Storia said without blinking.

"You don't know who you are Storia; you're confused," Carlee said.

"No. I'm not. You're in denial, and that is your problem.

"How did you get all of that stuff Storia?" Carlee asked.

"I prostitute," Storia said bluntly.

"Don't say that Storia. If anything, those men are taking advantage of you," Carlee declared.

"No, they're not! No robbery, no crime. It's a fair exchange. In the beginning, I was naïve. I had no idea that what Tommy was doing to me was wrong. I had no idea it was rape because I always associated rape with something forceful, something violent and painful. I understand that it was rape because I was young. I didn't know it was against the law. All I know is that I felt loved and cared for when I was with him. I felt safe, and then, I felt good. I know now that I wasn't supposed to feel that feeling with him and he was taking that opportunity from the one I was supposed to choose or allow to choose me. He raped me in many ways Carlee then he left me with someone he would never see or be a part of in life. I'm not knocking the latter, but that is not how it is supposed to go for me, but that's okay. I'm good," Storia refused to be a lifelong victim.

"Storia, dad wanted to be here with us growing up. That was our mom," Carlee said sadly.

"It may have been our mom, but when dad saw that mom was going to be ugly about him seeing us, he should have gone to court. He should have gone to the court and told them he would like to see Daniel and us regularly," Storia argued.

"Storia, you can't keep doing what you're doing," Carlee fussed.

"Life for me is what it is right now, and it is what I want it to be," Storia confessed.

"Storia you're only 16," Carlee said thinking that would make a difference.

"And?" Storia said thinking she should of have said what's your point.

"And you can get those men in a lot of trouble," Carlee said not caring about the men being in trouble.

"You don't think those perverted ass pedophiles know the law? Who are you trying to fool? It's what they like; this whole godforsaken town is full of men who want to sleep with little girls. They love it, Carlee. Why do you think I'm telling you I want out? I want out, especially for my daughter. This town will only make a fuss about it if I do and then, they will try to make as many excuses for him as possible so that he won't have to serve time. You see how they did Tommy? Carlee, don't be stupid."

"Why are you doing this?" Carlee asked upset.

"Did you not hear what I just said? BECAUSE I want out of this town and if letting someone taste what I have is what is going to get me out, then so be it," Storia confessed.

"So they don't put..."

"NO!" Storia interrupted. "I play dumb and scared. I tell them theirs is too big and I'm not ready. Mostly, I touch it. I might suck it every now and again," Storia said candidly.

"What?" Carlee asked blushing at how blunt Storia was about the content.

"They put a thingy on it, and I put some stuff on it that I got from a friend. No big deal," Storia explained.

"You are flipping crazy," Carlee said embarrassed.

"I know you've been in my closet and seen what I have. I also saw the envelope I told you to give back to Mr. Hunklebee," Storia said changing the subject.

"He said no expectation Storia. He wouldn't take it back," Carlee said quickly detecting Storia was about to go off on a tantrum about it.

"Whatever Carlee. You don't believe that, do you? Anyway, I have a little house outside the city. When I turn 18, I'm moving into it. I have the deed and everything," Storia said whispering.

"You can't own a home," Carlee said doubting Storia is telling the truth.

"A terrific friend of mine put it in his name since he's 18. My lawyer friend wrote up some documents stating the property isn't his, he has no interest in the property, and he will sign it over to me when I'm 18," Storia said proudly.

"Why didn't you have grandma do it? She wouldn't have said anything, "Carlee asked.

"Are you crazy? Grandma is cool, but she is not I'm cool with you hooking cool. It will be fine. The person I'm talking about is a cool customer, and not a customer as in we're having sex," Storia said looking at Hannah who is beginning to whine.

"Are you talking about Kory?" Carlee asked curiously.

"I'm not talking about anything else anymore. I am going to be late for my shift. I have to get going," Storia said as she watched the shadow at the bottom of the door.

"One last question," Carlee said looking back at the door to see what caught Storia's attention.

"Yeah," Storia said indulging her.

"Is that why Jimmy gave you the car? Did you have sex with him?" Carlee whispered.

"No. Mr. Franklin sincerely cares. He wanted me to steer clear of Georgia. He gave me that car because his daughter bought something else and it was just sitting there. He is 100% perv free as far as I know. He's like having another father; he's such a cock blocker," Storia said at first whispering but gradually getting loud.

"A what? Where did you hear that term?" Devon said bursting through the door.

"Dad the kids at school say it all of the time. It's when a boy you don't like hangs around and discourages a boy you do like from coming around," Carlee explained innocently.

"I know what it means young lady and that definition is a little on the kinder side. Why are you two talking about it?" Devon asked taking Hannah from Storia.

"Because I was telling Carlee that Mr. Franklin is like my second father. He stops guys from trying to talk to me," Storia said honestly, as she handed him Hannah's things.

"I'll make sure to thank him when I see him," Devon said looking at his girls.

"Oh no need, daddy," Storia said. "I'll see you all later because speaking of Mr. Franklin; I have the early shift today. More weekend day shifts, less weekday evening shifts," Storia said as she walked towards the door.

"What's going on with you and your sister, Carlee?" Devon asked once he heard Storia's bedroom door close.

"Well dad, Storia has changed since the incident. She has a real purpose that she is trying to fulfill. I only wish I knew what I wanted now that she is in full swing with Hannah," Carlee didn't want to talk about Storia too much.

"What does she want to do?" Devon asked wanting to hear what Storia said to her.

"She wants out of this town dad," Carlee said shrugging her shoulders.

"Oh?" Devon said trying to act as if he hadn't heard it before.

"She is going to be fine," Carlee thought about what Storia said regarding the house.

"You seem to be sure as though you know," Devon said still fishing for information.

"Dad, I don't have much more to say about it. I'm not going to share with you what she has told me. I hope that is not what you think. I am Team Storia. I want her to succeed and get out of this town because Lord knows she needs too. I need to get out of this town too, and I don't know how I'm gonna make it out," Carlee said thinking about all of the money Storia has in her closet.

"So what was going on with Hannah? Was Storia going to take her somewhere?" Devon asked concerned.

"She was going to bathe her until I walked in confronting her," Carlee confessed.

"Confronting? Why the confrontation?" Devon looked troubled.

"Because I became jealous when I heard Hannah say, mama, as Storia was holding her in her arms. I was mad cause Storia hadn't done anything for her in nine months then the time she goes in there and spends five minutes with her Hannah says, mama. I felt pissed beyond what I could comprehend, and I didn't understand why cause it was beautiful hearing her little voice," Carlee's voice cracked.

"She said, mama? What did Storia say?" Devon asked.

"She didn't say anything as far as I could tell. I wasn't in the room with them, I was peeking in the door crack, and for the record, this is a great start, but Storia still needs some time. Instead of me thinking along that line, I jumped down her throat," Carlee revealed.

"Oh Carlee," Devon said shaking his head. "You need to lay off your sister."

"You're right, dad. I am working on that," Carlee walked towards the door. "See you later."

Devon took Hannah downstairs with her clothes, a washcloth, and a towel. He bathed Hannah in the kitchen sink, dried her off and dressed her then put her in her playpen. Devon noticed the things Hannah had like the clothes, covers, and furniture. Devon thought nothing of it though. He figured Storia was spending her whole paychecks and tips on the things for Hannah. Carlee and Storia were downstairs to eat breakfast talking to one another. Storia agreed to drop Carlee off at the mall before going to work. They grabbed their purses and walked out the door. The girls got in the car with Carlee going back into her questioning.

"So all you do is oral, huh?" Carlee asked as though she wanted to get into the business.

"Yes and no. Well, I do that more than anything except for these two guys, Carlos and Ian. This one guy, Ian, wants to be exclusive. He likes catering to me and taking me out. He gives me money so that I won't do what I do, but I don't accept his money because he won't let me do what I do. He is really; I want to say mean, except, he's not mean to me," Storia answered.

"Then why do you say that?" Carlee asked confused.

"He is the only one I'm afraid of getting into a situation with entirely. He gives me this vibe that makes me feel like once I say yes, he's going to be controlling and abusive or something," Storia answered as she turned to enter the freeway.

"Why do you go out with him then?" Carlee asked trying to understand.

"Because I get the feeling that if I don't something will happen to me or I'll miss something; I don't know. It's complicated," Storia hit the steering wheel frustrated to be stuck in traffic.

"It must have been an accident or something. This freeway is never so jammed that no one is even moving. So, what about the other guy, you know, Carlos?" Carlee asked curiously.

"Carlee you can't be shy about these things. You just have to say it and to answer your question Carlos puts his mouth on me all of the time. When he does it, it feels so different than any of the others," Storia said as she eased up in the traffic.

"Why do you say that?" Carlee asked.

"Well, you're just full of questions aren't you? I hope you're not trying to or thinking about getting off into the field I'm in because I'm just sayin', this is not for you. Now, the reason why I say it's different is that Carlos takes his time like we have all night and he is not concerned about taking me home. Like I said, Ian never wants to do anything. He just says he wants me exclusively. We go to the movies, plays, concerts, dinner, parks, amusement parks and sometimes we will do something romantic, but we don't kiss, touch, taste, fuck or even dry hump (laughing). So, if I had to choose, it would be Carlos because he gives me a lot of money and Ian once I'm ready to settle." Storia explained.

"Storia, I swear I don't even know who you are anymore, but I can't stop listening," Carlee said laughing intently.

"Carlos drives me insane, but Ian is so different than the others. That is why I said what I said about not wanting to leave Ian alone," Storia said wide-eyed, smiling as she pressed the speed dial number to call her job.

"I would never have thought you would be telling me this not in a million years. So this guy, Ian, was he the one who opened the door for you?" Carlee said surprised.

"No. That guy is just your run of the mill perv. He dropped me off a few blocks from my work. Ian is nice looking and always seems to be around more than I would like. I think he is stalking me, I mean, I don't know. Someone is stalking me," Storia said waiting for someone to pick up the phone at her job.

"What a minute... Jimmy's little cousin Ian?" Carlee said thinking about the day she saw the other guy.

"Yeah, he buys me whatever and takes me wherever. He took me to this beautiful hotel, and all he wanted to do is lie next to me and talk to me about being with him, and him only. He is so weird, but I love being around him even though it is something about him that scares the crap out of me," Storia said switching to a lane with fewer cars before coming to a stop.

"Woooo, that's crazy Storia," Carlee said intrigued by what her sister is saying.

"Yeah, he said he wants it after I've stopped messing with everyone else. He said he just wanted me to experience what it would be like to be with him. Isn't that something?" Storia said naively.

"Wow Storia, you're an idiot," Carlee said laughing.

"I know. I guess. I just want out of this town. That's why I won't take anything from Ian (sigh) I like Ian, but he is just scary and creepy. Like he said to me, he wanted to be exclusive you know his usual spill, and I said that's not possible, then he says make it possible or I will. I'm telling you that's when I knew I was in trouble. The things he says - but I really, really feel like I like him," Storia said concluding.

"I think you're scared of the commitment and not him per say. I think you want him, but you don't want to because you don't want him clashing with your emotions especially with you doing what you are doing right now with the sex stuff," Carlee explained.

"You may be right, and then you may not understand. I feel safe with Ian, but there is something that is about him that makes me scared that he is going to do something but maybe not to me – YET. I mean I was with him the other day, and I told him to drop me off, and he wanted to take me to the door. I was like no, and while he was at the stop sign, I got out because that was the only time that I would be able to get out. He intended on taking me straight to the door. After I got out, he slowly drove along the side of me talking to me while I walked. Mr. Craver yelled at Ian for him to leave me alone because I guess he must have thought Ian was trying to pick me up," Storia said sounding annoyed exiting off the freeway.

"You'll have to go all the way around now," Carlee said referring to Storia taking the first exit off the freeway she got to due to the traffic jam.

"I know, bummer. Oh well, it gives us more time together. I may as well call off because, by the time I get to work, it will be time for me to get off give or take a few hours. I mean why go in for two and a half hours?" Storia said calling her job back.

"This is going to be fun," Carlee said happily. "So what did you do to him to make him like this? Why isn't he like the rest?" she asked.

"I first saw him at Burger – Burger. When I saw him, Carlee, I was so rude because I couldn't take my eyes off of him. He is gorgeous. I wanted to be with him like right there," Storia said reliving the moment.

"I have to meet him someday maybe, I mean you'll have to introduce us, and jeez Storia, you don't have to be blunt," Carlee said blushing.

"Well, I did. I apologized to Ian for staring, and I lied and said I thought that he was someone I knew. I should have just told him the truth and told him that he is someone I want to know. He said it was okay and after I breathed a sigh of relief I continued staring," Storia laughed along with Carlee. "His dark hair and those gray eyes on that olive like skin tone – oh boy; then he smelled so good, and his shirt was like thin cotton or something, and you could see how the wind was blowing the shirt up against his muscular frame. He was alluring for sure. I had to get out of there. I placed my order and played with my phone to keep from looking at him.

"Then what happened?" Carlee asked feeling like she could live through her sister's juicy stories.

"They called my number. I picked up my food, and I slow burned it out of there. When I got to the car, I put my drink on the hood so that I could open the door. I placed my purse and food on the passenger side seat and bent up to get my drink and there he was standing there. In the sun with the breeze hitting me in the face with his cologne and pushing his shirt up against his body. I said okay, stay calm, but it was too late. I was completely over the top in my mind. Then he spoke, and I heard his voice without all of the background noise from the restaurant. He told me his name, and I melted. I mean it was over," Storia explained as they turned off headed for the mall.

"I have to see him in person. He sounds yummy, I don't remember what Jimmy's cousin looks like," Carlee pictured what Storia said in her mind only needing his face to complete the thought.

"I know right? I looked at his bracelet as he was explaining something about his cousin; I don't even know what he was saying. His skin tone is so perfectly tan like a kiss from the sun. His eyes in the sun, his lips, everything about him; I had to get the heck out of there. I told him I had to get going and I left," Storia explained.

"You didn't get his number?" Carlee asked surprised, as they pulled into the parking lot of the mall.

"No I didn't at that time, but check this out! I was out with this guy, and we were at this place where you could eat, and dance and it was so nice. While I was sitting in this booth with the guy waiting for the food we ordered, I had to use the restroom. I went to the restroom, on my way back, Ian, out of nowhere asked me if I wanted to dance. I said no because I didn't want to be rude to the guy who brought me to the place. I went to sit in the booth noticing the guy wasn't there. I assumed he went to the restroom too, so I waited. In the meantime, Ian asked me again to dance. I told Ian no; then I told him the reason why. Ian said okay and left. So, imagine me sitting there waiting for this guy, and when he finally showed up, he told me that he had to go. He gave me money and told me to have dinner and get a taxi back home. I was like, okay. The guy high tailed it out of that place so fast that it was kind of funny. After that, Ian walked over to me and asked me to dance again. I looked at him for a moment, and then I danced with him. While we were dancing, he asked me what I was doing. I asked what he meant, and he said he noticed the guy had left and wanted to know why I was still there. I was thinking at that time that he said something to that guy, but I didn't mention it at all. I just continued dancing with him," Storia explained as she and Carlee sat in the parking space.

"Wow, that was killer. What else happened after the dance?" Carlee was listening to every word.

"He said that he wanted to know me, and wanted to know if I wanted to know him. I was thinking yeah I want to know you real good, but I said to him, let's exchange numbers and get to know one another. He, strangely, was pleased with that idea. We exchanged information and then; someone bumped into me with something because I was feeling wet. Ian told me the waitress spilled tea on my blouse, so I went to the bathroom to see. I started to rinse it off with some water, but I came out of the bathroom and told Ian I had to go," Storia explained as they walked through the parking lot headed to the mall.

"How did you get out of there?" Carlee asked curiously.

"I called for a cab while I was in the bathroom, then I washed my hands, brushed up my makeup, secured my bun and walked out," Storia said unbothered.

"Did Ian have a problem with you leaving?" Carlee asked.

"Not at all, when I walked out of the bathroom, I went to the counter and asked the waitress to place my order in a to-go bag. The waitress gave me my drink then walked to the back. When she came back, she had my order in her hand. I tried to pay for my meal, but the waitress told me that it was courtesy of some man that was sitting by the door. Just as I looked the man's way, I saw the taxi pulling into the parking lot. I got the hell out of there without saying one word to Ian or the guy who paid for my meal," Storia whispered as they were entering the mall.

"What happened to the guy you were there with in the first place?" Carlee asked with a lower tone.

"I called him, but his phone went straight to voicemail. I have been calling him since that day, and to this day, the calls are still going to voicemail, but the voicemail is full. He may be married. I think I'm just calling a burner phone or something. I haven't even seen him since" Storia said sounding concerned.

"Wow, that is deep," Carlee said looking at a blouse on the rack.

"Come to think of it, I called someone else I deal with to book an appointment, and he's disappeared on me as well," Storia said talking low.

"Oh my god. What?" Carlee said trying to figure out what was happening in her mind.

"I'm telling you, I haven't told you the half. I can't put my finger on it, but I know Ian has something to do with it because he always seems to be where I am nowadays. It is not a coincidence," Storia said examining the situation in her mind.

"Ian? What do you mean?" Carlee was thrown off entirely by Storia's assessment.

"One time I was on my way to the apartments to see someone that I know. Ian came out of the dive that is right across from them fussing at me as if we really know each other. I was so embarrassed," Storia began to explain.

"Yeah that sounds like that's a nice area," Carlee noted in her mind all the places she knew with a bar on the same block as where people live and how those places looked.

"The apartments aren't bad per se, but yeah, it is controlled rent housing, and most people who live in them are considered low income, but it is very diverse, and they aren't bad people," Storia defended the neighborhood where the apartments are located.

"Okay I'm sorry, and I'm not saying the people are bad, but what I am saying is that's not always the best area to be in conducting certain types of business," Carlee said trying not to be offensive.

"Girl the streets don't talk in that area. That is the best place to be," Storia was proud to be known in the area. She talked about the apartments as if she was bragging.

"Wow, this is cute," Carlee said looking at a skirt.

"You should try it on with that blouse over there," Storia said pointing to the coral blouse on the rack by the wall.

Storia and Carlee shopped. They purchased a few things; then stopped to have lunch. The whole time, Storia didn't see Ian following her and Carlee. The girls took in a movie to top off their time together. Ian waited in his car. While the girls watched the movie, Ian took a nap. The girls came out of the theater talking about what they viewed. They were loud as they laughed and joked. They walked through the parking lot headed to the car when someone Storia knew approached her from behind. She explained she was spending the day with her sister and suggested they meet up later that evening. Carlee startled, asked Storia if she liked how people just walked up to her. Storia said she didn't but didn't seem to be as frightened as Carlee. Ian watched the girls get into the car. He started his car and drove off in the direction where the girls were parked. As Ian turned the corner, the guy that Storia had planned to meet came back to the car and talked to Storia as she sat in the driver's seat. Ian turned on the searchlight and pointed it in Storia's direction. Carlee, Storia and Storia's friend put their hands over their eyes covering their brows trying to prevent the bright light from burning their eyes. Carlee shouted it's a cop and Storia told her friend to get away. Storia's friend stooped away so that whom they thought was the police wouldn't see him. Ian continued driving and doubled back trying to catch up with Storia's friend. Storia pulled off and headed home talking about how weird what happened was not realizing it was Ian. They laughed getting back to what happened in the movie they watched.

Ian placed a call. He explained what he was doing and then made a few suggestions and ended the conversation. Ian was asked for his location. He agreed to go check out a situation on the other side of town. He headed toward the disturbance when he received a call. The caller gave Ian information about a person Ian inquired about earlier that day. He wrote the info down then pulled up to the house to handle the issue. Storia pulled up to their house and popped the trunk. She left gathering the bags to Carlee. Storia closed the trunk of the car as Carlee struggled with the bags up the porch stairs. Storia looked on slowly backing out of the driveway. Once Carlee went into the house, Storia took off.

CHAPTER 18

Carlee unlocked the door, and subtlely peeked in to see where her father and grandmother were in the house. They were in other areas she assumed, so she walked into the house and dumped the bags on the floor of the doorway. She went to the mailbox and took the mail out wondering why her dad had not done it. As Carlee thumbed through the mail, there was a letter for her from the university. She opened the letter and read the content. She could not get past the words "You've been accepted..." She was excited and happy and overwhelmed simultaneously. She went into the house where her father greeted her with questions.

"Carlee, what's going on honey? Where's your sister? Where did all of these bags come from?" Devon did not give Carlee a chance to answer his question.

"I got accepted, dad! I'm going to Amber Dean," Carlee said not caring about the other questions her dad asked.

"Well I'm not surprised by that bit of news, but I thought you were going away to college? Where's your sister?" Devon tried to be happy about Carlee's acceptance letter but was more concerned about Storia.

"No, remember I said I was going to the local university so I can take care of Hannah?" Carlee ignored her dad's question about Storia hoping she would pull up soon.

"No. I don't remember that and by the way, had you told me that, you would have heard me say to you, that it is unacceptable for you to go to a local university. Do you remember me saying that?" Devon looked out the window. "Carlee, where is your sister?"

"No, dad, I don't recall hearing that, but I know I said it," Carlee picked up the bags.

"Well, you didn't say it to me. Hannah is not your responsibility," Devon realized Carlee wasn't going to answer his question.

"Dad? Hanny is my niece. I want to be there for her," Carlee picked up the remaining bags from the floor.

"She is - not - YOUR - responsibility! Besides, Storia is coming around. Speaking of Storia, Where. Is. She?" Devon was irritated having asked a question purposely going unanswered.

"Dad! I am not Storia's shadow. Stop asking me about her location. She has a phone – call her," Carlee shouted.

"Look, honey, you do not get to speak to me in that tone. You should allow Storia to take care of her responsibilities which by the looks of all these bags, including the baby shop ones, she doesn't have a problem doing. Yes, Hannah is your niece, and you can spend time with her, but to change your life to accommodate a child that is not yours not only relieves Storia of her responsibility but is not fair to you."

"Dad – Never mind," Carlee struggled with the bags towards the steps.

"Carlee. Please. Listen to me. Go to college. Live there. Do what freshman, sophomores, juniors, and senior college students do. Go to parties. Join a sorority if you want. Meet people. Network. Do your assignments. You know? Get a job on or off campus and experience college life. Have fun. I hope that you'll meet someone who will become your college sweetheart. You can't do all of that going to a school where you already know everyone. You're smart enough. Get out," Devon said on a serious note.

"But dad, what happened to Storia wasn't her fault," Carlee said still holding on to her idea about school.

"It wasn't your fault either. Apply to some schools, not in this town! Understand?" Devon said sternly.

"But dad," Carlee tried to negotiate.

"Understand?" Devon said firmly.

Carlee dropped her head and moped as she struggled up the stairs with the bag. She thought about how her dad saw her fighting to get up the stairs with the bags and didn't even think to offer her help. When Carlee finally got to the top of the stairs, she dropped the bags and grabbed Storia's doorknob to open the door, but it was locked. Carlee shuffled down the hall with the bags. When Carlee got to her room, she looked in the bags and took out what belonged to her. She put her belongings away by folding them placed them in drawers then she put the other items on hangers in her closet.

Carlee grabbed the things Storia bought for Hannah, took them to Hannah's room, and put them away. Then she walked out of Hannah's room back down the hall to her room. Once she got to her room, she looked through the things Storia bought her. She was fascinated by Storia's life as she twirled around in the mirror holding a sweater up to her chest. She tried on some pieces she had again and then she hung them up. She thought about going to church, so she took out the best outfit of all the sets purchased. As Carlee decided, she became excited about how beautiful the pieces were and how awesome she would look once she pulled the whole ensemble together. It was pink, cream, and girly. It was delicate and lacy. The buttons were like real pearls. She wanted to thank Storia for the dress repeatedly because it was perfect. Carlee looked at the shoes. She grabbed them out of the box, put them on her feet and danced on her back all over her bed with the shoes up in the air. She loved how they accented the dress and how sexy the pearl-like embellishments swept across her ankles. She was sure she wouldn't be able to walk in them because she walks in flats most of the time. She never had anywhere to go that required her to wear heels. She would try she thought. Carlee turned over on her side until her feet were hanging over the bed, and then she stood up. As Carlee walked, she fell off the side of her new shoes. She tightened the straps across her ankles hoping to be able to keep her foot in them. It didn't work. She would continue to fall over to the side two more times, but after walking from one side of her wall to the other, she was getting the hang of having to balance her weight on the heel and ball of her shoe. Carlee repeated the word balance in her head.

Carlee went to jump in the shower. She used the shampoo and conditioner Storia left on the shower caddy. Her scalp felt tingly. It felt warm and had the sensation of several fingers massaging her head. She rinsed off, got out of the shower, and then put on the oil Storia gave her to use. Storia told her the oil would secure the moisture in her skin so she could maintain her youthful look. Carlee didn't believe Storia, but she loved how Storia smelled, and it was what Storia used all of the time. She put on her dress and then slipped her new heels back on her feet. She walked to her room slowly balancing herself gently on her new shoes. Carlee looked in the mirror and was impressed. Then she picked up Storia's bags and walked them down the hall to Storia's room. Carlee didn't want Storia coming into her room scaring her during the night trying to get her packages. As she got just about to Storia's door, she could hear what sounded like arguing. It seemed like Storia was walking back and forth and occasionally yelling. Storia must be on the phone Carlee thought to herself. She walked up to the door and confirmed Storia in a heated conversation with someone over the phone, but who, Carlee asked herself. Carlee could hear Storia telling someone to leave her alone. She noted that Storia sounded upset. Carlee wondered if it was Ian. As Carlee was about to knock on the door, she heard Hannah whimpering. Carlee didn't realize Hannah was in her room, so she set the bags down and just as she turned to walk to Hannah's room, Storia opened the door and stormed down the hall angrily as though she wasn't standing there. Storia walked into Hannah's room and talked to Hannah when Carlee stuck her head in the door.

"You alright, Storia?" Carlee asked.

"Yeah," Storia said as she changed Hannah's diaper. "I bought a baby monitor so that I can care for Hannah from now on if you don't mind," Storia added a hint of attitude in her voice.

"I kinda heard you as I was walking towards your door. I wasn't eavesdropping, I swear, I was gonna put your bags at your door," Carlee said looking at Storia with concern.

"Yeah," Storia said walking over to the mini-fridge with Hannah.

"Storia, you have to talk about it," Carlee waited for Storia to respond.

"Look, Carlee, I know you're concerned, but I got this. I'll be fine," Storia said placing Hannah's bottle in hot water she took out of the microwave.

"Why don't you just put the bottle in the microwave?" Carlee asked as she walked into Hannah's room and shut the door behind her.

"Because it breaks down the nutrients in the milk and makes it a radioactive mess," Storia answered as she looked at Hannah.

"Oh," Carlee said with a surprised frown.

"Yeah, it's not good to put the bottle directly in the microwave. Even though it's more convenient, it is not as healthy," Storia held Hannah's hands to see if she would walk.

"You think she's ready?" Carlee asked looking at Hannah as she stepped slowly.

"Naw," she tries though. I give her another month or two," Storia said picking Hannah up and grabbing the bottle out of the hot water.

"Maybe by her birthday," Carlee watched Storia check the milk.

"That would be cool," Storia walked to Carlee now sitting on the ottoman.

"That would be awesome," Carlee received Hannah.

"So what all did you hear and where are you headed dressed like that?" Storia asked Carlee as she sat in the rocker.

"Not much. I mean I heard you telling someone to leave you alone. Was it Ian?" Carlee asked.

"You see the thing about it is, I'll be 17 in two days, and Hannah will be a year in a month. I need to focus on getting out of here, but instead, I have to focus on some lunatic, pervert, stalker who I told some months ago, several months ago as a matter of fact that I wanted nothing to do with him," Storia complained.

"Tell him to back off, or you'll go to the police," Carlee suggested.

"I can't go to the police; this is a small town. Everyone will know. Hell, everyone probably already knows somewhat. (sigh) Daddy would not only be embarrassed but who knows. I mean how does a father feel when he finds out his daughter is selling her body for money, property, jewelry, and anything else of value?" Storia said holding her head.

"Well, there's gotta be a way out of this," Carlee said thinking.

"Well, don't you be concerned; this is not your business," Storia said looking at Carlee trying to be nice. "Shouldn't you be on your way wherever you're going?" Storia asked.

"What do you mean? You're my sister. Of course, I'm going to be concerned rather it's my business or not," Carlee said seriously.

"Oh, Carlee, you have your life ahead of you. Unlike my life, which by the way I have jacked up completely, you don't need to get involved. I'll be fine," Storia touched Carlee's knee then took Hannah.

"I'm going to an out of state college. Dad is making me," Carlee stated with disdain.

"Oh cool," Storia said excitedly.

"No, wait. I want you to go with me," Carlee had an epiphany.

"What?" Storia frowned shaking her head.

"Yeah. As you said, you'll be 17, Hannah will be a year, and I'll be turning 19, you can live with me and go to school to do your last year," Carless explained.

"You'll be living on campus Carlee. Daddy will never go for that. Besides I told you, I have a house just outside the city. When I turn 18, I'll be on my way," Storia reasoned.

"No. I'll apply to different colleges, and once I'm accepted, we can look for an apartment that is close to the university. We have the car, Storia. We can make it work. You can go to a school with daycare, and you have enough money and prepaid cards to support you and Hannah," Carlee explained.

"How do you know that?" Storia interrupted.

"Because when I went into your room to get a blazer a few weeks ago, I stumbled across your closet. I saw all of the boxes of shoes among other things, and when I opened the box to see what the shoes looked like, I saw cards. I heard someone coming up the stairs, so I hid in the closet. I leaned against all of those clothes until I didn't hear anything, but once I stood up, the clothes pushed the boxes, and the boxes fell. When I went to stack the boxes back the way they were, I saw that the boxes full of cash and prepaid cards. Storia how long have you been doing what you do?" Carlee questioned Storia rocking Hannah.

"A while," Storia answered.

"Since Tommy?" Carlee tried to get a better answer.

"No. I started long after Tommy went to prison and weeks after I started working at Jades," Storia answered.

"What made you start doing it?" Carlee asked taking Hannah from Storia and walking her over to her crib.

"Georgia," Storia answered honestly.

"What?" Carlee asked surprised but feeling angry.

"Yeah, she does it. She convinced me," Storia said.

"Georgia fucking Cunningham convinced you to sell your body Storia? Georgia, the cunt that ruined Natalie's life? Really? That bitch!!!" Carlee was incensed. She saw red.

"Listen, Carlee. I'm pretty messed up. For Pete's sake, I didn't even know she was using me because she couldn't get anyone to pay her. The funny thing about it is now she is missing. The community in the apartments has missing flyers of her stapled next to the missing cat ones. It is really crazy. I was on a mission to show her how she played me. We argued outside of Jades about me not working with her anymore, and now, she is nowhere to be found, so so much for showing her. The bottom line is I'm selling a service that happens to be my hand, my mouth, my vag, my breast and my time and that's what I do. Carlee, get out of this town go to school elsewhere. Do you. Have fun meeting people," Storia rocked back and forth in the chair.

"Storia, who can say that had what happened to you had not have happened you wouldn't be doing this? Who can say that someone you are seeing didn't murder Georgia? Who can say that this person won't try to come after you? I'd like to think that you wouldn't be hooking. Storia I have a strong feeling that something is going to happen to you if you don't stop," Carlee looked at the ceiling to prevent the tears in her waterline from falling.

"Nothing is going to happen, Carlee. How do you know Georgia was murder? Did the cops find her body?" Storia asked.

"Umm, I don't know. Are you going to do this for another year?" Carlee asked.

"I don't know, maybe. I might move to Vegas, hire security, and have my own little business prostituting," Storia said laughing.

"Are you flipping kidding? That is not funny," Carlee yelled at Storia.

"Carlee calm down. I was only kidding. Get over it! This is my life by the way," Storia was a little snotty.

"You're coming with me, Storie. Period," Carlee said firmly.

"Carlee, I need to save myself."

"Do you think I'll be able to live my life knowing it's a possibility you're not going to be alright? Are you crazy to think that?"

"You're not my savior, Carlee," Storia declared.

"I'm not trying to be your savior, but with that said, perhaps He's using me to get you out of this situation," Carlee said softly.

"Hmmm, I can't call it," Storia stood up from the rocker.

"I'm going to apply to colleges tonight," Carlee said touching Storia's arm as they walked towards the door.

"Let me know when you're accepted," Storia put her arm around Carlee's waist as they walked to the door.

Carlee opened the door; there stood Grandma Ellie. She looked at Carlee and Storia and then turned and wobbled to the bathroom.

"How much do you think she heard?" Carlee whispered.

"I don't know. What is grandma doing up here anyway?" Storia shrugged her shoulders.

"Good question," Carlee and Storia watched Grandma Ellie walk into the bathroom.

"If she heard you, do you think she would say something?" Storia asked Carlee whispering.

"Hell yeah. Grandma holds nothing back; you know that. Will she tell dad is the question," Carlee looked scared.

"You know what Carlee, did you set this up?" Storia asked pulled away from Carlee.

"What? No! I swear," Carlee answered surprised.

"Yeah, I think you did. This is too coincidental you coming in asking me all of those fuckin' questions," Storia panicked.

"Storia, please. You have to know and believe I would never do anything like that to you and this is a hard secret for me to keep. I've known for awhile Storia, so why would I choose now to tell? Think about it Storia. Please consider the move with me. If grandma knows, she'll say something, and we'll deal with it but, don't panic. She may not have heard anything," Carlee pleaded.

"Yeah, you're right. I have some homework to do, then I have a few phone calls to make, and I wanna jump in the shower. Can you listen out for Hannah?" Storia asked calming down.

"Sure, just let me get out of these clothes," Carlee said turning towards her room.

"Yeah, about your outfit, you look beautiful. Where were you going? Storia asked smiling.

"I was going to church in hopes of seeing Kory, but that can wait," Carlee walked down the hall and changed her clothes. She looked in the mirror brushing her hair to make a ponytail and then walked out of her room down the hall to peek in on Hannah. Right before she walked down the stairs, she grabbed the baby monitor out of Storia's room.

Carlee walked down the stairs looking to see if her grandmother was sitting in her favorite seat, relieved when she saw she was not there. Carlee got on the computer and searched for out of town colleges. She came across a couple she was interested in then looked for apartments and daycare centers in the college area. When she found something where all three were right, she applied.

Storia lay on the bed reading for her homework assignment. She noticed she wasn't focused. Storia rolled over on her back and looked at the ceiling thinking about what Carlee said when her phone rang. It was Ian. He was calling to ask her how she was doing and when he could see her. Storia wasn't interested in seeing Ian anytime soon. She was seriously thinking about moving in with Carlee just to get away for a while. She knew she did not want to break it off with Ian entirely for some reason, so she asked if they could spend time with each other sometime next week. Ian agreed but asked her why so long. Storia explained she needed a break to think and wouldn't be going out. Ian was happy to hear that to Storia's surprise. He ended the call with a simple goodnight.

Storia got up from her bed and went to her closet. She got on her knees and pulled the boxes she had from the back. As she opened them one by one, she took the prepaid cards out and put them all in one box. She wanted to figure out just how much money she had versus how much she would need. Storia must have taken the lids off dozens of boxes as she looked around stunned that she had no more space to open any more boxes. She put money in the open boxes. As soon as one was full, she moved to the next. Then she separated bills and folded the cash that wasn't already wrapped by the thousands and placing a rubber band around the bills.

Storia felt herself getting sleepy. She was concerned because she had only read her school assignment; she hadn't done the actual homework related to what she read. Storia thought to distract herself so she wouldn't fall asleep, so she reached into her drawer for her planner. She looked at the dates. She was expecting her cycle in the next three days, and she knew it would be on time because of how she was feeling in her body. She slowly put the denominations together and placed them in the boxes based on the note of the bill from the largest to the smallest. Then, she stacked the boxes back the way she had them. She put the rest of the cards on the floor in the box and piled those.

As she stacked the boxes, Storia thought of the project she created that would need at least a week to complete now getting off the floor of her closet. She looked at her clothes and pulled some of her darker pieces to the front. She hated being pretty on her cycle days because those days were drab she thought. She had four jogging suits that she planned to wear with the hoodies to match all week.

She scribbled notes for her assignment and then wrote a paragraph to get her homework started. As she was writing what would be the last sentence, she gently pushed her papers to the side and fell asleep.

The next day, Storia awoke to the ringing of her phone. The caller let the phone ring twice and hung up. She thought it might have been Ian because he liked to call her to say good morning, but she did not look at her phone to see who called. Instead, Storia got up and walked into her closet. She opened the door and grabbed one of the outfits she purchased from the mall with the shoes and belt to match, some jewelry, and a large handbag. She thought to look as pretty as possible since she would be dressed down for the rest of the week. She started thinking about what would happen if her father or grandma saw all of the things she had; she would have to answer to them without knowing what she would say. She had only lied on purpose once to Ian when he caught her staring at him. She hated lying. She wouldn't be able to lie to her father or grandmother so was she ready to tell them the truth, she thought. She stood in her closet and began to cry. She walked over to the hanging items and looked. She had so many things too much, in fact, she thought to herself. She flipped her hair from her face, leaned against the wall of her closet, and bent over placing her hands on her knees. Without realizing it, she had a full-blown panic attack.

After about thirty minutes in the same spot breathing heavily, sweating profusely, and heart racing Storia heard the phone ringing. She felt like she could stand up straight, but her body didn't agree. She slowly pulled her torso up and leaned against her closet doorframe; she felt dizzy, so she kneeled down to her floor. Then inch-by-inch made her way to her bed on her hands and knees. She was having trouble breathing. Her heart was beating at a rate she thought was out of control. The phone had stopped ringing with her thinking about whom it could have been calling so early. She tried to make her way onto her bed but could not muster the strength. She dialed Carlee's number but hung up before the phone rang. She thought she was about to die and in her mind, she didn't care. She lay on the floor and struggled with her breathing until she passed out.

Storia regained consciousness with her sister kneeling above her head as though she had bent down to see if she was breathing. She opened her eyes more extensively to see Carlee hovering over her asking if she was okay. Storia read her lips because, for some reason, she couldn't hear Carlee. Carlee took a notebook Storia had on her bed and used it to fan Storia. Then Carlee grabbed Storia's pillow and put it under her head. She didn't want Storia to move. Storia lay on the floor for what seems like forever. When she got off the floor helped by Carlee, she felt dizzy, and her coordination was off. She asked Carlee to take her to the hospital. The two snuck down the stairs slowly and walked out of the door on their way to the hospital.

After being seen by a doctor, Storia learned that her blood sugar was low, she was dehydrated, and the anemia wasn't helping. In all of the running around Storia was doing, she wasn't taking care of herself. She was ordered to take iron three times a day, and she would need to drink small amounts of clear fluids often to hydrate. As for her blood sugar, it was a reaction to Storia fasting. She hadn't eaten, and the stress of the anxiety attack along with the other issues happening in Storia's body was the reason for the fainting. The doctor suggested Storia go home and get some rest. Instead, Storia went to school, and Carlee participated in Senior Skip Day.

CHAPTER 19

Carlee walked into the house battered by the ordeal with her sister. She got on the computer and continued looking for colleges, apartments, and day care centers. When her dad approached, she clicked on another screen she had opened just in case he inquired about why she was looking at daycare centers. Carlee figured he might go for an apartment because in actuality it would be cheaper than a dorm room including meals. She thought she would convince him to buy her a small car and to lease the apartment, and she would talk about saving money while learning to be responsible with utilities. Rehashing what to say to her father in her mind, Carlee looked for cheap, used cars. She had only a couple of weeks to figure out those details.

Suddenly like a flood, Carlee thought about Kory. His organization skills were flawless especially with the things concerning his life. She thought about how many people she knew that were like him and there was none. She thought about going to another state. She wondered how this whole thing would play out with Storia. Carlee felt guilty. The shopping she had done with Storia and the items she purchased. How was Storia handling all of this mentally, Carlee thought. Carlee's tear ducts begin to swell. She felt the time she had been keeping this secret hadn't been worth the hassle. She thought, sure, she had cool bags, shoes, and clothing to die for, but at the end of the day, Carlee had to hide most of it and act as if friends let her borrow those things and what was the fun in that she thought. As she became consumed with the details, she was startled by her father's touch. Carlee must have jumped to the ceiling. She apologized to her father and confirmed that she was okay. When asked where Storia was, Carlee looked around not realizing the time. It was late. Undoubtedly, Storia was out of school, and her work shift was over. Carlee quietly told her father Storia met with a friend to exchange something and would be right back. Carlee struggled with that answer then thought if what she said was indeed a lie. Okay, Storia exchanged sex with a trick and not a friend, but she is coming back. That wasn't a lie Carlee thought to herself. Then a voice came to her mind and asked her if she was kidding. The voice told her it was a lie and explained that omission of the truth and falsehood is the same because she knew and had known yet didn't reveal. What is my inner voice, a lawyer or something, Carlee thought to herself. What nerve Carlee felt as she got upset – with herself. "What am I doing? What am I saying?" Carlee said aloud without realizing. Her father interrupted her thought to ask her if she was talking to him. He had asked her a question, but Carlee had it all confused.

"Dad, I didn't hear you. Can you repeat your statement or question?" Carlee held her head with her left hand as she typed using one finger from the right.

"I said how is the college search coming?" Devon repeated.

"Oh. Good. I've applied to four. I am going to wait to see who says what. You know dad, I was thinking," Carlee felt unsure about what she would say to her father.

"Yeah, you were some miles away in thought," Devon giggled.

"I was thinking about getting an apartment instead of living in a dorm," Carlee looked towards the other room where her father was sitting.

"And why is that?" Devon got up from the couch.

"Well dad, have you seen my room? Have you compared my room to a dorm room? Dorms are really not that big, and I'll have to share. I will have to sleep in a twin bed, and my whole experience will be crappy because my environment will be cramped and not at all what I've grown accustomed to dad," Carlee explained.

"When did you become such a snob or is the right word diva?" Devon asked as the bottom of the palm of his hand went across his eyebrow.

"Dad before mom got remarried we were poor and lived in poor conditions. We had to sleep in these small uncomfortable beds. When she married Bill, we moved into this spacious house, and she bought all new furnishings. We've been here with you and look at this space. I can breathe. I rather go back and forth to the local university than to live in a dorm dad," Carlee hoped to inspire her dad to say okay.

"I think an apartment would be good for her. The money you've set aside for her room and board can go towards the apartment expenses, and she can get a job to cover the extras," Grandma Ellie said to Carlee's surprise. "She can get an apartment with some utilities included and laundry in the building. Maybe the laundry room should be on the same floor or perhaps in the apartment; you know the hookups? It should be a secure building, and if it's not so close to the college, it may be even more inexpensive. She'll stay on your plan so she won't have to be without a phone. If Carlee searches right, she may come in under budget," Grandma Ellie continued as though she had been thinking about this transition for a while. "Then she can take that money and buy food. It will teach her how to manage an apartment and money," Grandma Ellie concluded to Carlee's surprise.

"True. It may even be cheaper than dorm living. Well, Carlee research and see what you come up with," Devon said rubbing his hands together.

"Also, dad, um, Nana pretty much took the words right out of my mouth, which was my complete argument. (I guess I am an attorney Carlee thought to herself) I was also going to mention a car. You know a small, used one. You know like Storia's? One to get me back and forth to school and work," Carlee prayed that her grandmother would argue that point as good as she did for the apartment.

"Work?" Devon said confused.

"Well, that was also a part of my argument for the apartment. I was going to look for a job on campus or at the local mall or theater there and work part-time...you know, for the extras," Carlee said.

"That a girl," Devon smiled. We can take a look at some cars, but I don't like the idea of you being in another state by yourself in a used car," Devon said with concern.

"Dad, I won't be able to carry the insurance on a new vehicle. If I can find work, it wouldn't be paying enough for me to pay for apartment extras and insurance.

"I'll cover the insurance as a 'graduation/off to college gift.' Hell, I'll even buy the car," Grandma Ellie said with excitement.

"Oh my God," Carlee said holding her hands up to her mouth and tears coming to her eyes as she ran over to hug her grandmother.

Carlee suddenly felt overwhelmed with guilt that overcame her. She slumped down on her knees, put her hands on her face, and cried. She wasn't able to control her emotions. Her concern was real. She felt as though she was letting Storia down because it was hard to keep this particular secret a secret. Carlee took some tissue out of the box her grandmother handed her. She had to tell them she thought to herself.

"Dad, grandma, I have something to say," Carlee said regretfully between sniffling.

"What is it, honey?" Devon asked concerned as he rubbed Carlee's shoulder.

"You know Carlee, why don't you go and wash your face, collect your thoughts and then tell us what you have to say," Grandma Ellie said prompting Carlee along as she was standing up from her kneeled position.

"Yes Nana," Carlee said with tissue to her mouth and nose.

Carlee now knew for sure her grandmother knew what was going on with Storia. She didn't know how to handle her knowing, but she wondered if her grandmother would agree or convince her father to allow Storia to move with her when she went away to college. Carlee turned on the faucet and felt the water. Once the water was warm, she allowed the water to fill her cupped hands and splashed the water on to her face. Carlee avoided the mirror, pulled the paper towel off the row, and dried her face. She thought about her grandmother knowing about Storia and for a short time panicked thinking about her dad discovering she knew and didn't tell him.

Carlee walked out of the bathroom not wanting to talk. She thanked her grandmother who hugged her tight afterward. Her grandmother told her she wanted to shop for the car soon to give Carlee a chance to get adjusted to driving it before she left for college. Carlee agreed and calmly went over to hug and thank her dad for allowing her to get the apartment. Suddenly, Storia sped into the driveway. Carlee wondered what Storia would say when she walked into the house, but as she witnessed Storia pull up, she knew something had gone wrong.

Storia slammed the car door. It was so loud that everyone in the house heard. They all looked at each other and then looked out of the window as Storia stomped up the stairs and into the house slamming the door. Then without speaking to anyone, the three-watched Storia storm up the steps looking at each other until Storia got to her room slammed the door. Carlee looked at her father and then went up the stairs. She bypassed Storia's room and went to check on Hannah who was still sleeping. Devon and Grandma Ellie looked at one another, then came together, and whispered to one another. Carlee walked out of Hannah's room closing the door behind her and walked down to Storia's room. She could hear Storia yelling at someone demanding whomever it was to leave her alone. Carlee had never heard Storia this mad. She was scared to approach her door. Carlee continued tipping down the hall until she reached Storia's door. She knocked, but Storia didn't answer, so Carlee knocked harder. Storia still ignored her. Carlee tried to turn the doorknob, but Storia had it locked. Carlee called to Storia and received no reply.

Carlee spoke to Storia through the door asking her to open the door. Storia didn't respond so Carlee banged on the door. She continued pounding nonstop until Storia finally answered. Carlee could see that Storia was angry, so she didn't say a word. She just walked into Storia's room, closed the door, and saw a deck of cards on Storia's dresser. She picked them up and went over to the bed where Storia laid fuming. Carlee still not saying anything shuffled the cards and put the deck down on the bed. Storia responded by dividing the deck of cards in three. Carlee picked up the cards and dealt. Storia picked up the cards, and she and Carlee played. When Storia's phone rang Carla politely took the phone out of Storia's hand turned it off, and the two continued playing.

After about an hour and a half of playing, Storia won by a few points. Carlee picked the cards up off the bed, organized them in her hand until they were straight, and then placed them back in the box. By that time, Storia had calmed down, stood up and took her pants off. Carlee walked to Storia's dresser and set the cards back where she got them from then went into Storia's drawer and got a gown. She turned around and walked over to Storia who was pulling her top off, placed the garment over her head, and helped Storia pull her arms through the gown's arm shelves. Once the nightgown fell down Storia's body, Carlee hugged her sister, pulled the bed sheets back, and watched Storia climb in the bed. Carlee pulled the sheets up to Storia's chest, pressed her face on the side of her sister's face, kissed her on her forehead and continued in silence as she picked Storia's phone up went over to Storia's nightstand and placed the phone on the charger. Carlee picked Storia's clothes off the floor and put them in the clothes hamper. She then turned off the light leaving on the nightlight plugged into the wall. Carlee turned around and walked towards the door.

"Carlee, (Carlee turned to look at her sister) thank you. You are the best big sister I could ever be so blessed to have. I love you." Storia stated turning to her side.

"You're welcome," Carlee opened Storia's door. "I love you," Carlee said as she had one foot out of the door.

"This guy makes me fucking furious!" Storia started her back facing Carlee still in the doorway.

"Who?" Carlee asked walking back into Storia's room and closing the door.

"He interferes with the things I'm doing and gets downright postal and indignant as though because we were together, he owns me and has a say in what I do. That makes me so mad. I mean to even, think about it, we never did anything; I was there. Georgia is the one who had sex with him. Well, I let him... well anyway, it was about nothing. I never liked him," Storia said without answering Carlee's question now lying on her back.

"Who are you talking about Storia?" Carlee asked hoping to get an answer this time.

"Oh, Carlee. I'm sick of it," Storia said throwing her hands in the air.

"Okay," Carlee said realizing Storia just wanted to vent.

"He is not even, sex worthy. He's lousy doing the things I like," Storia said.

"Wow, Storia," Carlee giggled.

"He thinks because he owns a few stores I'm just going to flock to his calls. He'll never get inside of me," Storia declared.

"You're not about to get descriptive are you?" Carlee asked.

"No," Storia said smirking. "You're so crazy."

"So what happened?" Carlee asked thinking this time Storia would answer.

"Well, I met with this guy from another city in another city. We chat, have a snack, exchange looks, then he slides me the money. I go to meet him around the corner where the room was and low and behold I run into Paul," Storia explained angrily.

"Who's Paul?" Carlee asked.

"Paul is a damn stalker, that's who. He owns those businesses around by Jades. When I was hanging out with Georgia, he was one of the first I let blow me," Storia said strikingly stark Carlee thought.

"Blow you, Storia?" Carlee's facial expression showed she was not only shocked but also embarrassed.

"Yes, Carlee, blow me. That's what guys say. Why can't I?" Storia said confidently.

"Wow! Okay," Carlee answered.

"Anyway, Paul sucked me so hard I was swollen and in pain for several days," Storia complained getting worked up about the situation all over again.

"You are a trip. Well, will you look at the time? It is 12:04. You are officially 17 today. My 17-year-old sister! What you're doing has to stop Storia!" Carlee had a bewildered look on her face.

"Anyway, I steered clear of him and his advances since that time, and since that time, he has been getting more and more violent or downright aggressive. He trashed a guy's car, and tonight he was trying to do me in the parking lot. The guy I was meeting got into a fight with him. I ran because I didn't want to be involved and I didn't want the guy to get in trouble. It was really crazy," Storia explained.

"Okay. It seems like your time in this business in this town is ending. It's getting too dangerous Storia," Carlee was baffled and didn't know what else to say.

"And Ian, Oh my god, Carlee. I think I'm in love," Storia confessed.

"In love? I thought you said he was a pest and people disappeared whenever he is around," Carlee said confused.

"No. What I said was Ian wants to be exclusive," Storia said correcting.

"Um (sigh) okay," Carlee shook her head. "Why are you in love?"

"On my way here in a fit of rage, I saw him at the light, so we pulled over to the side, and he spoke to me so calmly even though I trashed him and probably made him feel like crap. He held me even though I was fighting him until I calmed down. He smelled tremendous. He is so muscular," Storia described Ian with her hands on her chest, turning her head back and forth with her eyes closed.

"Oh god (sigh)," Carlee said watching her.

"He is so flippin' hot. When I looked at him before, I didn't realize just how hot he is really, and his eyes, they are so dreamy," Storia went on.

"I thought you said he scared you," Carlee asked still puzzled.

"He does when he talks commitment. I don't have time for that, but I'm thinking about it so I can have him," Storia said deviously.

"What?" Carlee said jumping up from the bed.

"He wants to take me out of town for the weekend, you know, to some water slash amusement park for my birthday. I'm like great, okay, let's go. I'm thinking about telling him I'll be exclusive so I can see what he's like... you know? In bed," Storia said with a devilish look on her face.

"Who have you become Storia?" Carlee asked.

"I am a young woman, who would like to have sex with a guy, who doesn't want to if there are others in the picture, so, I am going to lie and say he is the only one, so I can have what I want," Storia strangely explained.

"When did you become a liar?" Carlee asked.

"First off, I'm not a liar. I am just choosing to lie to him. I tried to tell the truth, and he is not going for it thus the reason why I'm going to lie. Besides, men do it all of the time. Why do women have to be pulled over by the truth police, yet men lie on purpose constantly and daily to get what they want, and no one takes issue with it?" Storia said without pause.

"Storia you were not raised to do the things you're doing for one. Secondly, you're a teenage girl and not a woman. My last point, how are you in love, but you're going to lie to Ian?"

"No. I wasn't going to at first, but now I'm going to do it. I wasn't raised to know when someone is lying to me or when someone is raping me, but it happened too. So don't bring up my upbringing. I got caught up, not you. All my life before Tommy happened to me I wanted to be married and have children," Tears began rolling down Storia's face. "I didn't want to be a doctor, lawyer, or nurse. I wanted to be a housewife, with children. That dream is dead for me now. I wanted to be a virgin when I got married. I wanted to give myself to my groom. That dream is dead for me now. I have nothing special to offer my groom because what I thought would be special to share with him is gone. Our first child from my virgin womb gift is gone. I am a defiled, bastard having, young woman, with nothing special happening. So what, I wasn't raised this way. No one took the time to raise us for that matter. I just got caught believing a bunch of bull crap. My fault, but anyone else who wants me will beg for it and will pay major for it, unless, I want them. As far as I know,

I might commit to Ian. I love being around him. I love that he only wants my company. I love that we laugh, talk, and joke around and I would actually want to sleep with him after we have sex," Storia wiped her eyes and face.

"I love you Storia, but you are not a woman, you are a teenager. You have been on this Earth for seventeen years now. That is hardly being a woman. Yes, through no fault of your own, you had a baby, and I'm sorry that happened to you, but you having guys begging and paying is just you getting molested over and over again. If Ian likes you, you shouldn't take advantage of him." Carlee explained.

"Not really Carlee. You see this is what I chose to do. None of the men I've dealt with are violating me, Carlee. This time I know what they want and I know what I want, and there is no robbery; it's a fair exchange. I would have given it to my husband freely and willingly, but since they are not my husband or husband worthy, well, except for Ian since he won't even have sex with me, they must pay and pay big. My husband would have been my provider, and since that opportunity is no longer available for me, the men I meet have to pay for my missed opportunity," Storia said adamantly.

"Well, dad said I could get an apartment," Carlee said excitingly changing the subject.

"Great Carlee! Which college did you choose?" Storia asked gladly going with the subject change.

"I applied to about four of them. I wouldn't mind going to any of the colleges I applied to, so whoever accepts me first is where I'm going. Where we are going, Storia," Carlee explained.

"Cool," Storia said.

"I repeat, you're going with me Storia," Carlee said.

"Ah, I don't know about that Carlee," Storia looked through her fingernail polish.

"That wasn't me asking," Carlee said firmly.

"Carlee, don't start with me," Storia turned on her phone.

"You and Hannah are coming with me when I leave," Carlee reaffirmed her first statement. "You can start fresh, go to school and do whatever you wanna do like go to college once you get out of high school."

"That's interesting. Carlee my life is not your life," Storia looked at her newly polished nails.

"I didn't say it was, but Storia you're not going to stay young. How much longer do you think men who like little girls will continue putting up with you? You're growing out of the little girl stage, girl" Carlee yelled. "You need to get out of what you think is revenge mode and start thinking about your life," Carlee continued.

Storia continued polishing her nails.

"You can act like what I am saying is not the truth, but you're smart. You're really, really, smart, brilliant even. You know better. You are dealing with pedophiles and perverts. You're about out of their age range, and I know you know that. Paul is fighting about you because you're ignoring him. Give him what he wants, and I bet you'll never see him again. It's about conquering the quest. You know that I know," Carlee continued.

"Are you done?" Storia looked at her ringing phone. "Yeap, we're done," Storia answered her phone.

As Storia conversed with the caller, Carlee walked towards the door, and as she neared the door, she turned around.

"Oh and grandma knows what you're doing no fault of mine," Carlee said catching the look on Storia's face which gave her confidence that Storia heard what she said as she walked out and closed the door behind her.

Carlee went downstairs hoping everyone was gone. "Not a chance," she said to herself aloud as she got to the last stair and could hear her grandmother talking. She walked into the room and saw Hannah drinking from her sipping cup now realizing one of them probably heard everything she and Storia were talking about in Storia's room.

"Wow. Storia is moving her along," Carlee said as she walked into the room looking at Hannah run and fall with her sippy cup in her playpen.

"Yeah," her grandmother said ending her call. "Hannah responds very well to her mother. I never saw anything like it."

"Well, I'm glad. Hannah needs her," Carlee said looking in the refrigerator.

"So why didn't you tell me Storia was prostituting?" Grandma Ellie said cutting to the chase.

"Prostituting?" Carlee acted as if she was still looking for something in the fridge.

"Don't BS me, girl," Grandma Ellie pressed.

"Where is my dad?" Carlee said changing the subject.

"He's out with Lucy. Answer my question," Grandma Ellie said.

"Nana, I have no such knowledge," Carlee said closing the refrigerator door.

"BS," Grandma Ellie said insistently.

"Nana, why don't you ask Storia? I mean, I don't want to be in the middle," Carlee said sincerely.

"Because your sister is a ticking time bomb that we have to deal with delicately," Grandma Ellie explained.

"Does my dad know?" Carlee asked.

"Shit no! He doesn't need to know. If he were to find out, it would probably kill him," Grandma Ellie said sternly not wanting to let her cat out of the bag about how much she knew about this situation. Grandma Ellie knew how close Carlee and Storia were; she didn't want to take the chance of saying too much. "That is why I'm all for you getting an apartment and she going with you," Grandma Ellie added.

"How did you figure it out?" Carlee asked curiously.

"Have you seen the type of jewelry she has? Have you seen the bags and shoes? None of that stuff is cheap. I know the good stuff when I see it. Devon thinks its costume. He's a man, you know, the kind that doesn't pay attention. Oh, she's doing it right," Grandma Ellie said in affirmation finally confessing her knowledge of Storia's activities.

"Grandma you almost sound like you're gloating."

"Well, if you're going to do it," Grandma Ellie said. "Listen, I'm not condoning this by a long shot. I'm simply saying, girls, have boyfriends and get less. Hell, girls have husbands and get nothing," Grandma Ellie schooled.

"That's true," Carlee said thinking of the girls she knew.

"Carlee, Storia is smart. She goes to the doctor a lot because I see the mail. She is certainly on her A game. That's all I'm saying. She still is going to school. She is working, and she is interacting with her daughter now. Do I think she has an emotional challenge? Hell yeah. Do I think that one day this is going to end badly? Yes. I do indeed. That is why I want her to go with you," Grandma Ellie said coming to grips with reality.

"You can feel it too?" Carlee asked looking at Hannah and feeding right into her grandmother's game.

"Yes, yes I can," Grandma Ellie said glaring as the thought resurfaced in her mind.

#

The next day, Storia got up, took a shower, and dressed. She put on makeup, jewelry, and perfume then headed down to Hannah's room, picked her up, bathed and put a cute little outfit on her, brushed her hair and put it in two ponytails. She brushed her own hair as Hannah sat on her lap. Once she finished styling her hair, she and Hannah went downstairs. Storia placed a bib on Hannah, strapped her in her high chair, and turned on her favorite music box. She went to the kitchen and grabbed a bowl. As she talked to Hannah, she poured fruit rings on to Hannah's highchair tray. While Hannah crunched on the cereal rings, Storia made Hannah some warm cereal. She warmed apple juice slightly and poured it into Hannah's sippy cup with a little water, then shook it. She fed Hannah several spoons of the cereal, then took her out of the high chair, kissed her, put her in her playpen and, gave her the sippy cup.

Carlee came downstairs and joined Storia. They didn't speak to one another. Storia grabbed her book bag and went into the living room. Then she pushed Hannah still in the playpen to the family room and turned on the television. Storia turned the channel to one of her favorite cartoons when she was a child. Hannah stood eyes not entirely over the top of the playpen watching the characters sing and count. Storia got up and turned a chair around until it faced the television directly, picked up Hannah and together they watched the animated program. Storia told Hannah to say one. Hannah tried but couldn't quite say it. Storia encouraged Hannah then held and kissed her. She played with her making her laugh then watched television again. Devon came into the family room and spoke to her. Storia said good morning and looked at her watch. She kissed Hannah one more time then put her in her playpen. Storia said goodbye to her dad, grabbed her book bag and walked out of the door.

"You and Storia not talking?" Devon asked Carlee.

"Nope," Carlee said with an attitude.

"She's getting good with Hannah," Devon said smiling at Hannah now chewing on the frozen ring Devon gave her.

"Yeah. I will and can say that about your daughter. She has done a complete turnaround," Carlee conceded.

"Yes, she has," Devon agreed.

Carlee and Devon talked about another subject when in walked Lucy wearing Devon's shirt.

"What the fuck is this?" Carlee said looking at her father then Lucy.

"Well, sweetheart, 19 doesn't constitute disrespect. I was getting ready to tell you, me and Lucy got married yesterday," Devon said happily.

"Married?"

"Yes,"

"Married dad?" Carlee repeated. "What do you mean, married?"

"What is there to mean sweetheart? We flew to Vegas, got married, gambled a little, then flew back," Devon explained.

"This whole fucking family is crazy. I cannot blame Storia. Her parents are completely fucked up in the head! Dad, how do you leave and get married without saying anything?" Carlee yelled.

"First of all young lady, you will watch your mouth! Second, I do not need your permission. You knew we were dating," Devon retorted.

"I know that you all were seeing each other; okay, I get that and maybe even sexing but marriage, dad? Come on," Carlee said rudely.

"Well, we weren't sexing, not that I have to explain that to you; she was an honest woman," Devon proudly proclaimed.

"As far as you know or is this based on something she told you, dad?" Carlee gave Lucy an evil eye. "Did you get a prenup dad?"

"Carlee, that is enough! You will not stand her and be blatantly disrespectful and offensive!" Devon shouted.

"Well did you? I have to protect my, Daniel, Storia, and Hannah's inheritance you know," Carlee retorted not backing down.

"Carlee, you will not disrespect my wife, and I won't repeat it. If you don't like it, find a friend's house where you can sleep until you figure out what college you're going to and make no mistake about it, you're going to college," Devon grabbed his wife's hand.

"How much will she get for popping out how many kids dad?" Carlee continued trying hard to be disrespectful.

"Find another place to go that is not in my face young lady. Go!" Devon pointed in the other direction from where he stood.

Carlee stomped out of the room, took her phone out, and called Storia.

"Hello," Storia shouted.

"Storee, you're on speaker. Did you know dad got married yesterday?" Carlee asked.

"Why am I on speaker? Who told you that?" Storia asked without answering Carlee's question.

"She's here in dad's shirt! Dad told me," Carlee declared.

"That Lucy lady, you say? I can't really hear you," Storia asked.

"Yeah her," Carlee replied getting impatient with Storia's questions.

"Well, I didn't know, but I'm not surprised, Carlee. She has been doing a lot for dad."

"Are you saying this because you're on speaker Storia and someone is riding with you?" Carlee asked disgruntled.

"Wait, did you tell me why I am on speaker? No, I'm not just saying anything, and no one is in the car with me. She has been helping dad with like all of his stuff. Especially the business stuff and they were seeing each other like going out to dinner and the movies, and crap and he would talk to her all night. Didn't you notice any of that?"

"That's bullcrap," Carlee said pissed.

"Well, whatever, I'm just saying, I'm not surprised, you should ...”

~ SMASH ~

"Storia! Storia! – STORIA!!!" Carlee yelled.

"What's wrong, Carlee?" Devon asked running into the family room.

"There was a big boom dad, Storia's not answering me," Carlee panicked as Devon took her phone.

"STORIA!" Devon called as he could hear background noise. "Get the baby honey," Devon said to Lucy not waiting as he ran out the door, jumped in the car, and drove off using the app on his phone to find Storia's location.

"For goodness sake, what is going on?" Grandma Ellie said coming from her room.

"Storia?" Carlee continued trying to call, but the phone hadn't disconnected.

"Storia may have been in an accident," Lucy said answering Grandma Ellie's question as she wrung her hands looking at Hannah.

Devon drove the route of the GPS speeding the whole way until he arrived where he saw Storia's car. Devon opened the door and got out. He ran over to the scene and dropped to his knees. Devon continued to blink thinking that the car would look different with each blink. The police wouldn't allow him to go any further and the way the car looked, Devon wasn't sure if he wanted to go any further. He told the officer he was the driver's father. The officer said the paramedics were working on her, and he wouldn't be allowed over there. Devon felt like everything was in slow motion. He looked around, and he could see the other car involved and the man who apparently was the driver as his head was bleeding and he was in handcuffs. Devon could see Ian handling the guy. Ian had his back to Devon, so Ian didn't know he was there Devon thought. He could see people talking to the cops and officers writing down what they were hearing; then he saw Storia. She was bloody. Devon couldn't tell where it originated, but it was on her head, neck, and chest. It looked like the bone was sticking out of her leg. Devon was overwhelmed with grief. He fell to the ground rolling onto his back and wailed at the top of his voice.

Carlee and Lucy pulled up. They saw Devon on the ground rocking back and forth and ran over to him. Carlee looked up to see the paramedics putting someone in the back of the ambulance and then, Carlee saw Storia's car. Carlee ran over to Storia's car. She looked in and saw a lot of blood and then she ran over to the ambulance. As Carlee ran towards the ambulance, an officer grabbed her. Carlee tussled with the officer trying to break loose. She continued fighting with the officer as he grabbed her arms and tried to calm her down. She saw a man covered in blood and handcuffed sitting on the ground and as she grew tired of fighting, she thought about what Storia told her.

"Is that guy's name, Paul?" Carlee asked the officer.

"Huh?"

"That guy over there, is his name Paul?"

"Oh, yeah," the officer replied. "You know him?"

"You look very familiar. I know you in some way," Carlee said as she calmed down completely now trying to figure out what was going on. "What's your name?" She asked the officer.

"Agent Allister," he replied.

"No, your name?" Carlee insisted.

"Ian," he whispered.

"You're a cop?" Carlee said surprised.

"Shhh," Ian said.

"You're a cop? Where's your uniform?" Carlee whispered.

"What are you kiddin' me?" Ian asked.

"So you're in love with my sister?" Carlee asked as she stared rudely at Ian.

Ian looked at her, but he didn't answer her question.

"That's why you're waiting?" Carlee asked putting things together in her head. "That's why you want her to stop," Carlee continued in her mind. "How old are you?"

"I'm 22," Ian said.

"You're not a pervert. You're waiting for my sister," Carlee said to herself as Ian walked Carlee to her father's car. "You're waiting for her," Carlee whispered to herself.

"Come on sweetie. I need you to drive your father's car. We're going to the hospital," Lucy said to Carlee softly.

"Okay," Carlee said as she looked over to Lucy's car. She could see her dad. He was hysterical in the passenger's seat.

Carlee took the keys from Lucy. They rushed to the hospital. Storia was in critical but stable condition. The doctor induced a coma to monitor the swelling in Storia's brain. She looked bad. Carlee stared at her and in that instant bust out in tears.

"I'm sorry, Storia. I'm sorry. I was mad at you for such a stupid reason," Carlee said as she was being pulled off of Storia by her father.

Devon held Carlee as she cried as though Storia had died. Carlee was inconsolable. Lucy took Carlee by the hand, and the two walked to the hospital chapel Carlee weeping the whole way while Lucy talked about solace and how she had to find it through God. Lucy and Carlee arrived at the hospital chapel. Carlee continued to cry. She couldn't stop. Lucy lit three candles then fell to her knees and prayed. Carlee watched her as she rocked back and forth. Carlee tried to pray, but she was too consumed with emotion.

Devon stayed by Storia's side holding her hand with his head down crying in anger. He took comfort in the monitor connected to Storia. The machine made a sound every time her heart beat. He counted on that sound. He thought about his mother and then Storia's mother. He called both. He would have to leave a message on Jessi's voicemail telling her it was urgent for her to return his call. Then he called Bill. Bill answered. Bill explained that he and Jessi were no longer together and mentioned he had custody of the boys. Devon informed Bill of Storia's condition and asked that he tell Jessie if he spoke to her stating that she probably would not take a call from him no matter how urgent. Bill agreed. Devon then called his mother and cried the whole time he spoke to her. His mother tried to console him but found it wasn't helping.

Lucy came into the room and made Devon leave. She fussed at him for treating the situation as if Storia was dying or dead. She demanded he go to the chapel or elsewhere. Devon left, and Lucy walked over and sat in the chair next to Storia. She held Storia's hand and then prayed. When Lucy finished, she turned the chair around and turned on the television. She watched the news and was surprised when she saw a picture of the man handcuffed at the scene of the accident on the television screen. He was found dead in the back of the police car. The news anchor said they were investigating his death but so far had no leads. The news reported that the cameras at the scene didn't show anything out of the ordinary. "Paul Arkins was found dead in the back of the police cruiser. Chief of Police Evan Viles told Action 3 that there won't be a ruling on Mr. Arkin's death until after the autopsy is performed. Here is what he said when we asked."

"We are investigating what happened to Mr. Arkins. We know he meant a great deal to the community having owned several businesses in town and employed many. It certainly looks suspicious, but you can never be too sure with these things. Yes, he was fine moments ago but being involved in this type of accident, you never know. He could have had something going on internally from the car crash and succumbed to those injuries all while having the appearance of looking okay. We are going to look into his death. We certainly want to rule out homicide. We will inform the media once we have more to tell," Chief Viles stated.

There you have it. We're going to toss it back over to you. I'm Leah Campbell, Action 3."

Lucy continued watching the news. As the anchor continued, Lucy would learn about several men reported missing, each found dead in various locations around town. Lucy, so consumed with the news, didn't hear Ian walk into the room.

"How is she?" Ian asked.

Lucy jumped to the ceiling startled by Ian's voice. She turned off the television.

"Oh, she's... I'm not sure. You're the officer there on the scene?" Lucy noticed verbally.

Ian confirmed. He explained that he was stopping by to see how Storia was doing. Ian told Lucy he had to guard a prisoner on the same floor. Ian said someone shot the prisoner not far from Storia's accident. Lucy thanked him for stopping by then asked him if he knew about the man who hit Storia being dead. Lucy noticed his cryptic facial expression when he affirmed he knew of the man's death and spoke of karma. Lucy had a sick feeling in the pit of her stomach but thanked Ian again for stopping by to see Storia. Ian left returning to his post. Lucy figured Ian could have had anything to do with the man's death because it happened while Ian was en route to the shooting and now, Ian was at the hospital, but Lucy felt Ian could have had a little more diplomacy about the man's death.

CHAPTER 20

Ten months slowly passed. Storia had been out of the hospital for only two of those months. Her rehabilitation was going well, but she still couldn't walk without assistance. She was slow. Her hips had shifted due to the impact of the car crash. The doctor recommended rehab before reduction surgery to see if the physical therapist could work the bone back into place. The doctor also prescribed occupational therapy for Storia, something that she wasn't interested in at all. Storia's therapy sessions were going well, but it was excruciating, and Storia wasn't always up to the challenge.

Storia had full use of her arms, and her speech was not affected as the doctors declared in their prognosis. Storia was still as smart as she always was and now two months shy of 18, Storia's life had to take a different direction. Carlee got rid of Storia's phone, so she had no way to get in contact with the men she once knew. She hadn't been able to do anything but attend night school. Storia tested out of most of her classes, and as the months slipped by, only two subjects remained. She had one more week to go before she could graduate. She was proud of herself but couldn't wait until she walked without the leg braces because she didn't like depending on people, and she hated being slow.

Storia sat at the door waiting for Ian. He was on his way to drop her off at home. She still imagined being with him but now thought of herself as ugly with the leg braces and scares traveling across her torso and legs. As she waited for him, she thought about the things he says to her. She could feel he loved her, but there remained something secretive about him she still couldn't figure out. Though the fact that there were secrets that inadvertently stuck out like a blue jelly bean in a bowl filled with yellow ones, Storia couldn't shake the feeling of wanting and needing to be with Ian in every way possible. She hadn't given him anything since they met. He never pressured her either; things were always fun and light, and even though he always gave to her she thought to herself as she sat waiting, she wondered from whom was he getting affection.

Right after class, Storia met with Kory. It was late, but he was in town visiting his family and was ready to sign over Storia's deed to her home. Storia had three days to go before she would turn 18. She needed to look up the process to make sure she and Kory did it right, but she was sure it would be easy. As Storia finished her conversation with Kory, Ian arrived. Storia grabbed the arm of the braces and stood up. Ian came into the school and grabbed her book bag as usual then allowed Storia to put her arm through his arm and hold his arm while he grabbed her braces. She sauntered to his truck. Ian opened the door, and then Storia turned around and put her butt on the chair. As Ian stood in front of her, she pulled her legs around and took her book bag from Ian. Ian closed his passenger door, placed Storia's braces in the back seat, got into his truck, and drove Storia home.

Several nights later, Storia made it through all of her classes. The principle was proud to tell her she passed all of her subjects, and let her know that her diploma would be available in two weeks. Storia was elated. She spoke to Kory and asked him to meet her at the city hall in the morning so he could sign the quit-claim deed for the house. Kory agreed and to her surprise asked about Carlee.

Carlee went to the local university two months after Storia's accident. Carlee graduated high school but didn't go to the prom and spent most of her days in school or working. When Carlee wasn't working or at school, before Storia came home, she spent every day at the hospital visiting Storia and with Hannah. Carlee and Lucy continued to argue and fuss about everything and nothing, and at 20, Carlee still had dated no one. Carlee woke up one day and realized she was very frustrated and remembered what her sister said years ago and she knew just what she meant.

Storia didn't tell Kory all of the things going on with Carlee, but she mentioned that Carlee was the most fabulous sister in the world explaining how Carlee put her life on hold to care for her daughter. Kory told Storia it was always Carlee's plan to take care of Hannah until Storia got herself together. Storia thought about it and agreed then told Kory he should stop by once he got back in town. Storia could sense by Kory's silence he was thinking about it but didn't know how to decline. Storia let him off the hook by stating that it was just a suggestion for which he didn't have to oblige. They ended the call cordially, and as always, Ian picked Storia up on time.

Ian looked exceptionally good that night. Storia felt like she had never felt before; she felt insecure and did not like the feeling. As she sat in the passenger seat stewing, she noticed Ian was not taking her straight home, but she didn't question him. After driving for what seemed like an hour of verbal silence and a parade of love songs in the background, they finally arrived at a quaint little bed and breakfast. It looked like a cottage she thought. Ian took the keys out of the ignition then grabbed a bag and Storia's braces out of the back seat of his truck. He closed the door then walked over to her side of the vehicle and opened her door. He formed a bend in his arm and turned to the side so Storia could grab him and get out of the truck. She slowly moved her legs until they hung over the seat. Ian moved closer to Storia, and Storia grabbed his arm and used her other arm to put it around his neck. Ian braced himself for her weight. Storia pulled herself down slowly until her feet touched the ground. Ian moved slightly to give Storia enough space to get her bearings. She was stable. He walked her away from the truck as he closed the door and pressed the lock button on his key ring.

They slowly walked towards the entrance Storia inquiring every step of the way. Once they entered the building, Storia was speechless. She observed the place from the art hanging on the walls, the statues standing in place waiting for views, the colors chosen for the decor, the funny shaped indoor pool, and stylish lobby with the employees dressed in luxury uniforms with scarves and berets. She thought the other places Ian took her were beautiful, but by far, this place, she felt was the best.

Ian gave Storia a complete tour. She took pictures until she ran out of space on her phone. Then she used Ian's phone to continue memorializing the beauty of her surroundings. Suddenly Storia got nervous. She thought about sex as they arrived at their room. She hadn't had that feeling for a while and thought she might have lost it when Paul smashed into her. Ian talked to her about the hot tub. He felt the heat therapy would help her legs, and then he spoke to her about the pool and relaxing to take the stress of having to use the braces off her mind. Not one time did Ian mention sex nor did he insinuate that he wanted sex from her. That night they walked without the braces slowly through the flower garden and around the track. When she was tired of walking, they sat on a bench for a while. Once Storia was ready to go, Ian carried her back to the room on his back. After they entered the room, Ian undressed Storia down to her underwear and helped her into the hot tub. After an hour or so, he helped her out, dried her off, and helped her into a nightgown he bought. They watched movies the rest of the night with Storia falling asleep in his arms.

The next day Storia woke up feeling refreshed until she realized Ian was gone. Storia headed to the bathroom. She used the toilet, and slowly jumped into the shower. When she got out, she wrapped the towel around her body and headed into the room. As she walked around the corner, there was Ian. He looked as hot as ever standing in the middle of the floor with the clothes he had on from the day before with orange juice and hot cakes in hand.

He walked over to her, she looked up at him, and he kissed her. She dropped the towel, looked at him, and said, "Please." He looked at her body, then looked into her eyes and asked her if she would be his only. She eagerly said yes, and in that instant she remembered she said she would lie to have him, now realizing that she wasn't lying the moment she said yes. Her emotions were all over the place.

He looked at her and held her face between his hands kissing her gently, then pulled away from her arms and walked over to his bag. Storia saw a beautiful blue leather box in his hand when he turned around. As she stood there naked, he fell to his knee. She thought he was getting ready to do what she hadn't had done in over a year, but it wasn't why he was on his knee. She heard him in what seemed like an alternate universe say he loved her and wanted to spend the rest of his life with her. She heard him, but she felt like she was in a dream. She could feel the warmth of her tears running down her face seemingly in slow motion; she saw him looking up at her, she stood before him naked in disbelief that after all that she had done with other men he wanted her.

"Will you marry me?" Ian asked softly.

Storia looked at Ian as he opened the beautiful blue box to reveal the most significant diamond swimming in diamonds and white gold leaping out of the blue velvet foam slot. In all of the jewelry Storia owned, she had seen nothing as gorgeous in all the pieces she had.

Storia remembered every time Ian was with her. He never wanted to have sex with her and always wanted to be the only one in her life. He always treated her wonderfully unless she was with someone else, but even then, he never directed his anger towards her, he would instead attack the man with her. He was unique to her because he was so kind and would be the one who never had her even though she had been with a couple. Ian was the one she was supposed to have all of her first times with, Storia thought. It was Ian this whole time, she thought sadly. Storia wanted someone better than her for Ian. He could see in her eyes that she would turn him down.

"Look. I know you're not perfect in your eyes, but you're perfect to me. I want to be with you. I want to be who you get all you need from, and I want to take care of you and your daughter. I want to be the one you need. I want you to be my wife," Ian said so convincingly.

"But you deserve better," Storia declared passionately.

"What makes you think you're not my better?" Ian asked.

"Who have you been with because my reputation isn't stellar? You don't deserve to be known as the one who married the whore," Storia confessed.

"It doesn't matter. None of those girls were you. Do the men you've had matter to you? Have they all had you here?" Ian asked circling over her vaginal region with his hand.

"No," Storia answered. Her emotions were all over the place.

"Then what are you saying? Do you think you're bad because of the molestation? Do you think that you are a bad person because you touched and done things to men and allowed them to touch and do things to you for money? Do you think you're a bad person because you made some questionable decisions? Let's face it, yes you made some bad choices, but it doesn't mean you're a bad person. It is not like you robbed or killed people. For whatever reason, you sold yourself short. How long will you punish yourself for it or about it?" Ian gave Storia her clothes and sat on the bed.

"I never thought about it like that. I guess I have been punishing myself feeling that I was getting back at people who said something wrong about me or did something wrong to me, but I ended up no further. Except I was the culprit," Storia took her clothes from Ian.

"Well stop victimizing yourself and be my wife," Ian asked again not as beautiful as his first proposal.

"Why can't you just have me now? I told you there was no one else," Storia said frantically.

"Because Storia, I want it to be better, different, and MEANINGFUL for you when it happens this time. I want you to be my wife giving herself to her husband, not some whore putting out for cash," Ian said harshly.

Storia looked at Ian. She could see he was agitated.

(Storia speaking within herself) He did bring me to this beautiful place, and everything here is designed to help me feel better. He has been a gentleman the whole time I've known him since we met.

Storia scooted over to him in her bra and panties. He looked at her as though he was looking through her. She didn't know why she felt like he was someone else in disguise. She continued looking at him as he looked back at her. She hoped to see who he was to her. They stared at each other for some time all the while Storia felt more and more unsure, but she wasn't scared anymore.

"I would do anything to keep you safe," Ian said as he continued looking into her eyes.

Storia now saw it, she thought. He wasn't candid with her. He wasn't telling her everything. She could sense he was hiding something. She wanted to ask him about the men she was seeing. She wanted to know if he had something to do with their disappearance or deaths. Should she inquire as to if he killed them, she thought? She looked at him. His face was beautiful and full of youth. He wasn't like the older men she once dealt with by any means. She touched his face and continued looking at him.

She remembered Ian; his face appeared to her vaguely. He was graduating from high school the year Carlee went to homecoming; she was in the tenth grade. He was on the football team. Storia looked at Ian and recalled him coming up to her school when she was getting to the ninth grade after having Hannah. She remembered Ian. It's him. Sure, at the time, he was skinny, his hair was oily, his skin was terrible, and he had braces, but his eyes are the same grey that seemed blue at times. His smile displayed his dimples and his voice that made this so familiar. Storia's eyes grew wide as she looked at him. He continued staring at her now puzzled at her reaction.

"You told me you would wait for me. Did you know Tommy?" Storia asked troubled pulling away from Ian pressing her hands against the bed trying to get up.

"No. I didn't know Thomas, per se," Ian answered.

"What do you mean per se?" Storia questioned.

"I saw you the day you were leaving his house. I didn't know what happened, but I saw you. My uncle was one of the detectives working leads on the girl's who were murdered cases. He told me Thomas was murdering young girls, but he couldn't prove it. So, since that day, I started watching you because I didn't want you to become his next victim, but I was a recruit and college student. I regret that I didn't watch out for you as closely as I should have, but you were a young girl, and as a young adult, I was too old to be looking at you in that way, so I remained respectful and mindful of that fact. I just always said to myself, I would wait for you. You were a kid, you know, just getting to the high school where and when I was graduating. It was creepy, so I vowed to stay away from you. I even left town because I felt back then how I feel now, drawn to you," Ian explained. "When you started working at my cousin's place, he told me that you were, but you were still too young for me to get involved, so I stayed away. After you started hanging out with Georgia, my cousin, Jimmy, called me again and told me he thought you were starting to prostitute yourself. I knew I had to come back to make sure you were safe. When I was at Burger-Burger and saw you, I wanted to marry you. I've always wanted to be with you. I've always wanted to marry you since I saw you when you were only in high school," Ian continued to explain, as Storia slowly got dressed.

"Continue," Storia insisted.

"I saw you with Paul, so I threatened him. Then the other guy and the other guy and the other guy, I threatened all of them too. I met with your grandmother, and she told me about some other guy; I pulled up on him and threatened him too. Your father overheard your grandmother and me talking, so we ended up telling him what was going on," Ian revealed as Storia sat stunned to find out her father knew. "At first he was enraged. He calmed down as if we didn't say anything. That night you and I danced, and you went to the bathroom, I strong-armed the guy you were with and made him leave. Storia, your dad, was there," Ian said turning towards the wall wiping across his face with his hand allowing his hand to rest on his chin.

"What happened, Ian?" Storia asked heart beating fast.

Ian turned and looked at Storia.

"He followed the guy. I'm not sure what happened after that because that is the day I was coming out of Marneys when you were headed to the apartments. I guess you were headed to meet the guy from what I gathered because I beat his ass. I told him to leave you alone. Your grandmother knew about the apartments because as I understand it, the property manager knew her and called the moment she saw you. I yelled at you that night and told you to go home because I didn't want you in the apartments," Ian explained.

"What are you saying to me, Ian?" Storia asked shaking.

"What I'm saying? I forgot about you, Storia, well...I tried. I was out of town when my cousin called, but when he told me about you, everything that I thought I stopped feeling for you resurfaced. I told my cousin I would be there and I transferred over. I didn't tell you that because you never gave me a chance. You were so gung-ho about selling yourself to the highest payer, and that made me so mad," Ian said to Storia reaching out to touch her.

"What happened, Ian?" Storia allowed Ian to touch her and wipe the tears rolling down her face.

"I told my cousin I loved you, but you were too young. Everybody in this town is okay with having sex with little girls. I mean their planning for them as soon as the child pops out of the womb, and I wanted out because I didn't want to be that guy."

"I know, and that is what I like about you. Please, Ian, tell me what else?" Storia turned to look out the window at the beautiful sunrise then looked back at him.

"Your grandmother called me. She told me she spoke with your father and he was concerned about you keeping company with Georgia," Ian said pausing.

"Yeah," Storia turned her body slightly and looked out the corner of her eye. She could see Ian turned away from her with his hand covering the side of his face. "How many of my family's secrets are you keeping?"

"Georgia was a drug addict. She, her mother and her sister, were into some weird things," Ian began explaining as Storia thought back to Georgia telling her about her mother. "Georgia was whoring herself out so she could buy drugs. That's how Georgia died," Ian lied. "She overdosed," he confessed.

"Oh. I thought someone killed Georgia," Storia said confused.

"Anyway, I told your dad I was in love with you and always have felt like I loved you. I told him I wanted to marry you, but I was too old. When you were having the baby, I was turning 19. Your father asked me a bunch of questions then voiced his concern about you. He told me that I was not allowed to pursue you. He said as long as I wasn't trying to come after you, he was fine with the notion of me waiting for you to turn preferably 18 then it would be up to you to decide if you wanted to date me," Ian noted. "Your grandmother was completely different. Once she found out what you were doing, she said that you were a victim all over again, because of what happened to you when you were younger. Fair Shore is a small town. Things happen; people accept it or reject it that is the way it is; that is the way it has always been. Everyone loves a hero. Many people in this town have lost their daughters. You were lucky for some reason. If you think about your life, you are the only one who is still living. Have you ever thought about that?" Ian asked.

"No. I hadn't thought about anything. I guess I have been extremely angry for a while. It has jaded everything I do and how I look at things. I didn't know anything about Tommy. I just know it was fun, and then it was sex, and though my parents talked to me about inappropriate touching, I never thought it was inappropriate. Tommy was touching all of us. He bought stuff for all of my friends. He took us places, and it was never what my parents explained, so I just never saw it coming. Even when he wanted to do, quote, special things for me, unquote, there was no sex involved. I feel like I'm unprepared because I didn't know that was what I was supposed to look for you know? It is kind of like what you've been doing," Storia said as she slowly walked towards the hot tub. "I just want to put my legs in this time," Storia requested.

"When he started touching you, didn't you know that was wrong?" Ian asked walking over to the hot tub and preparing it for Storia.

"I don't know if I knew it was wrong at the time because of the way it happened. He was so gentle and nice. What he was saying made so much sense and I still had my clothes on, so I didn't think molestation or rape or inappropriate for that matter," Storia eyes filled with tears.

"I wouldn't think you would know like that I mean I don't know how it happened. I just know it was wrong and everything that has followed is just as wrong," Ian tried not to let on that he was still outraged.

"Ian, do you know who killed those men? I knew all of them," Storia asked as she leaned on Ian's arm.

"I don't know, and frankly, I don't care. All of those cases are cold. There are no leads, no evidence, nothing," Ian said. "No one is even looking into those deaths anymore," Ian continued.

"Oh my god, did you help to cover it up for my father?" Storia asked reacting to something that popped into her mind. "I know you know. Tell me," Storia begged.

"Storia..."

"Please tell me. I'm so tired of not knowing, people disappearing, people coming up dead, people flashing me with bright lights,"

"(sigh) (pause) (thinking) It was your mom," Ian diverted.

"WHAT???" Storia was shocked. "Ian, what?" Storia was hysterical and in tears crying uncontrollably in Ian's chest as he held her. "How? Why? Oh, Ian why? No." Storia was a wreck.

"Storia they all were beyond angry. You have to understand how helpless a parent feels to see their child misbehaving and the disgust when it is someone who has no business doing what they are doing. Some of the people – the men – have kids your age and younger and they guard them. They never let them out of their sight, so to do it to another's child is a slap in the face and stab in the back." Ian said justifying what happened.

"So you're the only one who knows?" Storia asked as she wiped her hands across her eyes, her cheeks, and mouth, shaking uncontrollably. She thought about what she heard. She was sure it was the hardest thing she ever listened to in her life. She thought it was worse than those mean and evil things Tommy said to her when she told him she was pregnant.

"Yeah, well, besides your family, there is a cop that knows," Ian admitted.

"My father, grandmother, and Carlee knew?" Storia wanted to know.

"Your father and grandmother know for sure. I am really not sure about your mother, and Carlee I've caught in some strange predicaments, but I don't know how much she knows. To be honest with you, I was only concerned about you. I really don't have much to say about your family members, I just know I wanted to keep you safe. I know William found out some things and divorced your mother, then she disappeared, some say she left town," Ian divulged.

"And you're willing to keep secret all the things you know?" Storia inquired.

"It never happened," Ian said looking directly into Storia's eyes.

"I will marry you," Storia looked up at Ian.

"What?" Ian said surprised.

"I'll marry you," Storia repeated. "Look. Let's do it now. My dad and his wife were married in Vegas over a year ago now. It's what (looking at the clock on the desk) 7:09. We can jump on a plane go to Vegas and get married, but we have to come right back because I have to meet with Kory to get my house back. What do you say?" Storia said ready to negotiate.

Ian jumped up and grabbed the ring from the box then slid it on Storia's finger. He kissed her and hugged her tight then grabbed her braces and the bag he brought in and ran out the door. Ian placed those items in the truck, then came back in, and picked up Storia. He carried Storia to the vehicle, put her in the seat, and then waited for her to swing her legs around so he could close the door. Once he had her secure, he went to check the room to make sure he hadn't forgotten anything, and then he went to settle the bill.

Storia's phone began to ring. Storia looked at it and saw it was Kory. Storia told Kory her plans changed and asked if they could meet later that afternoon before 4:00 or tomorrow morning so they could go to city hall. Kory was okay with the time change. He and Storia continued to talk briefly. Kory asked if he could stop by assuming Storia was home. Storia told Kory she would be at the house later and they could talk then. Kory told Storia he had something that he needed to say to her and he didn't want to forget. He asked that she remind him because it was important. Storia told him she would bring it up when she saw him. Storia told Kory she would call him once she made it home. The two ended their call.

Ian and Storia arrived at the airport. It took no time to get through security because they had nothing besides themselves to search. Ian hailed a carrier to take him and Storia over to the boarding area. Storia was excited riding in a golf cart for the first time, which seemed pretty amusing to Ian. Storia sat while Ian went to purchase the tickets. They were in luck. A plane to Vegas would be boarding in 30 minutes. They sat holding hands and talking until it was time for them to board the plane.

When they arrived in Vegas, Storia was like a child in a toy store. She was overwhelmed with the sights and excited that they were there. Ian told her he would have to travel with her often so she would see what God had allowed His creation to build. Storia agreed. Ian rented a car. The two drove around Vegas taking in the sights; then they grabbed something to eat. Ian stopped in a jewelry store and purchased wedding bands Storia picked out. They went to the nearby wedding chapel and got the most expensive package the chapel offered then said their I dos. Afterward, Storia walked over to the counter to sign the wedding certificate. The assistant told her to sign Storia Emily Anna Allister and not DeLuca. Storia repeated her name as she looked at the rings. She admired the wedding band Ian bought and how it complimented her finger in front of her engagement ring. Storia was over the moon. She hugged Ian as he swung her around.

"That was fast. We still have two hours and some change before we catch the flight back," Ian said with the biggest smile Storia had ever seen on him.

"Well, now that I am Mrs. Storia Emily Anna Allister. Can I partake in your magic?" Storia asked sweetly.

"Why do you feel you have to ask? Come on let's go," Ian said laughing and kissing her on the side of her head with his arm around her neck.

Ian and Storia went to a room adjacent the chapel. The rooms were cheesy as far as themes go, but Storia didn't care. Ian pulled out the stops with Storia she thought. He commissioned her to do nothing but breath. Storia didn't know if she was coming or going. Ian undressed. As he unbuttoned the last button on his shirt, Storia touched his muscular frame allowing her hand to rest between his chest and stomach. Ian took Storia's hand gently and raised it to his lips to kiss it. He touched her chin then raised her head up slightly to meet his lips. He kissed Storia passionately as she stood in the middle of the floor thoughts raced through her mind. Ian unzipped Storia's hoodie then pushed it off her shoulders. Then he lifted her shirt over her head. Storia swung her hair from side to side, as Ian whispered to her.

Ian unbuckled his belt, unbuttoned his pants, and then unzipped the zipper. Storia looked on as though she were watching an event. His pants fell to the floor. Storia went to pull her joggers down when Ian stopped her. She looked at him puzzled. Ian reached over and unsnapped Storia's joggers causing them to fall. Storia took one-step forward now only wearing a matching panty and bra set. Ian stared at Storia purposely.

"Is something wrong?" Storia asked.

"Nothing at all," Ian said seductively.

Ian stepped to Storia and kissed her passionately. He looked at her and pushed her hair behind her ear. He picked her up and carried her over to the bed.

"I want you in so many different ways," Ian said looking into Storia's eyes. Storia kissed Ian ready for whatever he was offering. Ian removed Storia's bra. He looked at her sweetly.

"Do you like what you see?" Storia asked smiling.

"I'm so glad you're my wife," Ian responded.

"Why is that?" Storia inquired.

"Because I can have you all of the time now, and by the way, I love what I see," Ian whispered touching Storia's breast and allowing his hand to travel downward.

Storia arched her back as Ian played with her emotions. He placed his mouth on her lower region; Storia pulled him up to her and kissed him softly.

Ian entered Storia gently, moaning, trying to look at her with every passing stroke. She looked back in her mind thinking it was more than she thought it would be. He took his time caressing every part of her body as he turned her around onto her stomach. Storia had never felt the intensity quite the way she was feeling it at that moment. She didn't know if it was because it had been over a year or if it was Ian's size. Just as Ian whispered to Storia to get on top of him, Storia turned around and crawled up Ian's body now lying opposite the headboard. Storia looked at Ian's manhood surprised that it was in her considering its size. Ian held Storia as she mounted him. She let off a moan unfamiliar to her. Ian moved Storia's hips and encouraged her to pull up as he pushed up. Ian could see Storia was having a hard time, so he sat up and pulled her into him. Storia felt as though Ian was bench-pressing her. Then, Ian laid Storia on her back and with her legs around his back, he gave her all that he had. Storia felt the hard thrust as he moved back and forth, in and out of her and suddenly, that feeling she missed. That feeling she thought she could only feel if the mouth prevailed was back. This time harder, stronger, longer, and more intense, nonstop as his body motioned back and forth looking at her with every stroke. Storia's eyes closed tight, and she let out a continuous groan in his ear that was like a sexy song to him explaining what he was also feeling. She held him tight as she could feel nature taking its course, and then, it was over. He kissed her humbly and moved off her gently breathing slowly in and out of his nose. Storia lay on the bed. She could still feel herself throbbing.

Storia was speechless. All of this time she waited for Ian and the wait was finally over. Storia thought it was well worth the wait, but she wanted more of him. She was so overwhelmed that she turned over and silently began crying. Ian asked Storia if she was okay. She told him she was and then Ian turned her over and held her, turned on his back and pulled her on to his chest.

"I'm not going anywhere Storia. You have me now," Ian said running his finger threw locks of her hair. He dozed off.

Hours later, Ian jumped up and startled Storia who had also fallen asleep. The two showered together, dressed, and left for the airport. They returned the car and took a carrier cart over to the boarding area. Storia texted Kory to let him know she would be in town in less than two hours. She wanted to see if he would be available to go to the city hall. He confirmed and told her to let him know when she was about there because he wasn't far from the place. Storia asked if he could go to the city once she arrived because it would be near closing by the time she reached the town. Kory agreed but told Storia to contact him if the plans changed. Storia confirmed then ended the call.

Ian and Storia finally boarded the plane. They slept the whole way home. When they got off the plane, they waited for the shuttle that took them to the parking lot where they parked their vehicle. Ian did his usual routine to help Storia in the truck. The two were on their way to the city hall. Storia texted Kory to let him know she was in route. Storia arrived in the city with ten minutes to spare. Kory signed the quit claim deed, then Storia paid and registered the document. Kory was surprised to see Ian but didn't say a word. Storia thanked Kory told him she would see him at her father's house later and the two parted ways.

Storia slowly walked to the truck where Ian met her halfway and helped her. She and Ian happily drove to the house. Ian thought the home was perfect, but Storia felt it needed work. Storia suggested they move in immediately. Ian agreed. Ian locked up the house. Instead of putting the key back under the mat, he gave it to Storia. They went to the hardware store, purchased new locks for the doors, and selected paint for each room.

While Ian loaded the truck with the purchased items, Storia sat in the vehicle. Once Ian finished, he walked over to Storia's side to close the door. Storia was hurting and very tired. Ian told Storia he would take her to her father's house figuring Storia had been way too active that day. He felt bad.

Ian pulled up to Devon's house to drop Storia off. He told her he would be back after he grabbed a few more things for the house and something for her to eat. Storia approved and asked Ian to take her up the stairs to her room. Storia pulled the keys out and opened the door. Ian took her upstairs to her room, kissed her, and then placed her on the bed. Storia lay in her bed looking at the ceiling thinking. She could feel her body getting heavy as she grew drowsy. She fell asleep.

#

Carlee walked in from school with Hannah. No one was home she thought. She walked up the stairs, and when she got to the top of the stairs, she could see Storia's bedroom door was open. Carlee walked pass Storia's room and saw her in the bed. Carlee was so happy to see her. She was worried because she had not seen or spoken to her since the day she left for school. Carlee went to Hannah's room and put her in the crib. Hannah didn't give Carlee any fuss; she went straight to sleep. Carlee walked back down to Storia's room. She touched her. Storia moved then turned over. Carlee saw the ring. Carlee blew a stack. She woke Storia. Storia asked her what was going on and inquired about Hannah. Carlee asked Storia if she was married. Storia was groggy and still very tired. She told Carlee she would talk to her later. Storia asked about Hannah again, and before Carlee could answer or reply to Storia in any way, Storia fell back to sleep.

Carlee stormed out of Storia's room and down the stairs fuming. She didn't know if she was mad because Storia said nothing to her about getting married or if it was jealousy because her sister the whore was married and she wasn't even seeing anyone. Lucy was coming in the door with groceries. Carlee was so mad she didn't help her or say hello. She walked to the family room, fell on the couch, and stewed as she tried to figure out who Storia married. Lucy thanked Carlee sarcastically and placed the groceries on the counter. Carlee didn't reply. Lucy put the groceries in the cabinets and refrigerator. Still working in her husband's business, she realized she had a meeting she needed to attend. Lucy didn't have time to put up the rest of the groceries, so she put up everything that was supposed to go in the refrigerator or freezer and left the rest. Lucy went into the bedroom and freshened up. She put on what she considered a power suit, her pumps, grabbed her suitcase, and then walked out the door.

Hannah's crying woke Storia. She swung her legs to the side of the bed and looked at her braces leaning against her desk chair. She had to get to Hannah she thought. She pulled herself up. She was slightly bent at the waist as she tried to figure out how she would get to the desk. She pulled her left leg. Storia's leg suffered a lot of damage, but she was glad that it wasn't so smashed that it was beyond repair; she wanted to walk a little faster. She finally reached her braces. She grabbed them and walked dragging her leg down the hall to Hannah's room. Storia was happy once she made it to Hannah. She had a newly discovered appreciation for her ability to walk. She spoke to Hannah and got close to her crib. She picked her up as she put most of her weight against Hannah's crib. Storia was praying there was something in the mini-fridge. She wasn't sure how she would get Hannah down the stairs. Storia put Hannah on the floor. She used one brace to walk over to the mini fridge. There was a bag of cereal. Storia had no idea how long the cereal had been in the frig. Storia had to go downstairs.

Storia sat in the rocker and looked at Hannah walking around, falling and laughing. She asked Hannah to come to her and kissed her on her forehead. She grabbed her leg brace. She put her weight on her right leg then grabbed Hannah's hand and slowly walked out the door and to the steps. Storia grabbed the stair rail and sat on the top of the stair with Hannah doing the same. The two went one step at a time going down the stairs. Just as they reached the bottom, Carlee raced around the corner.

"I'm sorry Storia. I didn't hear Hannah," Carlee grabbed Hannah.

"That's okay, just take care of her. I'm fine. I will make my way to the couch," Storia responded.

"Are you sure you're okay?" Carlee asked genuinely concerned about Storia.

"Yeah," Storia answered walking slowly over to the couch.

Carlee walked Hannah into the kitchen and placed her in her booster seat. Once in the kitchen, Carlee complained loudly about the groceries. Storia could hear Carlee slamming things around, so she gathered her strength and walked into the dining area to see why Carlee was complaining. Storia walked into the kitchen and over to the cabinet to grab the box of cereal rings. She walked over to Hannah and poured the cereal into a bowl in front of Hannah. She asked Carlee to give her a juice box over by her. Carlee gave Storia the juice box, and then Storia opened it, poured the content into a sippy cup, and gave it to Hannah. Storia leaned against her brace and waited for Hannah to finish eating before walking with her into the family room. Storia sat on the couch while Hannah played across the floor.

Storia noticed the back room door that led to her father's office open, so she got up, walked over, and closed the door. Storia rolled the gate over the opening of the kitchen and closed it off so Hannah would stay in the family room. Storia laid on the couch watching television while Carlee complained about putting up the groceries. Storia could feel her legs tingling. She rubbed them then called to see if she could see a physical therapist before her regularly scheduled time. There was a date available so she confirmed that she would be there. As she was finishing the call, she noticed Ian chiming in on the other line.

Storia answered the call and talked to Ian for about 45 minutes. Ian was at the new house getting things together and making appointments for workers to come out to the house. Ian let Storia know that they wouldn't be able to move in right away because the city inspector had stopped by and did a surprise inspection. Storia told him about the appointment and thanked him for working on the house. They ended the call.

"Storia," Carlee called.

"Oh Lord," Storia said under her breath. "Yes."

"Who are you married too?" Carlee asked with a frown on her face.

"Ian," Storia answered dryly.

"Why are you married to Ian, Storia?"

"Because I wanted to marry him, I wanted to be with him. I wanted him to be a part of my family," Storia shouted.

"You wanted to have sex with him so badly that you were willing to marry him, Storia?" Carlee yelled.

"Actually, for a change in my drama filled life, my decision to marry Ian had or has nothing to do with sex. I married him because I love him and I love my family," Storia said without thought. She looked at her phone to know the time.

"What do we have to do with it? Your family. What do we have to do with it?" Carlee asked placing her imaginary integrator hat on her head.

"You don't need to know. I don't know what your problem is anyway. Do you now have a problem with me because I'm married the way you still seem to have with Lucy? Carlee for the record, those are groceries. You eat them, why can't you put them away? Doesn't she still work at dad's company? I mean, she has practically doubled the volume of dad's business since she started working for him. I know what's wrong with you though. I have the solution too. Carlee put your best look on and be ready by 7:30. Now go, get ready. You don't have much time," Storia shifted her hair to the other side of her face.

"What? What do you mean? I mean, I do eat the groceries, but why couldn't she just put them away?" Carlee asked as she folded the paper bag.

"Where is she? Is she here?" Storia looked through her phone contacts list for Lucy's number to call her. "Hello, Lucy? How are you?" Storia asked. "Did you have an emergency that caused you to leave the groceries on the counter?" Storia listened to Lucy's respond. "I figured exactly. Well, that is all I wanted to know Lucy. See you, and if I don't see you, I hope to talk to you later, okay? Okay bye. She had a meeting Carlee. You need to stop being so hard on her," Storia shook her head.

Storia stood up to go to the bathroom. Suddenly, she felt a sharp pain that made her buckle over and screamed. Carlee ran over to help her, but Storia was in so much pain she did not want Carlee to touch her. Storia asked Carlee to run upstairs and get her pills. She explained she hadn't taken one since getting out of school and hadn't thought about them. Carlee ran upstairs, grabbed the pills, and charged down the stairs so fast she stumbled on the last two stairs. Storia cried out to Carlee to see if she was okay and was relieved to hear Carlee say she was okay. Carlee limped into the kitchen and got a bottle of water. She walked into the family room and handed Storia her purse and the water. Storia asked her again if she was okay and this time, Carlee said she wasn't sure as she sat on the floor next to Storia looking at her leg.

Storia took the pain pill and rolled on her knees. She crawled to the bathroom. Her hip hurt beyond any pain she had ever felt besides childbirth, she thought, but the pain was just about at childbirth level, and she couldn't wait for the pill to work. Storia got off the toilet and noticed her leg was straight. It didn't have the dragging feeling. She leaned over to flush the toilet and pivoted to wash her hands. She pulled out a piece of paper towel and dried her hands. She saw her ring. It was sparkling, seemingly flawlessly. She smiled. Storia went to walk out of the bathroom, but when she applied pressure to her leg, she felt a stabbing pain and yelled out then fell to the floor and stayed there with her leg in piercing pain. She slowly crawled to get out of the bathroom. She made it partially between the hallway and family room. Carlee limped over to Storia and helped her off the floor. Storia held her leg up and hopped to the family room and onto the couch. She watched television until she could feel the pain leaving her leg. Storia jumped up to see what was going on with her legs.

Carlee did what Storia told her and searched through her closet and pulled out a cute two-piece Storia bought her. She took a shower and put on perfume and makeup. She didn't have the extensive jewelry collection like Storia.

Her jewelry collection consisted of two pairs of earrings, a watch, and a bracelet. Carlee walked down to Storia's room and looked in her jewelry box. Storia had all kinds of beautiful pieces and knew them all. If one of her pieces of jewelry went missing, it would be hell to pay until returned, especially if you didn't ask. Carlee grabbed a pair of earrings and the matching bracelet and put them on. She walked back down to her room and took the heated rollers out of her hair. They were still warm. She turned on the curlers and curled the parts of hair still straight. Carlee put on the cutest flats she had. She wasn't sure where Storia was taking her, so she didn't want to be stuck in heels, feet hurting and not enjoying whatever activity. Carlee walked downstairs feeling gorgeous, and Storia confirmed by complimenting her.

Devon and Grandma Ellie arrived first, followed by Ian who arrived just shortly after but so close they all came into the house together. Everyone complemented Carlee as they walked into the house. Storia was just making it up to the top floor and into her room. She was walking much better but could still feel the pain though muffled by the pills. Storia jumped in the shower slowly and washed up quickly as she leaned against the shower wall. She sat on the edge of the tub and swung her legs around then stood up and took the shower cap off her hair. She brushed her hair then put one of her favorite hair potions in it making sure she pulled the cream down her hair shaft. Storia walked stepping on her leg easy not wanting to apply to much pressure. Storia went into her room where Ian greeted her. He was happy to see her walking without the brace. He noticed how she moved and made fun of her and they both laughed and hugged.

Storia walked into her closet and picked out something to wear. As she stood there, Ian walked over and looked over her shoulder. He commented on the stuff in her closet that he would have to move. Storia explained that it was just a bunch of shoes and clothes. She decided not to tell him about the prepaid cards, money, or all the jewelry she had in some boxes he was complaining about having to move. Storia thought to herself that she would get the rest of the prepaid cards she had together in one box and get a safety deposit box. Suddenly, Storia wasn't sure about Ian, and she felt insecure. In her thoughts, she focused on her body being healed completely, her daughter, her husband, and her new house.

Ian touched Storia bringing her out of thought. She smiled at Ian as he helped her get dressed. Ian had compliments and kisses for Storia. He decided the shoes Storia picked weren't the best choice for her with the stairs. The shoes went great with the outfit, but Ian was concerned since they had never been worn. He thought they would be too slippery. Ian feared her going down the stairs wearing them, so he told Storia he would take the shoes to the bottom of the stairs, and she could put them on once she got there. Storia agreed with Ian and placed her house slippers on her feet. She turned off the light to her room and walked towards the staircase. She could see her dad and Ian huddled in the corner talking. Grandma Ellie was sitting in her favorite seat not far from the conversation Ian and her dad was having. Carlee was sitting on the couch by herself.

Storia came down the steps. Ian ran to the stairs and watched her then went up the final few stairs and walked with her down to the floor. Everyone clapped except for Lucy, smiling from ear-to-ear with a drink tray in her hands holding drinks, was proud of Storia. Storia smiled to acknowledge everyone, put on her shoes, and went to the door. She could see the shadow in the window of the door. She opened the door already knowing who it was and looked back to Carlee.

"What are you doing here?" Carlee asked as tears instantly formed. She hugged him and couldn't help what she was feeling. She was so happy to see Kory. Kory looked at Storia and smiled.

"I was in town doing some business with your sister, and she invited me over," Kory replied sounding more relaxed than how he used to sound.

"Come in," Storia said standing by her husband waiting for Kory to get inside before she closed the door.

"I'm sorry. I know you're not the touching kind," Carlee said placing one hand in another.

"Well, you will be the first," Kory looked at Storia as if she was the only one in the room as he spoke to Carlee.

Storia gave the face of approval. "For her too," Storia said laughing with everyone else as Kory looked delighted after hearing that comment.

"Pay her no mind," Carlee said smiling and looking back at Storia mouthing something that was inaudible.

"Is it true?" Kory asked. Storia sauntered by Kory to check on Hannah who was sleep in her playpen.

"Yeah," (sigh) Carlee answered in embarrassment as she dropped her head turning it to the side.

"I don't want to sound arrogant," Kory began.

"Yes you do, or else you wouldn't say it," Storia stated laughing as she placed a blanket on Hannah.

"Your sister is funny... umm, were you waiting for me?" Kory asked lifting Carlee's head to look at her.

"I was ("Yes," Storia said mocking Carlee) waiting for someone like you. I didn't think you would be available," Carlee responded looking at him thoughtfully.

"Well, I am. . . available that is," Kory replied looking at Storia. He was as serious as he is seemingly all of the time.

"YES!" Storia said moving her fist up and down.

"So, do you want to see where we can go with this situation? I mean, I haven't been able to stop thinking about you, I mean it has been almost two years now," Kory confessed looking at Carlee while following with his eyes trying to figure out Ian and Storia.

"No one else has touched your lips?" Carlee said inviting. ("Didn't you hear the man, girl?" Storia said as she walked by winking at Kory.)

"NO ONE," Kory said smiling trying to be serious. "I was hoping your lips would be the ones permanently touching mine."

"So are you talking to me because you keep looking at my sister?"

"Yeah, well, she keeps saying things that seem to be funny. My apologies."

"Mine too Carlee. I'm just happy that's all. I didn't mean anything by it."

"The Bible says he who finds a wife finds a good thing and obtains favor from the LORD. Would you be my wife?" Kory proposed.

"Yes! Yes! Yes!" Storia said as though Kory asked her. Kory smiled then looked at Carlee.

Storia noticed Carlee's hesitation. "What is with the DeLuca women fucking up beautiful proposals, " Storia said to herself. "Oh my God. I didn't know you were going to do this. Why didn't you tell me?" Storia said excitedly trying not to draw too much attention to Carlee who looked faint.

"I didn't know. When I got your call, it made me think. I thought about many things, and it made me feel like I could commit. I especially liked the conversations about God. I have thought about it on and off the last couple of years. When I saw you, I thought about when she first told me what she was going to do once she got out of high school and I just thought it was so noble and selfless. I've just been doing a lot of thinking okay," Kory said as he smiled at Storia and she softly side nodded her head towards Carlee who was crying by this time after hearing what Kory said.

"So how about it?" Kory asked as he turned around to Carlee grabbing her hands and dropping to his knees to see her face. "Would you be my wife? My good thing?" He asked.

"Yes. Yes, I will," Carlee said as the household erupted in cheers.

Kory placed a beautiful ring on Carlee's finger that was a bit too big.

"No Vegas wedding for you honey," Lucy said sincerely. Carlee walked over to Lucy and hugged her.

As Kory turned around from proposing to Carlee and basking in the congratulatory hugs, claps, and cheers, his eyes met Ian's. Lucy refilled everyone's drinks then set the picture down and walked over to Storia to express her excitement about her standing and walking better. Storia told Lucy she was glad she was in her dad's life and said yes to her dad. Grandma Ellie made her way over to Kory to grill him about employment in which Kory was happy to report he owns property in another state and is gainfully employed making more than enough to support him and his wife if she decides not to work. Grandma Ellie was pleased with the news. Devon was saddened now knowing Carlee would not be living in the same state and Storia and Hannah would be in a different city though Storia would be closer than Carlee. Lucy and Storia were talking and giggling like school girls. They made plans for the wedding.

Now, Grandma Ellie, Devon, and Ian were quietly talking amongst one another privately. Storia looked at them conversing but couldn't figure out what was going on, so she spoke with Kory standing between the window and door. Carlee and Lucy talked about getting Carlee's ring resized.

"So what did you want to talk to me about?" Storia asked Kory.

Kory looked in the direction where Ian was standing.

"Yeah, you think we can go outside?" Kory asked feeling uncomfortable.

"Sure," Storia said walking to the door.

"Remember when you were doing your quote, in your words, bad girl, unquote?" Kory asked.

"Yeah. The prostituting I should have probably said, yeah," Storia answered.

"I wish we were able to talk before you two got married because I don't think it makes any sense to tell you now," Kory said looking at the door then back at Storia.

"He told me about the guys if that is what you are about to tell me," Storia said not knowing what Kory would say next.

"He told you he killed some of them, dudes; you were messing with?" Kory said surprised.

"He told me my mom – wait - - - - what?" Storia said looking at Kory like she didn't hear what he said.

"Well, your mom was sleeping with that one cat you were fooling with, and her husband found out some kinda way. I heard your mom left town, but I don't know. Your man has a terrible attitude. He was pretty furious when he beat that one guy at the apartments with another guy, but I couldn't see the other guy's face. He kinda looked like he was related to your dad you know like an uncle of yours or something," Kory said now walking down the stairs then turning around to face the door.

"Are you, yeah I know you, I know you're not lying," Storia said putting her hands on her head then sliding them down her face. "How do you know? I know you Kory, and I know you're not lying to me, but I want to know how you know?"

"The apartments, man. I was in the apartments when Ian came into the neighborhood and did it. The guy you were with was fumbling around with his keys. It seemed like, some way, the door jammed. Your dude walked up to the dude and said he thought he told him to stay the eff away from his girl – I'm assuming you. The guy starts popping off at the mouth, and your man pushed him into that alley by the apartments and beat the breaks off of dude. Your man left, and the guy went into his apartment. It seems like somebody was waiting because when the guy went into his apartment, suddenly you could hear that dude being worked over," Kory explained.

"Are you sure?" Storia asked still thinking her dad had something to do with that one, but the thing about her mother was unbelievable; she would never leave money for broke down dick sex she thought. "Which one was my mother sleeping with, do you know?"

"Word on the street is she was sleeping with the one you were dealing with that owns them properties around where you were working. I heard the cousin – Jim, I think, told your mom about him and how he tried to be with you and she started going around looking for him, slept with him, and then stabbed him in his junk. That is what street gossip says, but I don't know," Kory said.

"Well, she is gone and he some way is dead," Storia said looking at Kory. "Hey, look I am not sure what his or my mother's full involvement is, but I know my dad and grandma are involved in some way, and now you're telling me my husband has something to do with the murders too... I just need you to keep letting the streets talk without adding to what's said," Storia said almost begging.

"Naturally, I mean when I say the streets are talking, I'm not talking about me. The streets themselves and others who may or may not know aren't saying anything. I wanted to tell you only because I noticed you were hanging around tough with that guy. He has a horrible temper, but I think I said that already. I mean if someone commented on how nice you were to them when you were working at Jades, dude would come down on them with an iron fist telling anybody who was talking about you good or bad to keep your name out they mouth," Kory rehashed what he witnessed.

"You mean everyone knew what I was doing?" Storia asked naively.

"Yeah. What you mean, you didn't know? I mean you didn't think it was weird that of all the men you were with none of them wanted to penetrate you," Kory asked coyly. "I mean, so says the streets and another thing, that fool you were dealing with, the one who seems like he is mean mugging people all of the time, he is a cop. Your man threatened him too. The streets were waiting because that would be nothing short of a street war," Kory added.

"I never thought about it. I mean someone did, just not from this town, but I guess that is who you're talking about. I don't know what to say. This is so crazy," Storia said now thinking about every man she met.

"You never noticed that once you met them unless you had the encounter the same day you never really had the encounter? The streets say that dude, the cop I'm telling you about, you were dealing with; Carlos was falling for you and wanted to start a relationship with you. Well, when your man found out like I said, he was like hell in

327

the flesh, ever wonder what happened to that guy?" Kory asked recalling the crackdowns he witnessed Ian and some other guys he knew putting down on the men Storia knew.

"No. I mean yes. Ian knew Carlos, and I were close, but he told me Carlos found someone else and was moving on," Storia said rolling her wedding band around her finger dazing into nowhere.

"You believed that? Storia after that mess happened to you, your dude Ian snapped man. He was hosing dudes down if they had any interest in you even remotely. The day he found out that dude Tommy was molesting you; he tried to kill that guy the day the courts sentenced him to prison. The street says Tommy was recently in a fight where a jail gang jumped him and did him dirty, doggy style. A family member of mine tells me that dude is still in the infirmary. If he doesn't die, he probably won't survive beyond the month that he is released back into general population. Ian's family had to send him away according to the streets. Then, when you started that crap with Georgia, they called him back. All I know is dudes associated with you is dead, so you figure it out. That dude, Ian, used to put a gun into dudes faces telling them you were his and anybody assuming he was humorous or fictional would meet facts. I guess this doesn't matter now that you married him. One thing I know is he's a scary guy. When your dad and grandma co-signed his behavior, I knew it was water under a bridge. Everything is on the hush, so technically; I told you nothing. I just thought you should know," Kory shifted himself. He looked at Storia then guided his eyes to the door where Ian stood.

"I am so stoked that you are marrying my sister, and thanks a lot for helping me with the house. I'm glad that I was able to catch you before you left town," Storia smiled at Kory and waved as Kory walked towards his car.

Storia turned to look at her husband walked over and kissed him, then put her arms around him with pure fear in her heart.

"Welcome to the family, Kory," Ian shouted. He smiled at his wife and swept her off her feet.

"Thank you. Catch you all later," Kory got into his car and drove away.

== THE END ==

Thank you for coming along with us on this journey. We hope that you laughed, were angry, cried, and rejoiced throughout this read.

PERSONAL CARE

Anyone affected by sexual assault, whether it happened to you or someone you care about, can find support from online.rainn.org. You can also call the National Sexual Assault Hotline at 800.656.HOPE (4673) to be connected with someone over the phone that can help.

If you think you or someone you love is struggling with a mental health disorder, visit https://www.mentalhelp.net where you can find support based on your challenge.

If you're thinking about suicide, are worried about a friend or loved one, or would like emotional support, the Lifeline network is available 24/7 across the United States. 1-800-273-8255 or to chat with someone visit https://suicidepreventionlifeline.org/talk-to-someone-now/

MORE TITLES BY NINA R. RICCI

Naïve and Lethal
5 Minutes to Breathe (Naïve and Lethal, 2)
Showdown: Belong to No One (5 Minutes to Breathe, 3)
The Art of Revenge According to Carlee DeLuca (4)

Meltdown (Coming 2019)

About the Author

Nina R. Ricci, affectionately known as Reki, is a Michigander who is a unique talent always in search of ways to make her fellow neighbor's life brighter through her creations. On any day, one could find Nina creating different places for others to enjoy even if that space of enjoyment is in your mind. A self-proclaimed recluse and obvious introvert to those who know her always find it humorous as she always does the complete opposite when out in public. Nina is new to the world of writing. Completing her first book, Naïve and Lethal, has been both overwhelming and exciting. While Nina has served as a ghostwriter for many, she had never considered writing for herself until last year (2017). Nina wrote Naïve and Lethal in the summer of 2013. It was not until the winter (February) of 2018 while looking for a random item; she came across the book in a self-addressed envelope. Reading pages caused Nina to reprise her role as a writer. Nina considers writing a privilege and an honor to have the ability to express thoughts with words. Nina is working on a book entitled *Meltdown* available early 2019.

ONE LAST REQUEST

Please leave a review.
Thank you.

www.ingramcontent.com/pod-product-compliance
Lightning Source LLC
Chambersburg PA
CBHW030559180626
46816CB00005B/1601